Jo was too ~~strong~~ didn't fall for flowery words and touches. At least she didn't used to.

His hands, warm and strong, cupped her face as he brushed his lips over hers, whisper soft. Jo's eyes fluttered shut.

Levi kissed her again, longer this time, yet not nearly long enough. His lips caressed her, slowly, leisurely, driving her mad. Every touch shot warm shivers through her veins; every heartbeat was a burst of fire.

BOOK YOUR PLACE ON OUR WEBSITE
AND MAKE THE
READING CONNECTION!

We've created a customized website just for our very special readers, where you can get the inside scoop on everything that's going on with Zebra, Pinnacle and Kensington books.

When you come online, you'll have the exciting opportunity to:

- View covers of upcoming books
- Read sample chapters
- Learn about our future publishing schedule (listed by publication month *and author*)
- Find out when your favorite authors will be visiting a city near you
- Search for and order backlist books from our online catalog
- Check out author bios and background information
- Send e-mail to your favorite authors
- Meet the Kensington staff online
- Join us in weekly chats with authors, readers and other guests
- Get writing guidelines
- AND MUCH MORE!

Visit our website at
http://www.kensingtonbooks.com

CHARMING JO

LAURA DREWRY

ZEBRA BOOKS
Kensington Publishing Corp.
www.kensingtonbooks.com

ZEBRA BOOKS are published by

Kensington Publishing Corp.
850 Third Avenue
New York, NY 10022

All Kensington titles, imprints, and distributed lines are available
at special quantity discounts for bulk purchases for sales promo-
tion, premiums, fund-raising, educational or institutional use.

Special book excerpts or customized printings can also be created to fit specific needs. For details, write or phone the office
of the Kensington Special Sales Manager: Attn. Special Sales
Department. Kensington Publishing Corp., 850 Third Avenue,
New York, NY 10022. Phone: 1-800-221-2647.

Zebra and the Z logo Reg. U.S. Pat. & TM Off.

ISBN 0-8217-7859-5

First Printing: September 2006
10 9 8 7 6 5 4 3 2 1

Printed in the United States of America

For Ron.
Always.

With thanks to:
My editor, Hilary Sares for her patience and understanding;
my agent, Jenny Bent, for her support and direction;
the Debs, for always having the bucket ready;
and the L's—Laurel, Laurie and Lona—
for always giving it to me straight.

Chapter 1

Kansas, 1880

"No good sunsabitches—the whole lot of them. Just ain't right up an' quittin' like that."

Joanna McCaine nodded in agreement. "You're not saying anything I haven't already said. But cursing them out isn't getting me anywhere." She peered around the crowded saloon, biting back more useless curses. "Surely there's someone in town needing work, Lefty."

The old bartender shook his head slowly.

"All's I need is one man. Just one."

"That's a load of crap, Joey, and you know it." Lefty's whiskey-hardened voice always reminded Jo of wagon wheels over a rough dirt road. "You can't have more than a few hands left out there, can you?"

When she refused the bottle he offered, Lefty poured himself a long shot and downed it in one well-practiced swallow. All around them, the stench of stale whiskey, sweat, and tobacco hung thicker than an April fog. Blood from more than a few fights stained the dirt floor, and the door hung crookedly from its hinges.

Drunks—several of them once employed by Joanna herself—whooped and hollered over various card games while Lefty's working girls, adorned in tattered feathers and enough face paint to cover the entire building, slinked around the room offering their wares.

Above the ruckus, a lone voice sang with all the grace and tuning of a twenty-year-old tomcat. Sal.

God bless her, but the woman couldn't sing to save her life. How she'd ever convinced Lefty to let her do her caterwauling in his saloon was a complete wonder.

Jo re-rolled the sleeves of her father's threadbare shirt, then twirled her hat between her hands. Maybe if she pretended it wasn't so bad, it really wouldn't be.

And maybe pigs would fly, too.

"We've still got Walt, Simon, and Jimmy." She paused, swallowed. "Mac, of course. And Newt."

Lefty let out a rolling grunt that caused a few heads to turn their way. "Your Uncle Mac's been dead for ten years; just forgot to fall over is all. And Newt—how old is he?"

"Seventy. I think."

"How's his hands?"

"Would I be here looking for more help if his hands were any good?"

Another grunt. "So you've got a drunk, two half-wits, a corpse, and a cripple left working for you. You'll never get that fence built."

Jo blew out a long breath. "I would if I could get someone with a strong back and a will to work.

With three men out on the range that only leaves Mac to help me out." No point in adding Newt to the equation anymore. The man tried his best, but Lefty was right. Newt was too crippled up with arthritis to be the help she needed.

"Mac must be hatin' that." Lefty scratched the thick puckered scar under his blind right eye.

"On a good day he's only hating it. If I don't get him back out with the cattle soon, he's going to go loco on me." Jo laughed lightly, though there was probably more truth to that than she wanted to think about. "Since the others up and quit, Mac doesn't trust the three we have left. He figures they're either plain slackin' off or staying on long enough to collect next week's pay, then they'll quit, too."

Lefty clicked his tongue. "Wouldn't surprise me. And if Mac ain't out there ridin' herd on *them*, who's to know what the hell they're doing?"

"Which is exactly why I need him back out there."

Lefty scratched his ample belly and sighed. "Don't suppose you'd go out on the range an' have a couple of the other hands come in to work the fence?"

"Uh, no." Heat crept up her neck. "I wouldn't be much good to Mac out there."

"But . . ." Lefty trailed off, then grinned, showing off his tobacco-blackened teeth—or what was left of them, anyway. "Joey—you *still* can't rope?"

"Shh!" she eyed the tables nearest her and shrugged.

"But you can do everything on that damned ranch—what's so hard about ropin'?"

She couldn't help but laugh at herself. "If those

stupid animals would stand still, I'd be fine. But they just keep moving."

Lefty's laughter crackled through the room. "Yeah, I've heard they do that."

He downed another shot of whiskey, then set the glass down on the bar. When he looked up, all traces of laughter had disappeared from his face.

"Hate to tell you, Joey, but all these fellas here are already working."

Jo scanned the room full of card-playing, whiskey-drinking men, her brow raised in doubt.

"Well, they're not working right *now*," Lefty hurried to add.

"And even if they weren't working," Jo sighed. "None of them want to work for a woman."

Lefty offered her a quick shrug. "Don't matter how much you pay some men, they just can't abide bein' bossed around by no girl."

"I know. That's why I need someone who needs the money more than his pride. But I also need someone who'll actually do the work—not like those lazy grunts I hired last time."

Lefty shot a quick glance around the room. "There's this one fella I know of, but you won't want him."

Jo snorted—a sound that never failed to get her in trouble with her aunt. "At this point, Lefty, I'd hire the devil himself as long as he could help me get the fence built. Then Mac can go back out with the herd until roundup."

"But this fella's got himself a bit of a reputation."

"I don't care. If he's got two good working hands and a strong back, he's hired."

The old face looking back at her did not seem

convinced. "Mac'll have two fits sideways when he finds out."

Jo slid a coin across the bar. "It's my ranch, Lefty." Mac could have *four* fits if he wanted to. They needed the help. And as long as the fella didn't turn out to be . . .

"His name's Travers. Levi Travers."

Levi Travers. Of course. Papa always said the only kind of luck Joanna ever had was bad. Here was the proof.

A long groan ripped from her throat. "Not Travers," she said. "Anyone but him."

Lefty backed up, his line of vision darted away from Jo to something—or someone—behind her.

"Looking for me?" A low, deep voice jolted Jo upright. The ruckus around them paused for a brief moment—save for the echo of hiccups coming from the far corner. But once Sal hit the first key on the piano, the room filled again with curses, howls, and the clinking of glasses almost as though they were all trying to drown the poor woman out.

Jo swallowed hard, glared at Lefty, and slowly turned on her stool. Impossibly soft brown eyes, like a newborn calf's, stared back at her. He wore his black Stetson tipped a little to the right, leaving his too-long brownish hair to fall around his shoulders. Thick stubble covered his face, but did little to hide the fading bruise beneath his right eye, the inch-long scar on his chin, or the smirk curling his lip.

Clinging to his arm was one of Lefty's finest. Stella's white-blond ringlets, held back by some sort of red-feathered ribbon, swung with each movement of her head. Her bright blue dress, if you could call such a scrap of material a dress, boasted more of the same feathers in the most noticeable places—namely her bulging bosom.

"Hi ya, Joey." Stella's sugar-sweet smile never failed to nauseate Jo. "Whatcha needin' Levi for? He's kinda busy right now." She trailed her finger up his arm and across his cheek. The muscle in his lower jaw twitched, much like Jo had seen her cattle do against a buzzing mosquito.

Despite all the stories about Levi Travers, she'd expected him to look different.

A lot different. A lot uglier.

But seeing him in person made it easy to see why girls let him do what he did.

"You're Travers?"

He nodded. "Who wants to know?"

A voice called out from the dimness of the far corner. "Joey—is that you, girl? Does Mac know you're in here?"

She waved a dismissive hand toward the caller, but he continued.

"Come on and play a hand with us. I could use a little luck."

"Not a body alive who needs my kind of luck, Tip."

Travers shifted his stance a bit, bringing her attention back to him. Heat raced up her neck and over her cheeks. He did more than just look back at her, he seemed to look through her.

She cleared her throat and forced the words out. "Could we talk outside, please?"

Stella pouted. "Levi, stay here with me. Ain't I more fun than some dirty ol' cowgirl?" Her long finger swept the length of Jo's arm. "She's wearing her dead father's clothes, for pity's sake! Just the thought gives me the willies."

Jo cocked an appraising brow at the other woman and snorted again. "I don't think you're one to be handing out fashion tips, Stella."

Before Travers or Stella could answer, Jo jammed her hat back on and strode out of the saloon. There had to be someone else who could work for her. Someone who didn't keep all the tongues wagging in town; someone who didn't treat every woman as though her only purpose in life was to please him; someone who had at least an ounce of honor attached to his name. Was that asking too much?

Apparently so.

She stopped in front of Maggie's restaurant and, with a heavy sigh, slumped against the nearest post. People—no, men—wandered all through town, back and forth across the deep-rutted road, dodging horses, wagons, and yapping mutts. If there were so many men in town, why couldn't she find anyone to work for her?

Lefty had been her last hope. He knew everything about everyone else's business in town. If he said Travers was the only one, then that was the truth.

Damn it.

She'd have to send a wire to the neighboring towns. Surely someone was looking for work nearby. Of course, having to bring men in from out of town would take another week or so—time she could ill afford if she had any hope of getting her fence strung before roundup.

The heavy thud of boots scuffing against the boardwalk turned her head. Travers sauntered toward her, followed by a still pouting Stella.

"Are you going to tell me what this is all about?"
He leaned his boot against a nearby water trough
and looped his arm around Stella's shoulder. "In
case you missed it, I'm rather busy." With pro-
longed nonchalance, his gaze raked over Stella's
body, from toe to nose, with extended pauses in
certain areas.

"Yes," Jo snorted. "I'm told Stella can keep a man
busy for hours."

"That's right, sugar," Stella cooed into Travers's
ear. "So let's go back inside and . . ."

Travers's gaze locked on Jo for a long moment.
What did that look mean? It felt like he was about
to swallow her whole. He leaned his head toward
Stella, but never took his eyes from Jo.

"You go ahead, Stell. I'll catch up with you in a
while."

"But, Levi." The whine drifted on the air as he
waved her away. Jo waited until Stella disappeared
inside the saloon.

With a deep breath, she lifted her chin and forced
some starch into her voice. "I need an extra hand."

"Not interested. On my way out of town." He
tipped his head to the right a little and flashed a
dazzling smile of nearly straight white teeth.

"You mean you're being *run* out of town." Not
even Mac had teeth that clean.

A tiny sparkle danced in his eyes. "Six of one, half
dozen of 'nother."

"Not really, but regardless, I'm willing to pay you
very well." She crossed her arms over her old
button-down shirt and forced her best no-nonsense
look.

"How well?"

"Well enough."

His expression didn't change. "I'll ask again. How well?"

Jo ground her teeth together. Why him? Of all the men in town, why did he have to be the only one she could hire? If she'd been a man, she could have hired any number of good, strong workers. What was so bad about working for a woman? With a shake of her head, she relaxed her jaw.

"Fifty dollars a month plus room and board."

"No deal." He turned to walk back to the saloon.

"Sixty and you can have a cabin to yourself." When he hesitated, she nodded toward the restaurant. "Let me buy you a cup of Maggie's coffee and I'll explain."

Lord almighty, what was she thinking? Sixty dollars a month to have the likes of Levi Travers living on her ranch? Mama was no doubt dying a second long and painful death in her grave.

Travers shrugged, pulled open the restaurant door and waved her in ahead of him. Warm aromas of baking bread and fresh coffee made Jo's stomach gurgle. She pulled off her hat, nodded at Maggie, and made for the nearest table with Travers close behind. He held out her chair and waited 'til she was comfortable before taking his seat.

An eerie chill settled over her spine. Men didn't hold chairs for Joanna McCaine. They just about fell over themselves holding chairs for her sister, Carrie, but as for Jo—she was usually left to fend for herself. And that was fine with her; she didn't need to be coddled. She was more than capable of pulling out her own stupid chair.

Since Travers was her only hope, she could ill

afford to make a mistake and say something to scare him off, so while he settled himself across from her, his hat sitting on the chair beside him, she inhaled a few deep breaths and looked everywhere except at him.

Not much had changed in the six years since Maggie had taken over the restaurant. Yellow cloths covered each of the ten square tables, and the three tall, rectangular windows gleamed in the afternoon sun. There was nothing fancy about Maggie's restaurant—plain and simple, just like Jo.

The only other customers in the restaurant were Big Bill, who ran the livery, and his wife, Audrey. Their initial smiles turned to shock when they saw who Jo was sitting with. Big Bill's chair scraped back against the floor and, for a second, Jo thought he was going to come over, but Audrey patted his hand and the huge man shuffled his chair back in. But he positioned himself so he had a good view of both Jo and Travers.

Maggie poured two steaming cups of coffee, offered Jo and Levi menus, and then disappeared into the kitchen. Jo waited before speaking. For some reason, her mind was running in four different directions and her insides were jumping around like a frog on a hot griddle.

It would have been easier if the Levi Travers sitting in front of her had turned out to be short and squat, with a pockmarked, pasty face and thinning hair. Instead, this man made every story about him believable. It was no wonder women fell at his feet.

Jo wanted to kick herself. For goodness sake, he was only a man! Sure, he was nice looking, even as scruffy as he was with his long hair, stubbled face, and fraying black shirt. But none of that interested her. All she cared about was his ability to work—and work hard.

She looked him in the eye and spoke in a low, controlled voice.

"My name's Joanna McCaine. My sister and I own the Double M Ranch twelve miles north of here, just across the river."

"I'm familiar with the place." He took a slow sip of coffee, never blinking, just staring back at her with unnerving ease. "Heard you've been having some trouble."

She snorted. "That's one word for it. In the last month, three hands have quit and my foreman, Mac, is going to work himself into an early grave if I don't get some help out there."

Travers's eyes narrowed slightly. "Why'd they quit?"

As if he didn't already know. The whole town knew. Jo shifted in her chair and folded her hands on the table. "They had a problem working for a woman."

"You mean a woman who's hell-bent on fencing her neighbors out of prime grazing land." A slow smile spread across his face. "Yeah, I could see how that'd be a problem."

"It's my land, Mr. Travers, and—"

"Levi."

"Fine." Jo nodded slightly. "It's my land, *Levi*, and I'll do whatever I think is best. All I need is for you to help me get the fence built—two, three months tops—and then you can be on your way to . . . wherever it is you're running to."

"I'm not running, Miss Joanna."

"Call me Jo."

"Jo is a man's name."

The air thickened around her, her fingers clenched white. "It's also my name. I'm not a ruffles kind of girl, Travers, and I don't need a ruffles kind of name."

She swallowed a mouthful of coffee, hoping it would burn the rest of the spite from her tongue.

Travers shrugged his broad shoulders. If he'd only stop looking at her with that charming little smile, she'd feel much better about this whole thing. She raised her brow, took in a slow breath, and gave him a pointed look.

"Well?"

"San Francisco."

Jo cocked her right eyebrow. "Beg your pardon?"

"San Francisco. That's where I'm heading." He finally looked away from her and set his mug down.

What did she care where he was going? As long as he waited a few months. But if he wanted small talk, she'd manage it for a few minutes.

"Okay." She sipped her coffee, waiting for him to continue. He didn't. "What's in San Francisco?"

Travers tipped back in his chair, his fingers laced behind his head. "The ocean."

"*The ocean?* That's it?"

His chair fell forward with a thunk; the dreamy look that he'd had a moment ago vanished, replaced with disbelief and a little shock.

"Have you ever seen the ocean, Miss Joanna?"

"Jo. And no. But it's just water, Travers. We've got a great big pond out back of the spread that I'm sure you'll like just fine."

A soft, rumbling chuckle slipped through his lips.

"Believe me, Miss Joanna, your pond—no matter how big—is nothing compared to the Pacific."

She shrugged. Water was water—and salt water wouldn't do her cattle much good.

"Does your uncle know you're hiring me?" Travers's smile faded, but a small twitch lingered at the corner of his mouth. Was he mocking her?

"It's my ranch, not Mac's." Took more than a little willpower to keep from looking away.

"That's a no." Travers returned her pointed look.

"Listen." She rested her elbows on the table and folded her arms in front. "Mac's a big boy—if he has a problem with you being out there, he can take it up with me. Besides, you two'll hardly cross paths." She cleared her throat against the lie. "He'll be out with the cattle and you'll be working with me getting the fence up and tending to the yards."

"Believe me," he nodded, all traces of humor gone, "we'll cross paths."

"So you'll do it?"

He took a long sip of his coffee. "Not for sixty dollars a month."

"Sixty-five." She couldn't let him get away. It suddenly didn't matter that this was Levi Travers, the lowest of low, the subject of more scandalous stories than Jo had fingers and toes. He was a live body capable of work.

"Miss McCaine . . ."

"I'm being more than fair."

"I told you I'm on my way out of town."

"Seventy."

He hesitated, seeming to consider her offer for the first time. Jo pounced.

"Seventy-five—but I need your word you'll finish

the job." Like his word meant anything. Probably wasn't worth the bile that pooled in her belly.

"Seventy-five a month, plus my own cabin."

Jo nodded. Had she lost her mind? Nobody got paid that kind of money on her spread!

He tipped his head to the side, still not looking convinced. "I'd have a few conditions."

She nodded for him to continue. If it meant getting her fence built before she lost half her herd in the roundup, she was ready to concede almost anything. Almost.

"First—I get real meals—none of the usual crap they serve in bunkhouses. I want to sit down at a real table for my meals."

Jo wasn't about to argue that with him. Who cared where he ate? Besides, Cook had long quit anyway and Newt burned almost everything he put in a pot, so the hands pretty much fended for themselves. And having Travers in the house at meal times would give Mac and Carrie someone else to complain to. Or about.

Carrie. Jo worried her lip for a moment. Carrie might pose a bit of a problem.

"Second," Travers continued, ticking his conditions off on his fingers, "since you haven't started the fence yet and you seem to be losing help quicker than you can hire it, we need to bring in someone else."

She shook her head. "There isn't anyone. Lefty said—"

"I know someone who'll come."

She eyed him uneasily. "Who?"

"Someone who's not afraid of a little hard work—even if it's for a woman." The grin was back.

Jo challenged him with her own smile. "Even if it's for a woman who's *hell-bent on fencing her neighbors out of prime grazing land*?"

"Yup. Even so."

"That'd be a nice change." She looked down into her coffee—anywhere to break the hold his gaze had on her. "Who is it?"

"Name's Will Brennan."

"Never heard of him." Jo looked back at Travers. "Where's he from?"

"Doesn't matter. He's the man for the job." His gaze never wavered, his voice never hitched.

"You're sure you trust him? Or, more to the point, can *I* trust him?"

"I'd trust Brennan with my life."

"He gets the same pay as my other hands plus room and board."

Travers nodded, but Jo hesitated. Not only was she hiring Levi Travers, but now she was going to hire one of his friends? She'd be lucky if the two of them didn't turn her ranch into a giant whorehouse. She shuddered. Best not to think about it.

"Anything else?" When he shook his head, Jo nodded. "Fine. I have two conditions of my own."

"And they would be?"

"My ranch is not a saloon. There's no gambling, drinking, or *ladies* allowed. If you want to come into town on your own time and get into trouble, that's your business, as long as you're back at work on time and sober. Goes for Brennan, too."

"And?" His grin was back again, knocking a bit of the starch out of Jo.

She drained her mug, then pinned him with her fiercest glare. "And stay away from my sister."

Travers choked on his coffee. "What?"

"Let's not play games, Travers." Jo didn't even blink. "You've earned yourself a reputation that I'm sure your mother must cringe at."

"My mother's dead." Not an ounce of emotion showed in his face. Not a frown, not a tear, not even a sigh.

"So's mine." Jo pushed aside the quick pinch around her heart. "Doesn't mean we should be doing anything to shame them."

He eyed her slowly, almost like he was searching for something.

"What's your point, Miss McCaine?"

"My point is that I won't have you trying anything with Carrie. She might be young and pretty, but you'll be keeping your hands to yourself. Save your dazzling little smile and charm for someone like Stella. Got it?"

His dazzling little smile got bigger. "You think I'm charming?"

"I didn't say that." Or had she?

"*And* you think my smile is dazzling." He raised his brow a notch. "Never been told that before. The charming part, yeah, but never that I had a dazzling smile."

Jo rolled her eyes and sighed loud enough to attract Maggie's attention. When the other woman raised the coffeepot in question, Jo shook her head. The sooner this conversation was over, the better.

"Do we have a deal or not?"

"What about you, Miss Joanna McCaine?" His smile slipped away, but his eyes crinkled around the edges. "Can I flash my dazzling little smile and try to charm you?"

With a grin of her own, Jo plopped her hat back in place and stood. "The name's Jo, and save your breath, Travers . . ."

"Levi."

"Save your breath, *Levi*. I'm not interested in being charmed. And besides, once you've seen my sister, you'll forget all about everyone else—especially me."

She reached into her pocket for some coins, but stopped when he shook his head at her.

"Few things you should know about me, Miss Joanna." With slow measure, he rose from his chair, his gaze never leaving hers. "First off, I make no promises about your sister until I've actually seen her." With a flash of that smile and a wink, he continued. "Second, I'm taking it as a personal challenge to charm you—whether you're interested or not. And last"—he dropped several coins on the table—"I don't ever let ladies pay for my coffee."

Jo suppressed a smile. A lady. No one ever called her a lady. Hell, most people had long forgotten she was even human.

They walked back out into the sunshine, his hand against the small of her back, as though guiding her. The victory she'd felt at hiring him was outdone by the wave of butterflies brought on by his touch and that cursed smile. Good thing she was the sensible one in the family and not an airbrained dreamer like Carrie. Otherwise, she'd sure as sin find herself being charmed by this cad.

He squinted into the harsh sunlight before setting his twinkling eyes back on her. "When do I start?"

She quickly recovered her senses and forced herself

to concentrate. "Five minutes ago. Better go break the news to Stella that you'll be busy for the next few months. And wire your friend—the sooner he gets here, the better." She started across the road to the livery. "Hurry and catch up—the day's half gone already."

Levi's voice, deep and rich, laughed at her back. "I'd have done it for sixty."

Jo tucked her long braid under her hat and called back, "I'd have paid ninety."

With one easy leap, she mounted her horse and turned toward home, the home she'd helped build. She'd be damned if she was going to lose half her herd in roundup because she couldn't get a fence built.

Of course, by hiring Travers, she'd probably just damned herself all the way to hell and back anyway.

Chapter 2

Levi stood on the boardwalk, hands jammed deep in his pockets, and watched the fiery hellion ride away. Who'd have thought a woman dressed like a dirty old cowhand could be so damned attractive? Heavy denim pants hung straight from her waist and were rolled up enough that she probably could have made two extra legs out of the cuffs. Her blue cotton shirt, little more than a rag and tucked into the belted waistband, didn't fit much better. In fact, it looked more like an old potato sack hanging off her shoulders. And as for that sorry excuse for a hat . . .

Nope, he'd never seen such a God-awful getup in all his life. Yet somehow, on young Joanna McCaine, he couldn't imagine anything else. He'd heard all sorts of stories about her; how she ran her ranch with an iron will and sharp tongue, how she thought she was so damned much smarter than all the other ranchers in the county, and how, ten years after the fact, she still cried when she visited her mother's graveside. Even so, the girl from the stories didn't seem to do a damn bit of justice to the woman who'd just hired him.

The thick gray dust had long settled behind Joanna before Levi finally blinked. He hustled to the post office to send his wire to Will, then gathered his horse and few belongings he owned, and set out for the Double M. Stella be damned, he had better things to do this afternoon.

The vast Kansas prairie spread out before him in a million shades of green and gold. Wheat fields, cattle, crops, and new railroads were popping up everywhere. There was money to be made from the expansion and he'd do whatever he needed to if it meant it would put him that much closer to San Francisco. Even if it meant working for a woman.

At seventy-five dollars a month, he'd finally be able to leave town on his own, instead of being chased out. He could move on to greener pastures, cleaner saloons, and prettier girls than Lefty's. He'd finally have a life of his own, one that didn't constantly remind him of who he was and where he came from. Maybe he'd even give up the cards and whiskey and do something legitimate. Maybe.

Maybe not.

Until then, his life belonged to Joanna McCaine. And working for a woman was going to be *real* interesting. Wasn't a woman alive who could make a decision without changing her mind fourteen times—and if there were two McCaine girls in charge of the Double M, he could only imagine what kind of chaos was running rampant out there, regardless of how tough Joanna McCaine was said to be.

And speaking of Miss Joanna, she sure didn't

waste time playing coy, did she? He'd fully expected to catch up with her by now, but he was almost to the ranch before he had any clue she'd taken the same road.

Travers slowed his mount to a walk as he neared the McCaine house—a simple, two-story, frame and clapboard structure with a gabled roof and two brick-end chimneys. Joanna stood on the porch, leaning against one of the square posts, her arms crossed over her chest. She watched him through doubting eyes, her expression clear; she didn't trust him any more than anyone else did. And by the look on her face, she would have been just as happy to shoot him as hire him.

With a cock of her brow, Jo nodded toward the house.

"Come on in. You might as well meet Carrie while I'm here to keep an eye on you. Then we'll head out."

"Head out where?" Levi slid from his saddle and tossed the reins over the porch rail.

"The range." She narrowed her jade eyes at him. "Where did you think you'd find the cattle? In the parlor?"

He tried not to smile, but God help him, he'd never had a woman speak to him like that before.

"Even though you won't be working directly with the herd," she said as she pushed through the door, "you'll need to familiarize yourself with the setup just in case."

"Just in case what?"

"In case the rest of my men quit and I need you to take over the herd."

He stomped his boots on the porch, slipped his

hat from his head, and followed her inside. A soft scent of lemon hung in the air as he took a moment to look around.

The keeping room was by no means extravagant, but it was nicely furnished with a large, mossy-colored sofa and two matching wing chairs. A small oak desk sat under the western window, and in the far corner was a rather old-looking piano, with a fiddle set on top.

"This way." With a flick of her wrist, Joanna's hat tipped into her hand, releasing her long, thick braid down her back. It wasn't red, exactly, but more of a cinnamon-brick color. Not a curl or a wisp in sight, either. The single plait was a far cry from the hair-styles he'd seen on the women at Lefty's—or any other woman, for that matter.

Most women liked fancy styles, with those twists and ringlet things and fancy combs or pins—just like Stella wore. Hell, that's what he liked, too. Was nothing better than pulling those fancy combs from a woman's hair and letting it tumble over her bare shoulders. Especially when those women were blond. There was something about a blond. . .

"Travers, this is my sister, Carrie." Joanna's hard voice—and the sight before him—slammed him in mid-thought.

Standing in front of him was a girl right out of a fairy tale, draped in pink silk from the choker at her throat, to the tight bodice of her dress, all the way down to her tiny slippers. Her honey-blond hair was pulled back from her face, with a fringe of soft ringlets framing her face; eyes, the color of the Kansas sky, shone back at him from behind long blond lashes.

"It's a pleasure to meet you, Mr. Travers." The girl's voice was light as air, her lips curved in a soft smile. "I've heard so much about you." She held out her hand and waited for his response.

A long moment passed without a word, and before Levi could catch his breath, or take Carrie's hand, Joanna slapped him hard across the back of the head.

"Breathe, Travers." With an exaggerated eye-roll, she shook her head and moved past the other girl. "Close your mouth and stop staring. We made a deal, and you'll damn well hold up your end."

He didn't dare remind her that he'd made no promises with regard to her sister.

The blond girl giggled behind her hand and flounced up the stairs, leaving Levi to stumble behind Joanna to the kitchen.

"That's your sister?" He tried to hide his shock, but who was he kidding?

"Yes," she barked, "that's my sister. What's your point?"

It was Levi's turn to shake his head. "You two don't look anything alike."

"I'm aware of that," she growled. "It's not like you're the first to notice."

The kitchen turned out to be a large, bright room that welcomed him with its mouthwatering aromas and space to move. White lacy curtains fluttered in the open window and baking pans of various sizes covered most of the table and sideboard.

Joanna waved him in behind herself.

"Ginny, this is Levi Travers. He's going to help with the fence so Mac can get out with the herd."

A middle-aged woman with graying hair, and eyes

to match, smiled over the obvious shock of hearing his name. Flour covered her blue-checked apron and most of her right cheek.

"I'd shake your hand, but . . ." She smiled down at her hands, wrist deep in mucky batter. "Perhaps next time."

Levi took quick stock of the ingredients on the table. "Oatmeal raisin?" he asked hopefully.

"Yes," Ginny began. "They're—"

Jo elbowed Levi hard in the ribs. "She's Mac's *wife*, so you'd be wise to not even look at her."

"Joanna!" Ginny's eyes rounded as she flushed a deep crimson. "My niece forgets herself, Mr. Travers. Believes she's part man most of the time." After a brief moment, and a harsh glare at Joanna, she offered him a tentative smile. "It's nice to meet you."

He offered a slight bow while fighting back a chuckle. "Pleasure's mine. Your niece," he tipped his head toward Jo but kept his eyes on Ginny, "has given the order that I'm not to consort with females of any kind on your ranch, so pardon me if I seem a little . . . antisocial."

The corners of Ginny's mouth lifted, but she didn't laugh. How could such a sweet woman be married to someone as mean as Mac McCaine?

Jo rolled her eyes. "Travers thinks himself rather charming, Ginny. Don't be fooled by anything he says or does. And whatever you do, *don't* let him alone with Carrie."

A tiny wave of guilt washed over him, but he ignored it. They'd be smart to keep him away from that Carrie girl. Hell, if they had any sense, they'd keep him away from Joanna, too, though it seemed pretty clear she'd be the tougher of the two to win over.

The older woman looked between Levi and Jo then asked quietly. "Does Mac know he's here?"

"Not yet." A quick flash of something raced across Joanna's face, but she seemed to recover as quickly as it hit her, and she turned back to Levi. "Meals are at six, noon, and six. Wash bucket's outside the door there." She indicated the back door, then pinched a biscuit from the bowl on the counter and tossed him one.

"Do you do all the cooking?" he asked Ginny. One bite of that fluffy morsel had him hoping so.

"Carrie helps out sometimes." Levi caught the warning look she shot Joanna; he also caught that it went unheeded.

"But only if we're desperate," Joanna snorted. "You'd be better off eating Newt's sonuvabitch stew."

Ginny's eyes widened, her face pinked, and her lips tightened into a thin white line.

"Come on, Ginny." Joanna gave her aunt a quick hug. "I'm just making fun."

Fun? Joanna McCaine knew how to make fun? Levi chuckled softly. *Who knew?*

"You'd best go find Mac." Ginny's voice was soft and low, but the warning blared louder than a trumpet.

Joanna nodded, kissed Ginny on the cheek, and headed out the back door. If he'd had any sense at all, Levi would have turned tail and headed right back the way he'd come. The last thing he needed or wanted was to have to deal with someone like Mac McCaine. But the money was too good to pass up and damn if those McCaine girls weren't something to look at, especially that little blond one.

Lord almighty, someone should have warned him. He'd best get out of the house before she reappeared and left him looking like a mule's ass again.

He hurried out the door but Joanna was halfway across the yard already. She didn't just walk, she moved. Fast.

"Bring your horse," she called. "I'll give you a quick tour of the place and then we'll get started."

The layout of the ranch was typical of what he'd seen across the state. A couple dozen tall cottonwoods stood as a barrier between the main house and the rest of the ranch. On the far side of the trees, a large corral stood surrounded by the barns and stable, as well as the bunkhouse and two small cabins, which were set apart from the rest. Thin clumps of grass lay along the ground, with spurts of bright yellow buttercups popping up here and there.

Off to the east lay a huge spread of land, divided and sectioned off into smaller pens, and then farther on lay the open range. Or, rather, the open range Joanna was bent on closing in.

Hard to believe the McCaine girls hadn't been married off already. Both good-looking in their own ways, they obviously weren't starving, and given the expansion Kansas had already seen, they were sitting on a huge chunk of prime land.

Land. Theirs to do with as they pleased, with no one to answer to, and no one hunting them down for missed payments. It was a life Levi could get used to.

He blinked hard and shook the thought from his brain. There was no way in hell he was going to toy with that idea. San Francisco is where he belonged and San Francisco is where he was going to be in a few short months.

Too late, he caught Jo watching him.

"Go ahead and say it." She kept walking.

"Say what?"

"You have a problem with fencing."

He shrugged. "Not my place to say either way since it's not my land."

"I'm sure you have an opinion though." She looped her horse's reins around the top rail of the corral and waited. Her fingers ran along the animal's jaw, scratching his neck, around his ears, and down his muzzle. He nickered softly and pressed his nose into her hand until she pulled a bit of biscuit from her pocket and offered it up for him to nibble.

Levi secured his own mare as he swallowed back a chuckle. Damn, but she was ornery. A pushover with her horse, apparently, but ornery as hell with him.

"Of course I have an opinion," he said. "The entire state's got an opinion on fencing."

"And?"

"I don't like it."

Joanna pushed into the stable and started down the long row between the horses. She peeked into each stall as they walked by.

"You think it's a better idea to go on losing cattle every year to other ranchers who apparently don't notice the huge double-M on the backs of our herd? Guess they figure because we're girls, we're too stupid to know how to count or read."

She was something to watch when she moved. Long, determined strides, her hips swaying just a touch beneath the heavy denim of her father's pants. Levi blinked hard.

"You've been neighbors with these people for what—twenty years?" he asked. "Why would they start stealing your cattle now?"

"I'm not saying they're stealing them." But when she looked back, her green eyes said otherwise. "I'm simply saying that big parts of *our* herd seem to end up in *someone else's* herd every year. Is it intentional?" She shrugged. "Who's to say? But it's been happening for years and I'm tired of it."

They continued their progression through the stable, with Joanna pausing at every stall to peek in and around the various horses. "Pa always turned a blind eye to it, didn't want to believe his neighbors would do such a thing. But I'm not blind, Travers, and I'll be damned if I'm going to let anyone take what is rightfully mine."

She stopped at the farthest stall door, her expression softened. "There you are."

A young boy in tattered black pants and shirt scampered out, his arms wrapped around two squirming brown puppies. His coal-black hair didn't look like it'd seen a comb in a month of Sundays and his feet were completely bare. "I-I was j-just tendin' to the p-puppies, Miss Joanna."

"And doing a good job of it, by the looks of things." Joanna's voice took a slightly gentler tone as she lifted one of the pups from the boy's arms. "Travers, this is Clay. He helps out around here."

Clay's rounded brown eyes stared back, as he clutched the other pup tightly to his chest.

"Good to meet you, Clay," Levi said. "Do your folks work here, too?"

The boy ran a filthy hand under his nose. "Don't got no folks."

Levi's belly knotted. The boy couldn't have been more than six or seven.

"But M-miss Joanna lets me stay with Newt 'cause he ain't got no f-folks neither."

"Good idea." Levi squatted down in front of the boy and held out his hands until Clay placed the pup in them. "Being alone's not much fun, is it?"

"N-no, sir."

"How long've you been helping out here?"

When the boy shrugged, Levi turned his face to Joanna, who's brow was cocked in surprise. It seemed to take her a while to find her voice.

"Um, I guess it's been about six months or so," she said, turning away from him.

Clay stepped back into the stall and bent to fuss over the other puppies wrestling each other inside their crate.

Joanna leaned a little closer to Levi, but not too close. "Newt found him sleeping out by the pond last fall. Poor kid won't let anyone do anything for him, except Newt. You'd think they were sewn at the hip most days."

The knot in Levi's belly tightened. What would become of this poor kid—a boy whose only family was a crippled-up, ornery old man who could barely care for himself, never mind a child, and a litter of rag-tag puppies?

But then again, an ornery old man and a few puppies sure beat a house full of whores, rats, and a mangy three-legged cat, didn't it?

Levi pushed himself up to stand, placed the puppy back in Clay's arms, then nodded toward the squirming mound of fluff as it settled against the child's chest.

"It's a big job tending to a litter, isn't it?"

The worry began to drift from Clay's eyes. "Y-yes, sir. 'Specially since their mama's up 'n gone."

Levi crossed his arms. "Then I reckon they'll be needing a family, too."

A slight shrug. "Reckon." Clay wiped his nose again.

"Clay does a good job for us," Joanna interrupted with a smile, then handed her pup back as well. "Have you seen Mac?"

The boy winced. "In the b-bunkhouse. W-Walt's been drinkin' again."

Joanna's face turned to granite. "Saddle his horse."

She made for the far door, her boots kicking up a cloud of dust behind her. Watching her walk away made Levi's brain do a two-step for a moment before he regained his senses.

With a quick nod to Clay, he hurried to catch up. Again. She covered the distance between the stable and the bunkhouse in less than a dozen long strides, her arms swinging at her sides, her back straight as a rod.

This was going to be a show Levi didn't want to miss; here's where he'd see her in action, see how she held up against that uncle of hers, and maybe even have a chance to watch those eyes of hers flash and spark again. It should be good.

Joanna stormed up the steps and threw open the bunkhouse door. Levi hung back at the bottom of the steps and waited. No way was he going to follow her in—that'd be like going into a room with a cornered raccoon.

"Get him outta here, Mac." Her roar sent a flurry of yellow-breasted meadowlarks scattering from their perches high above the bunkhouse. "I don't want to see his face on my land again."

"Just hold on a minute, Jo." Levi couldn't see the man behind the voice, but recognized it as Mac McCaine's; hard, cold, and surprisingly weary. "We're already down three men, we can't afford to lose any more."

"I don't care if we lose the whole lot of them," she stormed. "I won't have drunks on my payroll. Get him outta here."

She charged back outside, her finger pointed right at Levi, and her voice splitting the air like an ax. "Tell me now, Travers. Is this what I should expect from you, too?" The faster she moved toward him, the faster he backed up until he nearly tripped over the bottom step of the nearest cabin. Joanna stopped mere inches from him, her eyes wild. "If this is how it's going to be with you, too, then you just get right back on that horse of yours and ride out the way you came in."

He didn't answer. Not because he didn't want to, but because he couldn't. He guessed he should have been a little intimidated by her, but all he could think about was the way her eyes flashed green fire when she yelled, the barely noticeable freckles dotting her face, and the way he'd like nothing more than to kiss that tight little frown off her mouth.

They stood in silence for a long moment, gazes locked on each other, his temperature warming up until it almost matched hers.

"I'll say it one more time just so we're clear." She

lowered her voice, but her eyes still blazed. "No drinking on my time. Not a drop. I don't even want to think you might be carrying a flask, got it?"

"Got it." His whisper barely reached his own ears. An odd feeling settled over him, one he couldn't place. But whatever it was, it didn't sit well. He'd never seen a woman so mad. Or so damned sexy.

If he didn't put some distance between them, some kind of distraction, he was going to haul her up into his arms and kiss every last ounce of that anger away. And a woman that passionate . . .

He stepped back, swallowed hard, and grabbed at the first thing he could think of. Cows. Thank God there were a couple of them bawling inside the barn—it gave him the perfect distraction.

"You don't think putting up a fence is a waste of money?" He cleared his throat and continued. "Wouldn't it be better spent somewhere else—like on hiring more help?"

The change of topic seemed to work; the color in her cheeks began to fade and the pulse in her throat slowed. A little.

"Hiring more help?" Joanna snorted—just like she had in the restaurant earlier. The sound made Levi want to laugh. Ladies didn't—or shouldn't— make noises like that. "In case you missed it, Travers, men don't want to work for me no matter how much I pay them."

"I'm here."

"Only because I'm paying you a small fortune and I couldn't get anyone else." As the last word settled on the air, Joanna's face flushed a deep pink. "Sorry, that was uncalled for."

Levi forced a grin and shrugged. "Truth ain't

always nice, Miss Joanna." Fact was, the truth was never nice about him, and up to that moment it had never bothered him one bit.

"Anyway," Joanna continued, averting her gaze, "once it's up, I won't be losing any more cattle. There's money saved already. I won't have to keep so many hands on the payroll because one man can do almost twice the job if it's fenced . . ."

"Not quite."

She was making sense, but he couldn't give in that easily—not when it meant she'd stop talking and her eyes would stop flashing those brilliant emerald flames.

She shrugged. "Close enough."

Two men staggered out of the bunkhouse—one propped against the other—just as Clay led a tired-looking old nag toward them. The drunk man barely made it into his saddle before Clay turned the horse and led them toward the road.

Joanna clicked her tongue before continuing. "Sure, the initial cost will be huge, but look at the long term. It's going to save us time and money. How can that be wrong?"

"How many miles of fence line are you looking at?"

"Thirty-nine." When he openly gaped at her, she smiled a little. And what a smile. It transformed her whole presence from a bossy, stubborn crank to a beautiful, soft woman.

"Okay," she continued, "so thirty-nine miles will take a while to string. But once it's up, we won't need to post as many riders out there. Instead of one man riding a six- or seven-mile stretch, chasing cattle on or off our land, he can cover twice that—easily—and still have time to do repairs and tend the cattle in his area. And best of all—no more roundups."

Which meant no more having to hire men like him. Levi shrugged it off. Didn't matter to him, anyway.

"I just don't think I could lock out my neighbors."

"They're not *your* neighbors. They're mine. And I don't think of it as locking my neighbors out. I think of it as locking my livelihood in."

With a toss of her head, Joanna dismissed any further conversation and turned toward the bunkhouse. A middle-aged man in dusty denim stepped toward them, his arms full of whiskey bottles, some empty, some not-so-empty.

"Mac," Joanna said. "You already know Travers."

Mac McCaine eyed Levi with a look meant to maim. "What the hell's he doing here?"

"He's working." Her back seemed to straighten as she spoke. "Or he will be once you start moving."

"He's not working *here.*"

Levi stepped forward. "Look, Mac, I know we've . . ."

"Stay out of this, Travers." Joanna put up a hand between the men. "This is my ranch, Mac, and as you just pointed out, we're down three men already."

"Four," Levi mumbled, casting a glace the way Clay and Walt had just gone.

"Right, four." She threw Levi a half nod, then wiped her sleeve over her brow and continued. "We need the cattle tended, the work done, and the fence built—all before roundup. Travers is going to help us make sure it gets done."

Mac made no attempt to hide his dislike. "Not him."

"Yes," she nodded. "Him."

"There's gotta be someone else—"

"There isn't."

"Did you talk to Lefty? He must know—"

"He's the one who told me about Travers."

Levi resisted the urge to wave his hand between them. Did they even remember he was standing there?

"But what about him and the Pearson girl?" It was pretty amazing that Mac could speak through teeth clenched that hard.

"What about it?" Joanna fisted her hands on her hips and jutted out her chin. "It has nothing to do with his ability to work."

Mac pointed one of the empty bottles toward Levi. "He got that girl in trouble and then turned tail and ran. We don't need his kind of help around here."

Joanna snorted. "Takes two to make trouble, Mac, and the LeeAnna Pearson I know isn't above getting herself—and plenty of others around her—into a little trouble."

Why was Joanna defending him? She didn't even know him—and those who did had never bothered doing it. Levi frowned. His mother hadn't even done it.

With a shake of his head, Mac set the armload of bottles in a pile by the cabin steps. "Doesn't make him any less responsible."

"I don't care. He's here, he's willing, and he's able—that's all that matters right now. He can deal with LeeAnna on his own time." Joanna led them back toward the corral where they'd left their horses. "When roundup's over, we'll have the luxury of being picky. Right now, we need help and he's all there is."

"But Jo, he's—"

"On the payroll," she said, with a note of finality.

Silence stretched between the three of them; Joanna and Mac stared each other down for long moments before Mac finally sighed and threw up his hands.

"So you're going ahead with the fence?" He rubbed his thick fingers over his face.

"Yes. You knew that."

"Your pa wouldn't want this, Joey. You know how he felt about fencing in the land."

Joanna's face turned the deepest shade of red Levi had ever seen. It almost bordered on purple. She wrapped her fingers around her horse's reins and turned to face her uncle.

"Yes, well, Pa's not here anymore, is he? If he were, I wouldn't be standing here in his clothes making decisions like this. And you wouldn't be all in a tizzy because I had to go and hire someone like Travers." She jerked her head toward Levi, sending her braid swishing from shoulder to shoulder.

If she weren't such a sight when she was mad, Levi might have been insulted.

"Jo." Mac's tone held more than just a little warning, but she stopped him with a raised hand.

Maybe the stories of Joanna McCaine were true—maybe she did rule with an iron fist. Because from the look falling over Mac's face, this argument was long over. Mac McCaine didn't lose arguments; it just wasn't done. Yet there he stood, facing down his niece and losing—badly.

"He's the only available body we can find to work and having him here will get you back where you belong—out from under foot and back with the herd."

"But . . ."

"I've made my decision, Mac." Then, as he'd seen her do earlier, Joanna mounted her horse in one graceful motion.

"Where are you going?" Mac asked, his voice still tight.

"Check on Clay. Put Travers to work and I'll see you at supper. He can do Walt's job until Chuck delivers the wire for the fence. Should be here in a couple days."

She shot a final warning look at both of them before kneeing her animal forward. "Try not to kill each other while I'm gone."

She rode off in the same direction as Clay while Levi stood watching her go.

"Is she always like that?" he asked, more to himself than Mac, since the only response he expected from Mac was a bullet between the eyes.

With a defeated sigh, Mac swiped the back of his hand over his mouth and shot a final glare at his niece's back before turning to Levi. "You mean stubborn?"

"Yeah, but . . ."

"Bossy?"

"Yeah . . ."

"Ornery?"

Levi snickered. "There's just something about her—what the hell is it?"

Mac jabbed a gloved finger at him. "You keep the hell away from her, Travers. She'll have you for breakfast. And if she doesn't, I will!" His voice lowered, but the warning remained. "Jo isn't like other girls."

Levi chuckled. "I noticed."

"Well stop noticing! That there's one woman you'd do well to leave alone." Mac spat on the ground and turned toward the barn, mumbling to himself. "Don't know why I let her grind me—she's never gonna change."

A low whistle escaped Levi's lips. "Why would you want her to?"

Chapter 3

Jo cursed up at the old windmill. Seemed like she'd just fixed the damned thing, but judging from the way the wheel was spinning so violently, she was going to have to climb up there again.

If only she didn't have to climb so high. People were inventing things all the time nowadays—so why couldn't someone invent a better way to fix a damned windmill? A way that wouldn't force her to climb thirty feet straight up.

She could go get Travers to do it. In fact, she *should* go get him. But she wouldn't. No way would she give him the satisfaction of thinking she couldn't handle her own damned ranch.

Besides, he didn't need to know she'd rather face down a den of rattlesnakes than climb that ladder. That was her own business.

She rode back to the stable, saddled a second horse, and searched around until she found Newt. The old man was perched on an upturned pail in the barn next to one of the milk cows that he'd somehow managed to tie to a rail.

But from the looks of things, his crippled fingers weren't about to get any milk from that udder—no matter how full it was, or how loud the cow bawled.

"Dammit, girl, just be still." Almost-white hair poked out from beneath his hat and his thin gray whiskers gave his weathered face a look of gruffness—like he needed any more of that.

If it weren't for his arthritis, he'd be the most sought-after ranch hand in the county. And even though he couldn't do most of the jobs that needed to be done at the Double M, Jo insisted he stay on. After all, it had been Newt who'd comforted her after her mama died; Newt who'd finally convinced her to accept Ginny and Mac onto the ranch; and Newt who'd stayed on even after Papa died and Jo had taken over.

"Hey Newt. I could use your help with something." Jo squatted next to him, gently eased his hands away, and pumped the teats just as he'd taught her so many years ago. Milk sprayed into the bucket in sharp bursts.

"Not so fast," he growled. "Find your rhythm. There you go."

Jo hid her smile as best she could. Newt might be old and tired, but he held firm to his code—do the job right or get the hell out of the way and let him do it.

"I have to fix that sucker rod again, and I need your help." Jo gave the cow's flank a gentle pat, eased the bucket out from beneath the beast, and set it aside. "All I need you to do is control the horses while I haul up the rod and—"

"I know what needs to be done." Newt fumbled with the rope for a long moment before he finally freed the cow and walked her back to her stall. "Just 'cuz I can't do it no more don't mean I don't know how."

"Newt . . ." Jo stopped. Nothing she could say would make it any better. "You get the tools and I'll run this up to Ginny. Meet you outside."

His only response was a loud grunt.

Half an hour later, they had the horses tied to the block and tackle and Jo was on her way up the thirty-foot ladder.

"Mac ain't gonna like this," Newt muttered. "He ain't gonna like this at all."

Jo swallowed her reply. It was Mac's fault she was up there in the first place. He was even more scared of heights than she was, otherwise she'd sure as hell have him up there doing it instead.

She hauled up the joint rod, fished around for what seemed like forever before she finally hooked up the plunger, then set to repairing the break.

Cattle milled below, bawling loudly.

"These here animals ain't sounding too happy, Jo." Newt didn't sound nervous—just impatient.

"I'm working as fast as I can, Newt. It's not exactly easy, you know."

"Don't start preaching to me about how hard it is, missy. I been fixing windmills longer 'n you been breathin'."

"I know, I know."

"Then you know, too, that you shoulda damn well got someone else to do this. I know you got that Travers fella workin' here now. He coulda done it."

Jo risked a glance down. "You know about Travers already?"

"For God's sake, girl, don't look down." Newt shook his head. "Didn't I teach you nothin'?"

Jo turned her attention back to the rod. "How'd you find out so fast?"

"Clay done told me." He almost sounded hurt. "Woulda been nice to hear it from you or Mac," he continued, "but no, I gotta hear it from the runt."

"Sorry, Newt—but things are a little crazy around here, in case you didn't notice."

"I noticed all right," he growled. "An' you think hiring Travers is gonna make them *less* crazy?"

Jo shrugged. "No." She set the mill to spinning again and began the long climb down. "All I'm thinking is that he can ease some of the workload for a while."

He clicked his tongue. "You're foolin' yourself, girl. Hiring a cur like him is just asking for more trouble."

The sounds of an approaching wagon turned their attention from the mill.

"And speakin' of trouble," Newt muttered, shaking his head.

Carrie pulled to a stop beside the other horses. As she fluffed her hair and straightened her skirts, she didn't even look at Jo or Newt.

"I thought Mr. Travers might be with you."

"He's not." Jo stepped to the ground and peeled her gloves off finger by finger. "And don't bother going looking for him, either. He's busy."

"But I brought lemonade." Carrie searched the surrounding land, as though surely Travers would pop out from behind a tree at any moment.

"Good," Newt said, stepping forward. "I'm damn near parched."

"Me, too." Jo chuckled as she lifted the cup and jug of cool lemonade from the seat beside Carrie and offered them first to Newt.

When he'd had his fill, he passed her the cup and she drank more than she normally would have—just to prickle Carrie. She set the near empty jug on the seat and wiped the back of her hand across her mouth.

"Go home, Carrie. Leave Travers alone."

"You're such a poop, Joanna," Carrie said, obviously unmoved by Jo's warning. "I just wanted to take him some refreshment."

"He's got a canteen," Newt said. "An' if he don't, that's his problem. Not yours."

He and Jo set about collecting the tools and unhitching the horses from the blocks. Carrie remained where she was, shading her eyes with one hand while keeping a firm grip on the reins with the other. Even Carrie wasn't stupid enough to let down her guard around the milling cattle.

"Will he be joining us for supper?" she asked.

"Who?" Jo and Newt both asked at the same time, then grinned at each other.

"Mr. Travers." Carrie's tone was becoming increasingly annoyed.

Newt eyed Jo for a minute, then sighed and clicked his tongue.

"Yes," Jo answered slowly. "That was part of our agreement. He'll eat his meals with us, Carrie, but if you think for one minute about carrying on—"

"I don't know what you mean." Carrie didn't even pretend to look offended.

Newt lifted the heavier tools into the buggy beside Carrie and frowned at her.

"I'm leavin'." He turned back to Jo. "Unless there's something else?"

"No, that's it. Thanks, Newt."

He climbed up into his saddle, nodded at Jo, and urged his horse back toward the yard.

When Carrie clicked to her horse, Jo took the animal by the bridle and looked up at her sister.

"I mean it, Carrie. Levi Travers is not someone you want to be toying with."

"I'm not toying with him, Joanna." Carrie rolled her eyes dramatically. "He's merely a means to an end for me and I intend to make good use of him."

"What are you talking about?"

Carrie smiled sweetly. "San Francisco. That's what I'm talking about."

"Wha . . ?"

"Milly Jean told me he's on his way there, and I intend to go with him." She looked so smug, it took all Jo's control not to leap up into the buggy and slap her.

"Are you out of your mind?" Jo managed to keep from yelling—but barely. "We're not going to let you go to San Francisco."

"Yes," Carrie answered dryly, "I know. You've made it perfectly clear where you will and will not allow me to go. But I'm old enough to make my own decisions now, Joanna. And I'm going."

Why did she have to be so infuriating? Why couldn't she go along with things—just once?

"You're not going." Jo released the reins so she could collect the remaining tools.

"Yes," Carrie answered, her voice more confident than Jo had ever heard, "I am."

"And what, exactly, are you going to do when you get there?"

"I don't care. As long as it has nothing to do with cows, chickens, or dirt."

"Where will you stay? You'll need to get a job."

Carrie shrugged, but there wasn't a trace of indecision in her voice. "I've already written Aunt Meredith and she's agreed to let me stay with her."

"Aunt Meredith?" Jo choked. "But she's an actress!" Aunt Ginny would die a thousand deaths at the thought of Carrie living with an actress.

"Yes," Carrie sniffed, "I'm well aware of her occupation, Joanna. Unlike you, however, I am not such a snob. It doesn't matter to me, as long as I have a place to sleep until I find something else."

"But *Aunt Meredith?*"

"Yes." She swatted at a mosquito. "Do you have a better suggestion?"

"You're damned right I do." But Carrie wasn't listening. She never did. "If you're so set on leaving, why don't we sit down with Mac and Ginny tonight and talk it over? I'm sure *if* we can find suitable arrangements for you, we'd all be more willing to let you go."

The look in Carrie's sky-blue eyes chilled Jo clear down to her toes.

"I really don't care if you're willing to 'let me go' or not," she said. "I'm going. I have some money saved and since Mr. Travers is heading that way anyway, I can use him as my traveling companion to ward off any trouble."

"*Ward off trouble?*" Jo dropped the gear she was holding and grabbed Carrie's horse again. "Do you have any idea what kind of trouble a man like Travers could *cause*? Think of your reputation, Carrie."

"Pish. San Francisco is big enough that no one will pay any mind to me arriving with the man and then parting ways. It'll be forgotten faster than yesterday's breakfast."

"That's easy for you to say, Carrie," Jo began, "but you have no idea what Travers is like. How do you know he won't . . . I mean, how can you be sure your reputation will still be intact by the time you reach Aunt Meredith's?"

"Let go, Joanna. I need to get back." Before Jo could step out of the way, Carrie snapped the reins against the animal's back and sent it off in the same direction Newt had gone.

Jo watched the buggy bounce away, silently cursing everything around her. Carrie in San Francisco with Levi Travers. What would Mama think of *that*?

"I'm not waiting anymore. Let's eat." Jo passed the carrots to Carrie who took half a spoonful and passed the bowl on.

Ginny set it down without taking any, a small frown puckered her brow. "A few more minutes won't make any difference."

"If they can't get themselves to the table on time, Ginny, that's their fault." With her fork jabbed into a huge piece of ham, Jo shrugged. "I'm hungry so I'm going to eat. You do what you like."

She continued to pile food on her plate while Ginny's remained empty. Carrie picked at her carrots without eating anything. For long minutes, the only sound was Jo's knife and fork scraping against her plate. The clock on the window ledge slowly ticked off the minutes and still no one spoke.

Just as well. Better for the digestion, that's what Mama used to say, anyway.

Jo had just stuffed her last forkful of potatoes into her mouth when the door opened and the two men came in, both of them stiff and tense.

Lines etched around Mac's pale blue eyes, and his mouth pinched together in a tight line. Travers didn't look much happier. The twinkle she'd watched dance in his eyes earlier had disappeared and his jaw clenched so tight, it made her own hurt just to look at him.

"Sorry, Gin," Mac offered, giving her a quick kiss on the cheek. "We had the darndest time herding one of the bulls. He was being as pigheaded as . . . well—"

"Joanna?" Carrie's suggestion was met with howls of laughter from both Mac and Travers. At least Ginny had the decency to hide her smile behind her napkin.

The tension drained from both Mac's and Travers's faces. Jo shot them each a glare before swallowing the thick lump of potatoes still in her mouth.

As the two men took their seats, Mac winked across the table at Jo and handed Travers the bowl of carrots. "I see some of you had the good manners to wait for us, this being Travers's first meal here and all."

His last, too, Jo mused, if he didn't stop staring at Carrie.

"I'm sure you must be famished, Mr. Travers,"

Carrie gushed as she lifted the meat platter and offered it to him.

"Allow me." He speared two big pieces of ham, passed the plate to Mac, then flashed her a bright smile. "Did you do the cooking tonight, Miss Carrie?"

"No, but I made pie." With a flutter of her lashes and a sugar-sweet smile, Carrie pointed toward the sideboard where the steaming pie sat cooling.

Jo rolled her eyes. She should have known it wouldn't just be Travers she need worry about—it was going to be Carrie who'd give her the most grief. That girl would flirt with anything in pants, except, of course, Jo. And now that she had it in her head to go west with Travers, there'd be no telling what she'd do.

"I see you got over your snit." Jo looked pointedly at her uncle, who offered no explanation other than a shrug.

She caught Travers looking at her, a small smile tugging at his lips. And even when he spoke to the others, his eyes kept shifting back to look at her.

"Smells awfully good," he said as he heaped more on his plate and nodded his thanks to Ginny. His hair fell in chestnut waves around his collar and over his forehead. Jo's fingers itched to brush it out of his face, but no sooner had she pushed the thought away than he did it himself—again flashing her a bright grin.

"Miss Ginny," he said, "I'm told you're the best cook in the county."

Before Ginny could respond, Carrie puffed up like a peacock.

"I'm learning all her secrets," she said. "I believe

every lady should know how to cook. After all, it's the way to a man's heart, isn't it?" Her voice dripped with enough sweetness to make everyone else's teeth ache.

"Or a man's coffin, if you're cooking," Jo muttered into her napkin.

Travers choked on his ham, swallowed a huge gulp of water, then grinned at Jo. Good God—had he heard her? No one else seemed to. Or maybe they were just used to it by now.

Carrie's lips curled into a forced smile. "I'm still learning, of course, but I help out when I can. Like with the pie." Again, she pointed toward the sideboard.

Jo swallowed her retort. No point in dragging this conversation on any longer. If Carrie wanted Travers to think she was a good cook, that was her business. And if he was stupid enough to believe her, that'd be a lesson he'd long remember.

"Do you cook, Miss Joanna?" Travers leaned back in his chair, a knowing grin daring her to answer.

With her mouth full of carrots, Jo's only answer was a glare hot enough to cook his hide.

Mac swallowed and nodded toward Jo. "Joey doesn't have time to cook. She's got a ranch to run."

"So if Joanna runs the ranch and Ginny does the cooking," Travers said, turning to Carrie, "what is it that you do?"

"She handles the books," Mac answered over his next forkful of carrots. "Smart as a whip, that girl."

"Mac." Ginny shook her head briefly as color flooded Carrie's cheeks.

"What? It's the truth."

"Yeah." Jo snorted. "But she doesn't like people

knowing it. She'd rather have people think she's pretty." She could feel Carrie's heated glare, but for reasons she didn't want to think about, Jo couldn't stop herself. "After all, men don't like smart girls, do they, Carrie?"

"Joanna!" Carrie's eyes looked like they were going to pop out of their sockets any second. "I'm sure Mr. Travers isn't interested in any of this."

"Actually," Travers interrupted, his grin becoming even larger, "I am." He winked at Jo. "In all your years, you never learned to cook at all? Not even a pie?"

Damn that grin of his.

She tried to shrug it off, but a little voice inside her head began whispering warnings. "Never had the need. Or the time to learn."

"Ever thought about switching places for a couple days?"

She wouldn't change places with Carrie for all the longhorns in Texas.

"Oh, no," Carrie said, toying with her choker. "I'm a little nervous around all those cows."

"Cattle," Jo ground out. Carrie ignored her, and Travers seemed to enjoy that even more.

"And Joanna," Carrie continued, "well, she can't sit still for any longer than it takes to inhale her meal, so she'd be of no use in the house at all."

As Jo opened her mouth to fire back, Mac's hand closed around her arm. A simple shake of his head made her slam her mouth shut again. For now.

Carrie pressed her napkin against her mouth, then smoothed back her hair. "I'm more of what you'd call an organizer. I help arrange the annual Isabella McCaine Fund-raising Ball."

"Yeah," Jo snorted again. "Takes her a whole year to plan one party."

"Joanna Belle McCaine!" Ginny warned. "You will stop making those noises at my table."

Carrie flashed Jo a triumphant look, then continued. "It's an enormous undertaking to bring the event together," she said, giving her ringlets a small toss. "Exhausting, really, but it's such a rewarding experience."

"Ha!" Jo had to cover her mouth with her napkin to keep the food from flying out. "Exhausting? Is that what you call it? I have another word for it—"

"Now, Joanna," Ginny began, her voice taking on the "poor baby" tone it always did when she spoke about Carrie. "You know she doesn't have the strength you do." She turned to Levi. "She was such a sickly little girl. It's a wonder she's survived this long."

"She hasn't been sick for more than ten years." Jo wiped up her plate with a piece of bread and smirked. "But heaven forbid one of Carrie's precious ringlets gets put out of place—whatever would we do?"

"Why, I never!" Carrie pushed back from the table and threw her napkin down with more theatrics than Jo had witnessed in a while.

"No," Jo agreed, "and you probably never will, either."

An exaggerated flounce sent layers of silk shimmering around her as Carrie whooshed out of the kitchen and up to her room, slamming the door hard enough to rattle the windows.

Ginny tucked her napkin under the edge of her plate and hurried after her niece. Jo just shook her head—that girl had been spoiled from the moment she was born, first by Mama and Papa and now by Ginny and Mac. Not that she was jealous, mind you. She didn't want or need that much attention.

"Well," Mac sighed. "Welcome to the Crazy McCaine's supper table, Travers. Don't know what Joey's paying you to be here, but I'd wager you're having second thoughts now."

Jo didn't wait to hear his response. She stormed out of the kitchen and headed back to the stable. As long as there was light, there was work to be done, and she much preferred the work to listening to anything else about Carrie.

Ankle-deep in horse dung, with a pitchfork in hand and a dusty bandana tied around her mouth and nose, the last thing in the world Jo expected— or wanted—was company. The stable was her sanctuary, the one place no one else, except Mac, dared set foot after supper for fear of being put to work.

The creak of the door didn't give her a moment's pause, however. She knew who it was even before she turned around. Travers leaned against the stall door with that damned smile of his making her mind trip over its next thought.

"You were a little hard on her, don't you think?"

He had to be kidding. Jo didn't even bother to remove her bandana. "Stay out of it, Travers."

A low chuckle. "It's a little hard when you carry on like that at the supper table."

"The way *I* carry on?" Jo fought the urge to snort. "And I guess Carrie's performance had nothing to do with it. I should have known you'd take her side." She shook her head. "Everyone else does."

"I didn't know there were sides to take." His velvety eyes sparkled in the lantern light. "All I said was . . ."

"I heard what you said." She threw down the pitchfork and pushed past him. Where the hell was that wheelbarrow? "So why aren't you up there with Ginny, comforting poor little Carrie and her ruffled ringlets? I'm sure she'd love that."

"What are you mad at me for?"

Frustration burned in her belly as Jo whirled around and jabbed a finger at him. "Because you make me sick! You're such a . . . a man!"

Despite her fury, he had the nerve to laugh at her. "Nice of you to notice."

She yanked the bandana down a little so it hung around her chin. "You're all the same—all you see, all you want, is a woman who sits like a china doll and does nothing but bat her eyelashes and swish her skirts." She did her best imitation of Carrie and ended it with a good loud snort.

His smile deepened until both his cheeks dimpled. "That denim just doesn't swish quite right, does it?"

"Can't you see what she's doing? Pretending to be so very ladylike and charming, with that sugary-sweet voice . . . ugh—forget it."

"So I take it you and your sister have different outlooks on most things?"

"Carrie's only concern is herself."

Travers shrugged indifferently. He obviously didn't see the problem with what Jo had just said. Probably because his only concern was himself, too.

With her arms waving madly, she pointed out every stall in the stable. "See these? Someone has to clean them out. Dirty stalls mean sick horses. Without horses, we have no transportation, no way to herd the damned cattle that pay our bills." She pushed into the end stall, yanked the wheelbarrow out, and stomped back. "Think darling little Carrie would ever stoop to do it? Not a chance in hell. Mac's got too much work as it is and poor Newt can barely hold the pitchfork. But with three hands gone . . ."

"Four." He took a step closer.

"Right. With four hands gone, who does that leave?"

Another step. "I guess that would leave you." With a slow tug, he pulled the bandana the rest of the way down, so it fell away from her face and hung around her neck.

"You're damn right it leaves me." Jo backed up. For some reason it was getting harder and harder to breathe. With every word, her anger subsided another little bit. "When was the last time I got to sit up in the house and read a book or plan a fancy party?"

Hell—she was whining. She hated whiners.

Another step. "I have no idea. When was the last time you wanted to do any of that?" A long, dark smudge crossed the front of his shirt and ran over his left forearm. Why was it so hard to look away from his arm? Sure, it was muscled and tanned golden brown, but who cared about stuff like that?

"I don't know." She swallowed, her voice a mere cackle. "What are you doing?"

"Nothing." He reached for the end of her braid and rubbed it gently between his fingers. "Just listening to you yell."

Damn, but her throat was dry. "I'm not yelling."

"You were." His eyes sparkled in the lantern light and that smile of his was making her knees tremble.

"I-I was mad."

"I noticed." His fingers pulled the ratty blue string from her hair and eased the braid apart.

"I'm not mad anymore." Her heart pounded against her ribs and echoed in her ears. She needed to step away, to slap him, to do something. Anything besides standing there, letting him touch her like that. Where was that damned pitchfork?

"I noticed that, too." Damn, but he smelled good; like a mixture of leather, soap, and sunshine.

"I . . ."

"Jo!" Mac's voice boomed through the open door. "You in there?"

Levi stepped away and Jo had to grab the nearest rail to steady herself.

"Uh, yeah," she forced out, her throat tight. "In here."

"What the hell . . ?" Mac stormed into the barn, then stopped when he saw Levi, his glare shifting between them. "Am I interrupting something?"

Jo choked out a dry laugh, her cheeks burning under his heated glare. "No, of course not."

"No," Levi agreed. "Not a thing."

One of the horses nickered softly, almost like he was disagreeing.

"What did you need?" She tucked her hair beneath her hat and steadied her knees. Damn that Travers— he'd tried to charm her! And damn herself—she'd almost let him.

"Carrie just told me you were working on the windmill today. Again."

Steam began to build in Jo's head. She should

have known Carrie would do whatever she could to get Jo in trouble, but if Mac thought he could waltz into *her* stable and tell her what she should and shouldn't be doing on *her* ranch, he had another thing coming.

"So? The sucker rod snapped again, and the blades looked like they were going to spin right off. It had to be fixed."

"By you." He crossed his arms over his chest and waited. Travers leaned back against the stall and grinned, though Jo found nothing amusing about this at all.

"Yes, by me. Who else? Clay?" She scoffed. "Or maybe darling Carrie would have come to help. Oh, that's right—she's too exhausted from writing out invitations."

"You could have found someone else to do it." Though the implication was clear, neither of them looked at Travers.

With a sigh even Carrie would have been proud of, Jo elbowed past him and retrieved her pitchfork.

"Yes," she said, "I probably could have. But in case you hadn't noticed, we're running a little thin on help these days. And in the time it would have taken me to go find someone else, I had it done myself."

"It's too dangerous." Mac's voice lowered to an even warning. "And why the hell would you put yourself through that, anyway—climbing all the—"

"Oh for goodness sake, Mac." No way would she let Travers in on her fear of heights. "I've been fixing that windmill since I was twelve."

"And how many times have you fallen?"

"I don't know." Four. "Doesn't matter anyway. It needed to be done. And it's a damn sight more enter-

taining than dealing with drunk employees or listening to stories about how frail our pretty little Carrie is."
Damn it, why did she have to bring that up again? "Besides, Newt was helping me."

Jo swallowed hard; why couldn't everyone just go
away and leave her be?

"You could have been hurt. Or killed."

With a loud snort, she tossed a forkful of muck
into the wheelbarrow. "I'm fine, the windmill's
fixed, and no one got hurt."

"This time." He stormed toward the door, then
turned. "Travers, I could use your help."

Travers nodded but made no move to follow. "Be
right there."

Jo shifted her position so her back was to him.
God help her if he flashed one of those damned
smiles again; she'd run the pitchfork clear through
him. She didn't have time for nonsense like that—
there was work to be done.

"Fixing sucker rods is a risky thing to do—especially when there's cattle milling around." Thank
goodness his voice came from a safe distance away.
"Were there?"

"There's always cattle around, Travers. In case
you hadn't noticed, it's a cattle ranch."

"You should have got me or Mac to do it."

She laughed again. She'd seen Mac try it once
and that had been all she needed to know she
could never ask him again. "Mac's just worried that
I'll get myself killed and then he'll have to take over
the ranch himself." She tossed another forkful of
muck just as the straw behind her crackled under
his weight. With the pitchfork at the ready, she
turned to face him.

"So why didn't you get me to do it?" He was close enough to touch, which was exactly why she positioned the fork between them, prongs up.

She shrugged, hoping her voice would carry the lie. "Didn't think of it."

There was that damned smile of his again. "Liar."

His scent surrounded her, muddled her thoughts.

"Next time," he said, his voice a low murmur, "come and get me. I'll fix the damned rod. And then you won't have to pretend."

"Pretend what?"

"That you're not scared to death of heights."

Jo's spine stiffened. Dammit—he was quicker than she'd thought. "I don't need to be taken care of, Travers."

"Levi."

"Fine. I don't need to be taken care of, *Levi.*" She rolled her eyes. She found herself doing that a lot around him.

"You might not need it, Miss Joanna," he began.

"Jo."

"Fine." It was his turn to roll his eyes. "You might not need it, *Jo,* but it'd sure be a nice change for you, wouldn't it?"

"Travers!" Mac's bellow made them both jump.

Jo cocked her brow at him and snickered. "Your mother's calling."

Travers tucked a strand of hair behind her ear, then tapped the tip of her nose. "We're not nearly done here, Miss Joanna."

"It's Jo." She forced a mocking smile. "And yes, we are. I make the decisions around here, Travers, and if I want to fix the damned windmill, I'll do it."

He leaned closer, but she shifted the fork to keep

him out of her space. "Nobody *wants* to fix those damned things." Another grin. "Besides, it's not the windmill we'll be talking about."

Jo shifted the fork again until the prongs touched his chin. "If you'll recall, I can't be charmed, so save your breath."

His low, throaty laugh caressed her ears. "Even snakes can be charmed. Just takes patience, that's all."

"I'm a snake?" she tipped her head to the side and opened her eyes wide in the best innocent look she could muster.

He chuckled. "I didn't say that."

"Uh, yes, you did."

He thought on that for a second.

"Okay, I did. But that's not what I meant." A wash of color crept up his face, making his grin even more tempting. "Just making the point that I've got enough patience for anything."

"Travers!" Mac bellowed again.

He backed out of the stall slowly, his eyes still focused on Jo's. "Patience," he repeated. "Something your uncle appears to lack."

Jo laughed as he turned and bolted for the door. It was a long time later before she was able to get back to her work, though. She'd never been one to believe any of that fluffy, bone-melting nonsense Carrie spoke of all the time—romance, love, seduction. Who had time?

But apparently time had nothing to do with it. She'd only known Travers for a few hours, yet whenever he came near, her brain turned to fluff and her bones did, in fact, feel as though they were melting. Too many hours in the sun—that had to be the reason.

Sure, he was nice looking. Okay, he was the best looking man she'd seen in a long while, even with that long hair of his. And sure, his smile knocked the starch clear out of her temper tantrum, but that didn't mean anything. He was a scoundrel of the worst kind.

A scoundrel who, despite his reputation, managed to stay within an inch of the law; a scoundrel who made her laugh just like he'd probably done with a hundred other women; a scoundrel who wanted to charm her. *Her*!

God only knew what he wanted to do with Carrie.

Chapter 4

"Chuck dropped off the first load of wire this morning." Joanna refilled her mug, then loaded it down with heaps of sugar. "So Travers and I'll get started on the fence today."

Levi only half listened as she and Mac nattered on about it, but for the most part, he was too busy studying the array of freckles across her nose. Mornings were the best time to see them—just after she'd washed her face and before the dust and grime from the ranch had a chance to dull them again.

There were lots of them, too, and scattered in no particular pattern.

He'd never figured freckles to be an attractive trait on a woman before. But on her . . . Levi shook his head clear. What was wrong with him, anyway? Since when did he ever think twice about something as boneheaded as a woman's freckles? There were a few other things he'd thought more than twice about, but freckles?

And this was Joanna, for crying out loud. Joanna who refused to have anything to do with frills or fanciness; Joanna who refused to be coddled or fawned over; and Joanna who refused to use her real name, preferring a man's name instead. How could any of that be the slightest bit attractive to him?

Hell if he could figure it out.

Carrie's sugary voice buzzed in his ear as it had at every meal for the last week. If it hadn't been for the way Joanna's eyes shot scorching emerald flames at both of them, Levi would have ignored Carrie altogether. But knowing it bothered the hell out of Joanna whenever he glanced Carrie's way was all the encouragement he needed to pay the younger girl any attention at all.

The McCaine girls were as different as night and day. Carrie about fell over herself trying to get his attention; she smiled and primped and spoke in those soft dainty tones girls were supposed to use. Joanna, on the other hand . . . well, she couldn't be more unlike Carrie if she tried.

She did all she could to avoid him, spent less time primping than most *men* did, and her voice—well, that voice wasn't near as soft or dainty as Carrie's. It was low, throaty, and sexy as hell.

Joanna was blunt, strong, and more often than not, plain mean to him, but any time he moved close to her, her pulse beat harder in her throat and she seemed to lick her lips a lot.

Levi swallowed hard. There was something about those lips . . . didn't look nearly as soft as Carrie's, not nearly as dainty or well-tended as Carrie's, either. But Lordy, what he wouldn't give to taste them. Just once.

Maybe twice.

Damn, he needed to get a grip. Joanna would

probably shoot him on the spot just for thinking these things. And if she didn't, Mac sure as hell would.

It must be the lack of Stella's comforts that had him thinking like a crazy man. He couldn't remember the last time he'd been so long without a woman's company and the stress of it was definitely beginning to show. He'd have to get himself into town right quick like—a good dose of Stella would straighten him out, all right.

Carrie's voice continued to buzz in his head and he tried his best to focus on it. But all she talked about was ribbons, lace, and some girl named Milly Jean Carlson. It was enough to drive a body mad. He'd much rather listen to Jo's throaty voice talk about the finer points of castration than hear one more sugar-coated word out of Carrie's painted mouth.

When her napkin slid to the floor again, Levi ignored it. He'd played along with her little game up until now, but if he bent over to pick the damned thing up, he'd have to look away from Joanna.

Carrie could pick up her own damned napkin. He had other things to do—like study the freckles on her sister's face. Or listen to Joanna talk about barbed wire, nails, and chopping down trees. Damn, she was sexy. Stella was gonna have to work double hard tonight.

"Travers!" Mac jabbed him in the shoulder with his fork.

"Hey!" Levi rubbed the injured spot. "What'd you do that for?"

Ginny smiled behind her hand, and Carrie's lip

came out in a pout, but Joanna's face turned the prettiest shade of pink Levi'd ever seen.

"If you're done making cow eyes at Jo," Mac said. "We've got work to do."

Levi straightened in his chair. "I don't make cow eyes at anyone."

"Right," Mac scoffed, "so what were we just talking about?"

Damn. "Well, hmmm." Levi scratched his chin and grinned. "I heard something about Chuck, and then . . ."

A painful moment passed with everyone staring at him, waiting for his answer. Everyone except Joanna. At long last, he grinned and shrugged.

"Exactly my point." Mac pulled Levi up by the back of his collar. "Let's get moo-ving."

Levi tripped over his chair, righted it, then winked at Ginny. "Thanks for the meal." He offered a brief nod to Carrie who continued to pout. He'd have to make it up to her. Couldn't have any of the McCaines thinking he wasn't interested in a pretty girl—what would that do to his reputation?

"Come on, Travers!" Mac shook his head before pulling Levi out the door behind him.

"Okay, okay, I'm coming."

They made for the stable, a strange quiet between them. Mac's boots kicked up a thick cloud of dust as he walked.

Levi pulled his gear off the rail and set about saddling his mare. He knew Mac was going to chew him out, but it was best to let the man start on his own. The less Levi said, the better, especially since he had no idea what the hell he'd say anyway.

Mac rested his elbows on the rail and stared at him. "You better not be playin' with her, Travers."

"Playin' with who?" he asked over a cough.

"Don't be stupid with me—you know exactly who I mean." He swiped his palm over his mouth. "She might come off as being tough as leather, but under all that grit, she's got herself a heart as soft as—"

"What the hell are you talking about?" Levi smoothed a blanket over his mare's back, then reached for his saddle, making sure he looked anywhere but at Mac.

"I'm talking about them cow eyes of yours." He positioned his own blanket and saddle on his horse, and kept talking. "You've got enough trouble on your plate as it is, what with Pearson's daughter and the money you owe him."

"Owed. It's in the past."

"What about his daughter?"

Levi's gut twisted. "What about her?"

Mac dropped the girth strap and let it dangle while he stared at Levi over his horse's back. "You know damn well what I'm talking about."

The twisting in Levi's belly tightened. "That's none of your business."

"It damn well is if you're planning on doing the same thing to my niece!"

Levi ran a hand down his mare's flank, then took a long moment to adjust the perfectly set girth. He could tell Mac the truth about LeeAnna Pearson, but why? Would Mac even believe him? Probably not—especially since he couldn't prove anything, which left it as his word against hers. Wasn't a man in the state who'd take the word of Levi Travers over that of a rich lady's.

And when it came to Joanna, Levi didn't have the first damned clue what he was planning to do with her. Hell, he could hardly think straight with her around.

The only plan he had—if he could call it that—was to try not to make a fool of himself before he could finish this job and get the hell out of town. San Francisco seemed twice as far away as it had a week ago.

Mac coaxed his horse to accept the bit, then said in a low voice, "I know about the other girls, too."

"What other girls?" Levi tried to sound innocent, then gave it up.

"Let's start with Stella."

"Good old Stella," he muttered. She hadn't crossed his mind in nearly a week, and yet today her name kept coming up—sort of like a bad penny. It's not that he wasn't interested in her anymore. No man, save for Mac, could resist Stella's particular talents, but he'd been too busy at the Double M to think much about her lately.

If he wasn't thinking about the job at hand, then he was thinking about the McCaine sisters; how could he get Carrie to shut up, and how could he get Joanna to talk to him about something other than cattle?

But maybe a night with Stella was just what he needed to put his mind back to normal.

"Then we're agreed." Mac cinched the strap, adjusted a crooked stirrup and waited for Levi to answer.

"Agreed on what?"

"You know damn well what." Mac pointed at him. "I've come to like you, Travers. You're not near the son of a bitch I thought you'd be. You're a hard worker, a helluva nice fella, and you've kept away from Carrie even though she's doing all she can to get your attention. But when all's said and done, you're still Levi Travers. And we both know what that means."

Levi knew all too well. He'd strived his whole life to build the reputation he had—work hard enough to keep your job, but not any harder; bet only what you can afford to lose, or just don't get caught cheating; love all women equally—but only one night each; and for God's sake, don't depend on anyone and don't let them depend on you.

It was a way of life that had served him well all these years, right up until he'd set foot on the Double M. In the last week, his ways had begun to lose their appeal. He couldn't rightly explain why, though, and that bothered the hell out of him.

Mac's voice cut into his thoughts. "All you want is a little fun and then you'll be on your way."

"You make it sound like a bad thing." He chuckled, but the hollow sound echoed in his ears. It didn't matter that Mac spoke the truth; it didn't sit right with Levi to have him point it out.

"Only when it affects Joey. She doesn't need anyone mucking up her life. What she needs is to get this damned fence built and to find some halfway dependable hands to help out around here."

Levi had nothing to say to that. After all, he had no intention of being anywhere near the Double M after the fence was up—and if Joanna needed dependable men, then she'd best look somewhere else.

"Besides," Mac said, "I'd have thought someone like you'd be after a girl more like Carrie—which would be worse since she's got all these romantic notions in that fool head of hers."

"Carrie's a little girl, for crying out loud." Levi led the horse outside and swung up into the saddle. "I'm not quite as bad as you're giving me credit for, Mac. I don't go after little girls."

"That there's no little girl, Travers. And neither's Joey."

"I see that." He couldn't help but smile. Joanna McCaine was nothing like the girls he was used to. Fact was, Joanna was no girl at all. She was all woman.

"So then I'll say it again. Don't be messing with her. You've got enough trouble with Pearson's girl—you don't want to be adding to it."

Levi turned his mount toward the range and kneed her into an easy trot. Mac rode up beside him, his weathered face stern and unyielding. Unease pooled in Levi's belly.

He probably shouldn't ask, but since it didn't really matter to him either way, there was no harm in it. "Why haven't they married? Surely there've been others . . ."

The laughter that shook Mac's shoulder pretty much answered that question.

"Carrie might like to play a little, but there's not a chance in hell she'd ever marry a fella from around here."

Levi frowned. "Why's that?"

"Our Carrie's a dreamer. She's got plans on going somewhere more exciting, with more people and less cattle."

"That sounds like Carrie." A few weeks ago, he'd have agreed wholeheartedly with her, too. But the longer he stayed at the Double M, the more he wondered about leaving.

He *would* leave, of course, but still—he wondered.

"Why hasn't she gone before now? There's trains heading out of here every day."

"Joey won't hear of it. Says Carrie's too young—too naïve—to be off on her own in a city."

"Naïve?" Levi choked. "Carrie?"

Mac shot him a look that told him everything he needed to know. Nobody in the family thought Carrie was naïve, they were all just scared to death of what she'd do once she was let loose.

After a long moment, Mac cleared his throat. "I hear from Ginny that Carrie's got it in her head to go with you to San Francisco."

"She *what*?" Several cows grazing nearby started at Levi's yelp. He gripped his saddle horn to keep from falling to the ground. "No way."

Wasn't a man alive who could travel such a distance with that kind of prattling and whining going on.

With a long shrug, Mac sighed. "She figures you could act as her escort since you're heading that way anyway."

"I hope you all told her that wasn't gonna happen."

"Joey told her, all right," he said with a nod. "Made it good and clear that there was no way she'd let Carrie travel halfway across the country with *you*, but we don't have much say in the matter anymore."

"Why's that?" Levi forced the insult to the back of his mind. He should be glad Joanna didn't want her sister traveling with him.

"Carrie's near a grown woman, Travers. There's not much we can do if she decides she's going."

"You could lock her in her room," Levi offered with a short chuckle.

"Believe me," Mac sighed, "Joey's tried just about everything. But Carrie's determined."

They rode in silence for a moment, a small knot in Levi's stomach getting tighter and tighter.

"I won't do it, Mac," he said. "No matter what she does or how often she asks, I won't take her west with me."

Though he didn't respond, Mac's brow raised in question, making Levi laugh.

"I can't believe I'm saying that, either," he said. "But despite what I've given people to think of me, I'm not that much of a sonuvabitch." He sobered, swallowed, and forced the words out; words he'd never imagined himself saying. "I've got too much respect for you, Mac. I won't be the one to ruin her—she's going to have to find someone else to do that for her."

It was Mac's turn to laugh, though he sure didn't sound like he thought anything was funny. "That's what worries me. Carrie's too pretty for her own good. She'll sure as shootin' get herself into some kind of trouble out on her own.

"She's never been on her own, never had to work a day in her life."

"And whose fault is that?" Levi asked, then immediately regretted it. Who was he to judge anyone? But Mac laughed again.

"Guess we're all a little guilty on that one. I just wish she was a little more sensible, a little more like Joey."

Joanna. Levi's knuckles whitened around the pommel. He glanced around casually, trying to pay attention to the land around him—the huge cottonwoods, the way the cattle moved, anything else but the way Mac stared at him, waiting for him to ask the question they both knew he wanted to ask.

The sun's heat blazed through his shirt, yet the sweat that trickled down his spine was anything but warm. He scratched behind his horse's ear, then rubbed her neck. When he couldn't stand the silence anymore, he shifted in his saddle and swallowed hard. Twice.

"And why hasn't Joanna married yet?"

With a drawn-out sigh, Mac scrubbed his face with his left hand.

"Joey's different."

Different? Levi fought the urge to roll his eyes. Joanna was more than just different. She was . . . well . . . how the hell could anyone explain her?

"There's not a man in the county—probably the whole state—who was ever brave enough to tangle with a wildcat like her. She's mean and ornery and about as friendly as a peeled rattler, in case you hadn't noticed." He laughed lightly, but stopped when he faced Levi.

"'Sides, once anyone gets a look at Carrie, they pretty much forget all about Joey."

Words died on Levi's lips. He could see how that would happen—Carrie was about the prettiest little thing he'd ever seen. But still, there was something about Joanna that went beyond being pretty. Hell, it went beyond a lot of things.

Mac's shoulders lifted in a tired shrug. "A woman like Joey needs a strong man—one who ain't afraid of her. But she also deserves a good, honest man who'll respect who she is and love her despite of it."

"And I'm none of those things, is that what you're saying?" Why couldn't he keep his mouth shut? Of course he wasn't any of those things—and they both knew it.

Mac shrugged again. Why did that irritate Levi so much?

"Have you seen me do anything out of line since I've been here?" he asked.

"Nope."

"Seen any girls hanging around my cabin? Hell—have you even seen any girls on the ranch—other than your nieces?"

"Nope. But you've only been here a short while, Travers. Gonna take a little longer than that to prove you've changed your stripes, is all." Mac took a long drink from his canteen. "Told you before, I've come to like you, but that don't count for spit when it comes to Joey. There's lots of folks 'round here that I like, but I wouldn't want to see any of them hook up with her, either.

"You got yourself a reputation and until you prove otherwise, I don't think you're near good enough for her. Not even close."

"That's not really for you to decide, is it?" Anger coiled deep in his belly. Or was it fear?

Mac shrugged. "Nope, I guess it's not."

Silence hung between them like a noose. The muscle along Mac's jaw twitched, his mouth turned in a deep frown.

"Does this mean you're thinkin' about courtin' our Joey?"

"No," Levi answered, maybe a little too quickly.

Mac didn't look the slightest bit convinced.

"Besides," Levi shifted in his saddle and grinned,

"Joanna's not going to let someone like me get away with anything."

"Prob'ly true," Mac nodded. "But I'm still gonna be keeping an eye on things. If you even think about hurting our Joey, I'll hunt you down like a mangy dog, Travers. Pearson and his boys'll seem like a bunch of quilt-sewing old women next to me. Mark my words on that one."

"Consider them marked."

So Mac didn't think he was good enough for Joanna. A week ago, that wouldn't have mattered a stitch to Levi. Today it bothered the hell out of him.

Chapter 5

That afternoon, after sending Mac out to the herd, Jo and Levi set about fencing in the ranch. Jo had never strung barbed wire, but apparently Travers had—which gave her ample reason to watch him work.

Starting at the barn, he paced out the distance between stakes and hammered them into the ground. He then worked the wire around them, attached the guy wires to boulders, and buried those deep in the ground.

He put everything he had into the job until it was done—and done right. Despite what everyone said about him, he was a damn hard worker and never backed away from any job, even when she'd sent him to help Clay collect dried patties yesterday.

Jo had to admit he was something to watch—the way he swung the ax with perfect accuracy, the way his muscles flexed beneath his shirt, and the way he winked at her every time he caught her watching.

It's not like she was enjoying herself, standing there in the heat of the day watching him work. It was something she had to do in order to learn. It just so happened she was a slow learner when it came to fencing.

When she'd watched as long as she could, Jo had Clay help her load a roll of wire and the other tools she'd need into the wagon and they rode off across the yard. No point in her and Levi working the same area; she'd never get the work done with that kind of distraction.

Jo pulled the tools out of the wagon bed and nodded toward the horses.

"Take them back to the stable and give them some water."

Clay nodded, his eyes solemn. He accepted each job she gave him with determination and pride, whether it was tending a litter of abandoned pups or collecting patties for fuel. As he set to work on the harness, Jo smiled.

"And Clay?"

"Yes, ma'am?"

"You be sure to tell Newt I said you could have an extra helping of dessert tonight."

A huge grin split the boy's face. "Yes, ma'am!"

Minutes later, he was leading the animals away, whistling.

Jo rolled up her sleeves, picked up the ax, and took aim at an old fallen cottonwood. As she'd seen Levi do, she chopped the trunk into long, even stakes and piled them beside the wagon. The wood split easily enough, but with the constant swinging, it wasn't long before her shoulders began to ache and her teeth rattled at each chop.

With a good sized stack of posts ready to use, she leaned back against the wagon and uncorked her canteen. Three long swallows later, it was half empty and she wasn't near as parched as she had been a minute before.

Jo pulled off her hat, leaned her head back, and poured the rest of the water over her face, leaving the liquid gold to run down her cheeks and into her ears.

"Hi." Travers's voice jerked her back to her senses. She pulled upright, blinking hard against the water that had pooled over her closed eyes.

How on earth did he get there? Jo was never one to be caught off guard, especially out on the ranch, but he'd walked right up to the wagon without her knowing. She'd need to be more attentive from now on.

She tipped the empty canteen into her mouth, wishing she had one drop left to ease the sudden dryness in her throat again.

"Need some help?" he asked, his gaze drifting from the canteen to her mouth.

"Got some?" She moved away from the wagon, shielding her eyes from the sun, and watched him approach. He moved like a cat about to pounce, with a sly little grin and a gaze that sent goose-bumps racing down her sun-baked arms.

"Some what?" His voice was low, deep, and all too alluring for her liking.

With the best disinterested look she could muster, she wiped a droplet from her lashes. "Water. I'm talking about water."

"I'm not." A strange look simmered in his eyes. She couldn't quite place it, but it made every last one of her nerves twitch. What were they talking about, anyway?

"You're not what?" she croaked.

He slinked closer, his gaze moving over her face, taking in every drop that slid from her nose and chin. "I'm not talking about water." With his next step, they stood toe to toe, his face a mere breath away.

If she'd wanted to, she could have leaned in and kissed him; could have pushed his hat off, filled her hands with that long dark hair, and held him long enough to discover what those rough, teasing lips tasted like once and for all.

If she'd wanted to.

"What were you talking about?" Why was she whispering? And why did it feel like a butterfly was fluttering its feather-soft wings over her heart? He was trying to charm her and she wouldn't stand for it. She'd back away . . . any second now.

He moved his face next to hers until they were cheek to cheek and his lips, those same rough, teasing lips, were brushing against her ear. Her lids drifted closed as he whispered against her skin.

"I was talking about the fence."

Jo's eyes flew open and she shoved him back, her face even hotter than before she'd splashed it with water. Travers leaned against the wagon, his arms crossed over his chest and a smug smile on his face.

"No, I don't need your help," she huffed. "What I do need is more water."

She jammed her hat on her head before tugging on her gloves and shoving past him to the back of the wagon.

"Dropped my canteen in the shade." He indicated the other side of the wagon. "Help yourself."

She started to sneer and then gave up. What was

the point, anyway? It'd just prove that he was, in fact, getting to her. She pulled the top from his canteen and guzzled half the water before corking it again.

Travers moved to the chopped-up tree and her pile of stakes, and was regarding them with a strange look on his face.

"Did you do all this?"

"No. Leprechauns came running out from behind the barn and did it for me." She pointed off toward the open range. "They ran like hell the second they heard you coming, though."

He ignored her. "That's a lot of chopping for a little thing like you." Gone was the smug little smile. Was he actually concerned? "You might want to take a break for a minute."

"I'm not a little thing and I just had a break." She had no sooner begun to tug the roll of wire from the wagon than he was beside her.

"Let me do that."

"I can manage just fine, Travers."

"Levi." His arms, bare from wrists to elbows, distracted her for a minute. A dozen or so new scratches stained his golden brown skin—no doubt a result of the barbed wire. God knew Jo had seen cuts and scrapes a lot worse than these; hell, she had worse ones on her own arms, but this was the first time she'd thought about tending anyone else's.

She shook her head clear and tugged the roll again. "Fine, *Levi*. In case I haven't made myself clear before this, I don't need to be coddled."

The roll bumped to the ground at their feet.

"I'm not coddling," he said, "I'm helping. There's a difference."

"Either way, it's not going to work." She had to give him credit for actually looking confused.

"What's not going to work?"

"I'm not going to turn into a brainless idiot because you show off your muscles and smile your little smile at me."

"No?" He flashed her that very smile.

"No." Well, maybe.

"But you said it was dazzling." With a quick wink, he picked up a stake and hammered it into the ground in four quick whacks. Would have taken her at least twice that.

She unrolled a length of wire with her gloved hands and twisted the end around the first stake. "Oh, it's dazzling all right. There's no question you're a nice looking man, Travers."

"Levi."

With a long roll of her eyes, she proceeded to string the wire along to the next stake while he continued to pace out and hammer more in. "My point is that a pretty smile isn't going to get you anything from me."

His brown eyes danced with his laughter. "And what is it you think I'm after?"

She shrugged. "Whatever you can get."

He stopped working for a moment and challenged her with a quirk of his brow. "And what *can* I get, Miss Joanna?"

Jo pretended to consider his question for a moment. "I've got a pretty good right hook I'd be happy to show you."

Travers's deep laughter filled the air around her. "Not exactly what I had in mind."

"Didn't think so." She unwound another length

of wire. "But you'll have to go see Stella for what you've got in mind."

"Stella?" He actually looked surprised, maybe even a little shocked.

"Come on, Travers." Jo snorted. "You've been out here over a week and not been back to Lefty's once. I reckon you must be missing Stella's company something awful by now."

"You've been keeping track of me?" He waggled his eyebrows, then whacked another stake into the ground.

"Don't be thinking you're special," she said as she pinched the wire around the next stake. "I make it my business to know where my hands are at all times." Sure, it was a lie, but he didn't need to know that.

"So do I." His hands closed around her waist, then turned her to face him.

"What are you doing?" she forced her voice steady, despite the quake that rattled her bones.

A low chuckle. "I'm making it my business to know where my hands are at all times." He pulled her closer, his face hovering just above hers.

Could he feel her heart pounding against her ribs? Did he hear the tremor in her voice? Damn, but her mouth was dry.

"Very funny, Travers." She licked her lips quickly and pushed against his hands, but he wouldn't be moved. And for a minute, she was glad for that. His fingers tightened through her belt loops, which somehow caused a tightening in her belly. "L-let go."

"Why?" His eyes warmed like golden fire, his voice a mere whisper, and dammit he smelled good—sunshine, leather, and something Jo could only describe as all male. Whatever it was, it was driving her crazy.

"B-because you're being an idiot." She couldn't stop staring at his mouth. What would it feel like to have him kiss her right there in the middle of the day, out behind the barn with the sun scorching their backs and her fingers wound through that hair of his?

"I can't help it," he murmured. "You have that effect on me."

His face lowered until the side of his nose brushed against hers. He was going to kiss her. Jo tried to swallow the panic rising in her throat, but couldn't manage to do even that. She had to stop him. One kiss would lead to another, and then before she knew it, he'd have her under his spell. And, God help her, she would not be his next LeeAnna Pearson.

She forced her mouth into a harsh grin and shoved his hands away. "No, Travers. You're a big enough idiot without any help from me."

The fire in his eyes smoldered a moment longer, then he stepped back, blowing a long breath over his bottom lip.

"Can't blame a man for trying." He retrieved the hammer and another stake and set back to work.

"No, but it does make a girl wonder." Jo slipped her gloves off and pretended to study them.

"'Bout what?" He didn't look at her, which was just as well.

"Why you bother. What do you think you're going to gain?" What was she doing? She did *not* want to have this conversation. She didn't even care why he bothered, so why ask?

His grin returned. "Believe me, Miss Joanna. You're no bother."

"But you know none of your little charming smiles are going to work on me, so why waste your time?" Again, her voice betrayed her, spilling the words she'd tried to swallow. "Why do you treat me like this?" She wished her voice sounded stronger, that it didn't tremble so. But it seemed to have taken on a mind of its own in the last few moments.

"Like what?" He paced out the next stake and hammered it into the ground.

"Like this." She waved her hand between them, hoping he'd catch on. He didn't. Or at least he pretended he didn't. "As though you . . ."

She stopped, shook her head, and reached for the shovel. Maybe if she got back to work, her tongue would stop flapping.

"As though I what?" Travers stopped hammering and sauntered back to her, standing close like he always did.

Joanna tipped her chin up and forced the twittering in her throat to stop. "As though you like me. We both know I'm not the kind of girl you usually pay mind to, so why bother with all this crap?" A slow burning sensation began in her throat, but she forced it back. "Why waste your efforts on someone like me when Carrie's right over there in the house?"

With his gaze still on her, Travers tucked his gloves into his pocket and pushed her hat back until it fell from her head. Then, as he'd done before, he loosened her braid and set her hair free.

"Stop doing that." She pulled away, trying desperately to rebraid her hair—anything to keep her trembling hands out of his sight.

His fingers closed around hers and eased her hands down again. Jo couldn't breathe. She tried, God help her, she really did, but the air was locked somewhere between her lungs and throat, and every time his thumb made another circle against her palm, the lock tightened.

"Maybe I do like you." His voice was a low, husky whisper against her cheek.

"Liar." Despite herself, she shivered. His hands were so warm, so gentle. "You don't like girls like me; you like pretty girls with ringlets and fancy dresses."

"You're right." He chuckled softly. "I *do* like pretty girls." He ran his fingers through the length of her hair, then spread it over her shoulders.

Fire burned behind her eyes, but she wouldn't cry—she never cried in front of anyone. Especially when she had no idea what she was crying for. But it couldn't be over something as silly as a man—especially one like him. If Travers wanted a pretty girl, he could go find one. In fact, he could have Carrie if it meant he'd stop toying with Jo.

He cupped her face in his hands,—rough hands that held her as tenderly as if she were made of fine china; rough hands that held her with such strength she could willingly trust him with anything—including her heart, her stupid, foolish, weak heart.

"You're a pretty girl, Miss Joanna." He stared deep into her eyes, the gold flecks around his pupils shining brilliantly, and for a moment, she almost believed him.

"No, I'm not," she choked. "Carrie's the pretty one. She's got pretty hair and soft skin and . . ." She couldn't finish.

"Sure, Carrie's pretty, too." A small smile tugged

at Levi's lips, but it didn't mock her. It was the most beautiful smile Jo had ever seen. "But not pretty enough that I'd give up time at Lefty's if she offered me a job here."

"No?" Jo forced a smile. None of this should matter to her, and she'd be damned if she'd let on it did.

"Nope." His eyes caressed her face as his thumbs moved in slow circles over her cheeks. "I've never wanted to string barbed wire with her, either. Never even considered it."

"Bet she'd be sorry to hear that." If Jo's throat had been any drier, it would have closed up completely.

Travers didn't seem to have heard her. His thumb traced the line of her cheekbone up to her ear and back again, sending a string of shivers down her spine. "And I've never once wanted to stand right up next to Carrie and kiss the breath out of her."

A tiny moan slipped from Jo's mouth. Surely this was a dream—or a nightmare. Heat exhaustion, maybe. Things like this didn't happen to her. She was too strong for nonsense like this; she didn't fall for flowery words and touches. At least she didn't used to.

His hands, warm and strong, cupped her face as he brushed his lips over hers, whisper soft. Jo's eyes fluttered shut, her mouth opened just enough to breathe, just enough to slide her tongue out and taste where he'd touched.

He kissed her again, longer this time, yet not nearly long enough. His lips caressed her, slowly, leisurely, driving her mad. Every touch shot warm shivers through her veins; every heartbeat was a burst of fire.

The ground tilted beneath her feet, her legs suddenly unable to hold her. If she didn't steady herself, she was going to collapse right there at his feet. In desperation, she reached out for the first thing she could find.

Him.

The warmth from his skin seeped through his shirt and into her fingers, his heart hammering against her fist. Thick fingers slid through her hair, taking handfuls of it and tipping her head back. She leaned closer, pressing against his chest, giving herself up to all he offered.

His lips were soft against hers—the kiss gentle and tender. He tasted like heaven, as though the warmth of the sun had mingled with his very essence. He shifted his weight, brought her hard against him, and deepened the kiss. He was hungry, seeking, ravishing her lips, leaving her breathless.

Jo spread her hands over his chest, aching to touch him—not his shirt, but him. She needed more of him, of all of him, yet it was already so much more than she'd ever imagined.

His hands moved over her back, pressing her even closer and caressing with every movement. Her body reacted in ways she'd never imagined; she melted into him, pressing her belly against the hard length of him. She tugged his hat off and buried her fingers in that silky hair of his. Heaven.

Someone sighed—was it her? The thought had barely registered when she felt his lips smile against hers. Lip to lip, they gasped for breath. Her mouth tingled from his touch; her fingers slid down and curled around his shirt again, refusing to let him go. Not yet.

"Wow." Levi breathed out a long, low whistle and rested his forehead against hers. His hands continued to move over her back, slowly, tempting her to lean in and kiss him again.

"Why did you do that?" she whispered, her fingers toying with a loose button on his shirt.

"I wanted to." His voice, low and husky, sang against her neck and through her hair.

"Oh." Jo swallowed a great gulp of air. What else could she possibly say? She expected him to laugh at her, expected to see that smile she'd come to know so well, but there was no trace of it. All she saw was her own desperate hunger reflected back in his eyes. She needed to taste those lips again, to savor the sensation of them whispering against hers, to feel his heart pounding just as hard as hers.

"I'd really like to do it again." His thumb brushed against her bottom lip until she tipped her face up to his.

He began slowly, leaving a soft, wet trail of shivery kisses down her cheek, then making his way to her lips, which were open, waiting and trembling.

She leaned into him again until they were pressed against the wagon. More—that's all she wanted. More.

His arms tightened around her, his lips coaxing, teasing, caressing all the while. She couldn't get enough—the more he gave, the more she needed.

Low whimpers slipped from her mouth. She should be horrified that she'd make such noises, but with every one, Travers's kiss deepened, his arms tightened, and his tongue—whew.

Just when she was certain she'd burst, he released her mouth and spread more soft kisses over her chin, her cheeks, and down her neck to just below her ear. He nibbled her earlobe, then moved back down her neck, kissing his way slowly across to her other ear.

Jo's breath came in gasps, her lungs searching for air that just wouldn't come. She found a small amount of comfort in that Levi's breathing sounded equally labored, and when she ran her fingers through his long, silky hair again, it was his turn to moan.

What was she doing, standing right there in the open, kissing Levi Travers? Sure, she'd thought about it, but never in her wildest dreams did she think it would be anything like this, or that—

Levi's arms dropped and he stepped away, leaving a gaping emptiness between them. Jo stumbled before bracing herself against the wagon again. There was something in his eyes—a look she could only describe as regret.

"Wh—"

"M-Miss Joanna?" Clay's trembling voice sent a crashing wave of dread to the pit of Jo's stomach. That was twice she'd been caught unawares in the same afternoon! What the hell was the matter with her?

Tomorrow she'd go farther out where people would have to ride out to her—that way at least she'd hear the horses coming.

She took a moment to collect herself before turning. Clay wasn't alone.

The tall man next to him had short, sandy colored hair, eyes as dark as pitch, and a smirk Jo would have loved to smack off his face. He twirled his Stetson between his hands and nodded toward Travers.

"Good to see you, Will." Travers pumped the man's hand, then began introductions, but his gaze never met Jo's. "Jo, this is Will Brennan, the man I told you about."

"Nice to meet you, Will." She shook his hand, reached for Levi's canteen, and downed all that was left. *Should have brought a flask, too.* "Travers assures me you're the man for the job."

Will chuckled uneasily, his gaze flickering between her and Travers. "Him and I go back a ways."

She nodded, swallowed past a small lump that appeared out of nowhere, and smiled. "You know what needs to be done here?"

"Yes, ma'am. But I'm wondering if I wouldn't be more help working the fence."

When she cocked her head in question, Will shot a quick look at Clay.

"This young fella's a hard worker, but I bet he's got other jobs he should be tending."

Jo glanced at Travers. "You left Clay to string the fence?"

"He wanted to help," he said with a shrug. Why wouldn't he look at her?

Will chewed the inside of his cheek for a moment, his hands pushed deep in his pockets. "I bet you've got lots more important jobs for him to do."

Silence followed his statement, then Jo laughed dryly. "Of course I do. Why don't you and Travers take over for Clay and I'll continue on here? Then Clay can get back to his regular chores."

Travers and Clay turned to go, but Will remained where he was.

"You're going to string this fence by yourself, ma'am?"

To hide her trembling hands again, Jo wound them through her hair, setting the braid in record time.

"Yes, as a matter of fact, I am. I was well on my way before Travers came by and interrupted me."

Travers kept his back to her. *Coward.*

Will half nodded, half shrugged. "But it's not exactly woman's work, if you don't mind my saying so."

From the corner of her eye, she saw Clay and Travers both cringe.

"As a matter of fact, I do mind you saying so, Will. It's my ranch and I'm not *nearly* as useless as you might think."

Uncertainty showed in his eyes, but he simply shrugged and nodded. "If you say so. No offense intended."

Jo gave up trying to smile. "Let's not waste each other's time, Will." She crossed her arms over her chest and stiffened her spine. "Are you going to have a problem working for me?"

Will rubbed his dirty fingers over his chin. "Well, now, that depends."

"On what?"

"Am I gonna have to collect chips?"

"Th-that's my job," Clay said with pride.

Will chuckled. "Okay, good. Will I get paid on time?"

Jo fought back a snort. "You do your job, you'll get paid on time. Yes."

The uncertainty faded from his eyes, replaced by a faint twinkle. "Then I reckon you and me'll get on just fine."

"Good." She scooped up her hat and dismissed them all with a wave. "I'll see you at supper."

The three of them walked off without another word. But the last look Levi gave her spoke volumes. He wasn't happy about their kiss—in fact, regret was probably a huge understatement. Well, that was fine with her. She didn't have time for such nonsense anyway.

She'd wanted to know what it would be like if he kissed her. And now she knew. In fact, it was a lesson she'd not soon forget.

His warmth remained on her palms, his taste lingered on her lips, and his scent hung all around her, on her clothes and even on her own skin.

Damn it all, anyway.

Chapter 6

To his credit, Will waited until they were back at the other fence before he upbraided Levi.

"What the hell d'you think you're doing, Travers?" His eyes were wide, his voice low but laughing. "She's the boss, for crying out loud!"

Levi hammered another stake into the ground. "I'm not doing anything. It was just a stupid kiss."

Will choked. "That was more than just a stupid kiss, my friend."

"How would you know?" He didn't dare look at Will, but the snort told him everything he needed to know. Will was having more fun with this than he'd had in a long time.

"You ain't never looked at any girl that way before. And you've looked at plenty of girls."

Levi picked up another stake and forced a look of indifference. "What's your point?"

"My point," Will began, carefully winding the wire into a knot, "is that you and her . . . well, let's face it, Travers, she's not exactly your type."

Levi tightened his grip on the hammer. He wiped

the sweat from his brow and tried to steady the stake against the ground. If his hands would quit shaking, it'd be a lot easier. "And what's my type?"

The know-it-all chuckle from his friend made Levi want to punch him. Hard.

"You know exactly what type I'm talkin' about. Top-heavy blondes who are long on time and short on brains." Will pulled another handful of nails from the tin.

"Yeah, well . . ." Levi had no good answer for that. It was true. By all that was right in the world, he should be spending his time trying to charm the pants—or skirt, as it might be—off Carrie, not Joanna.

Will stopped in mid-step and gaped at him. "You're not . . . oh, no—say it ain't so."

"What?" Levi bent to his job. *Don't say it.*

"You're not," Will stepped closer, his voice lowered to a laughing whisper. "You're not *in love* with her, are you?"

Damn it. Levi focused on the next stake to keep from hammering his own hand instead.

"What the hell are you talking about, Will?" The second swing of the hammer slammed against his thumb, but he'd be damned if he'd let Will know. "Can't I even kiss a girl anymore?"

His thumb throbbed, as did his head.

"Normally, yes," Will laughed, "but this one, I dunno. You tell me."

It took some doing, but Levi forced himself to breathe through the pain and look Will right in the eye. "It's nothing."

Will eyed him cautiously, his expression going from amused, to solemn, then back to grinning. "You're a lyin' cur dog, Travers," he said, pointing the hammer at him. "It ain't nothin', that much I know."

Levi shrugged indifferently and pulled out his trump card. "You haven't met Carrie yet, have you?"

"Who's Carrie?"

With three hard swings, Levi set another stake, keeping his thumb well out of the way this time. "Carrie's the younger sister. And once you see her, you'll believe me when I tell you that kiss wasn't anything more than a kiss."

"She pretty?" Will unwound a length of wire and set to working it around the next stake.

"Pretty?" Levi laughed, offering up silent thanks for the change in subject. "Pretty doesn't even begin to describe Carrie."

"So why aren't you kissing her instead?"

Good question.

"Pacing myself." He forced a laugh that didn't sound the least bit convincing to either one of them. "Besides, once we get this fence up, we'll be on our way to San Francisco, right?"

Will shrugged. "I might be, but I'm not so sure about you now. Doesn't matter what you say, Travers, or how pretty the sister is, that was no normal kiss going on back there."

"You don't know what you're talking about," Levi said.

"And you don't know what you're doing." All hints of humor vanished from Will's face. "Don't be gettin' yourself involved in something you've got no intention of following through on, Travers. You got enough problems."

"Shut up and get stringing," Levi grumbled. "We

might work for a woman, but in case you didn't notice, she's got the temper of a peeled rattler."

They worked in silence for a long while, the blistering afternoon sun giving them not a moment's relief. The heat seeped through to Levi's brain, searing Will's words there. What would happen when the fence was done?

He'd be more than ready to leave by then; that had always been the plan and he wasn't about to start changing things now.

Will had been right, though. That kiss was about as far from normal as Levi'd ever been. Sure, Joanna had responded in a way neither of them had expected, and sure, he'd never kissed a woman that way before. But Joanna McCaine was nothing more than a distraction, something to keep him occupied while he was working at the ranch. And since he spent his days working beside her, it was only natural, wasn't it? If he'd been working with Carrie all this time, he'd have kissed her instead.

Levi frowned. The thought of kissing Carrie held absolutely no appeal for him at all. In fact, it didn't even give him a second's pause.

What the hell was wrong with him?

Will would probably be more than happy to answer that question, and even though he was keeping his mouth shut for the moment, his lopsided grin and shaking head said everything he didn't.

Levi cursed himself with every swing of the hammer. How could he have been so stupid? He should have known kissing Joanna wouldn't be like kissing anyone else. She wasn't like any darned female he'd ever met. Sure, she acted tough and mean, but the way she responded to him was all woman—soft, warm, and sexy as hell.

He'd never been so fired up in his whole life. And dammit, but he'd never been so scared, either.

As he chugged from Will's canteen, the picture of Joanna, dripping wet, haunted him. Damn near drove him crazy watching that water drip from her skin. And if only she hadn't looked at him with those beautiful, trusting green eyes, if only she hadn't trembled when he went near, he might have been able to walk away without kissing her.

But now that he'd done it once, now that he knew what she tasted like, knew where to touch her to make her sigh, he was going to have to do it again. And again.

Levi licked his lips, her flavor still there, taunting him. Her soft sighs echoed in his ears, and God help him, he could still feel her long fingers sliding through his hair.

He needed a drink. No, he needed the whole bottle.

He shouldn't have done it. Mac was probably going to skin him alive—if Joanna didn't do it first. Hell, she probably wanted to castrate him right along with the herd. And while the thought of that made him wince, the thought of her hands on him pushed a long groan from his throat.

Why *her*? He didn't toy with girls like Joanna; girls who were strong enough to know what they wanted—and what they didn't want. He liked girls who played along with him, who enjoyed his ways and returned the attentions.

Granted, those girls were usually the ones who charged for their services, but that's what made it so easy for him to walk away. The only attachment he had with them was the jingle of coins in his pocket.

So why Jo? She knew what kind of man he was and the stories that followed him. And even though she'd kissed him back, had nearly come undone in his arms, she obviously wasn't happy about it. And from the look she gave him before he left, she wasn't likely to let him kiss her again.

That tiny piece of knowledge sent an icy chill through Levi's gut. Hot damn, he was completely taken by an ornery cuss of a woman who could—and would—no doubt get on quite nicely without him. In fact, she could probably go the rest of her life without giving him a second thought.

Levi swiped his bare arm over his forehead and took one more swallow from the canteen before handing it back to Will. He'd left his with Joanna—but she'd emptied it when Clay and Will arrived.

She must be damn near parched by now, and knowing Joanna, she'd still be too fired up to stop working long enough to find more water. But how could he get it to her without raising Will's suspicions? The last thing he needed was Will hounding him day and night about some dame.

"You okay here for a while? I'm just gonna go fill the canteen."

Will shrugged. "I'm good."

Without a second thought or a glance back, Levi hurried toward the house. He filled two extra canteens from the huge water barrel, then dodged his way back to Joanna, careful to keep out of anyone's sight.

Her progress on the fence was slow, but considering

she was the only one working it, she'd done a damn fine job.

"What d'you need?" She didn't stop to look at him, just kept hammering. There was no surprising her this time.

"Nothing." He stepped closer, holding out one of the canteens. "Thought you might be thirsty."

"Clay brought some water a while ago." She raised the hammer above her head and brought it down with a hard crack on top of the stake. "Anything else?"

Levi edged closer, careful to avoid the crazy way she wielded the hammer like a weapon. "Listen, Joanna, about before . . ."

"What?"

"You know what."

"You mean when you kissed me?" She shrugged, but something flicked across her face that was anything but indifference.

"Hate to remind you," he said with a chuckle, "but you kissed me back."

"It was nothing." She scoffed. "So we kissed. Big deal." She wasn't kidding either one of them. It was a *huge* deal. "Don't have to explain anything to me."

"I think I do."

She shrugged again and kept right on swinging.

"I shouldn't have done it," he said slowly. "Kissing you, I mean." He caught her arms as she brought the hammer up one more time. "Will you just listen for a minute?"

Her face turned his way, but her eyes, now clouded and flat, looked past him. When he released her arms, they fell limply to her sides, the hammer dangling from her fingers.

Levi inhaled a long breath. "I've got no business kissing you like that. I'm sorry."

"Yes, you are." She laughed—a dry, humorless sound that ripped through him. "You're the sorriest sonuvabitch I've ever met. Well, you know what, Travers? So am I." She moved out of his reach, swiped her sleeve across her mouth, and glared right through him. "I'm sorry I was so desperate I had to hire a skunk like you, and I'm sorry you wasted a kiss like that on someone like me, when it would have been better spent on someone like Stella.

"But I swear to God," she moved forward again, stabbing her finger into his chest, "if you so much as think about doing the same thing to Carrie, I'll tear you limb from limb—you got that?"

Levi stumbled back a step. "Carrie?" He frowned. "What does she have to do with this?"

"Oh, come on, Travers." Joanna rolled her eyes. "If you're able to catch me off guard and kiss me like that, I can only imagine what you've got planned for my sister."

He moved closer. She backed away. "This has nothing to do with Carrie," he ground out. "I meant what I said before—I've got no interest in doing anything with her."

"Right." Sarcasm dripped from Joanna's one word. She stepped around him and reached for another stake. "That's why you nearly tripped over your own tongue the first time you saw her."

"It wasn't that bad," he lied.

She rolled her eyes again—something she seemed to do so often around him. "Yes it was. And you look the exact same way every time you're anywhere near her."

Levi swallowed. So she'd noticed. Good. No, *not*

good. He didn't want Joanna to think he was like everyone else—looking through her to see Carrie. But he also didn't want her thinking he was anything but what his reputation led her to believe—a skunk. If she kept that opinion of him, it'd be a helluva lot easier to leave once the fence was up.

"I have work to do," she said, waving the stake in her hand. "And so do you."

Damn, she was ornery. "Joanna . . ."

"Look, Travers." When she looked up at him, he could see the battle raging behind her eyes. Her jaw tightened for a moment, her chest heaved in a deep breath. "I'm not going to wilt away because you don't want to kiss me." She chuckled, but there was nothing happy about it. "I'm not one of those women who needs a man, and sure as hell not one like you."

Her throat bobbed against a hard swallow, then she turned away. But not before he saw the tears glistening against her eyes.

"Like me?" Of course not like him, that's what he wanted her to think, wasn't it?

"*Like you*. If and when I decide I need a man, he won't be one who's kissing me but ogling Carrie." She hammered in another stake. "And he sure as hell won't be one who gets a girl in trouble and then leaves her on her own."

Fire ignited in Levi's belly, but he held his tongue. His knuckles whitened around the canteen, his teeth ground together until his head began to pound again.

Jo lifted her shoulder in a careless shrug. "He'll see me—and only me—exactly as I am, and that'll be enough for him."

God, if only she knew.

And God, if only he weren't such a coward. He should tell her—confess everything he felt, everything he wanted, everything he needed from her. He should pull her back into his arms right there and then and kiss her senseless again, until she begged him to stop—or do more.

He should—

"I'm not paying you to stand around, Travers." Joanna cleared her throat against the cracking of her voice. "You've got a fence to build, so get back to work."

He'd seen women cry before—hell, he was responsible for it most of the time—but this was the first time he'd ever felt guilty about it.

He dropped one of the canteens on the ground and walked back to Will. Joanna was right about one thing—he had work to do. And the faster he got it done, the sooner he could get the hell off the Double M and out of town.

Coward.

Will had managed to string most of the standing posts by the time he made it back. Without a word, Levi scooped up his hammer and an armload of stakes and went back to pounding his frustration out on those stupid pieces of wood.

Will raised his head enough to squint up at him from beneath his hat. "How's the queen rattler doing?"

"Shut up, Will. Just shut the hell up." He drove the next stake in with two swings of the hammer, the sound of Will's laughter echoing in his ears.

* * *

"The fund-raiser ball is only a few weeks away, and there's still so much to do." Carrie groaned over the lists in front of her. "I could use your help, Joanna."

Jo snorted. Would be a cold day in hell before she'd agree to help organize a party she wouldn't attend.

Carrie ran her finger down the first list. "Was that a yes?"

"No." Jo finished her pie, then swallowed the rest of her coffee.

Carrie, of course, continued as if she hadn't even spoken. "I want to build a dance floor. We can't have another episode like last year, for goodness sake. The way Milly Jean carried on, you'd have thought her leg had come clear off."

"No." As Jo carried her dishes to the sideboard, she pinned her sister with a glare before repeating, "No."

Carrie tipped her perfectly coiffed head to the side and smiled sweetly. "Now, Joanna, you know this fund-raiser brings in a great deal of money for the school and church, and it *is* named for Mama."

"No." With supper long over and the kitchen put to rights, Ginny and Mac had set out on a walk, leaving Jo alone with Carrie. There couldn't be a worse fate.

All sweetness drained from Carrie's voice. "Look, Joanna, by this time next year, I'll be as far away from here as I can get."

"So you've said. Over and over and over."

"Well, since this is the last year I'm going to be organizing the ball, don't you think it would be nice if we all pitched in and helped? It would be even better if we would *all* attend this year, too."

"No."

Carrie sighed, but not in her usual dramatic way, more to show her impatience. "But come next year, if you and Ginny aren't willing to organize it, the town will probably change the name of it."

"So what?"

"So," she sighed, "it's the last time all the Mc-Caines will be together for a fund-raiser named for a McCaine—doesn't that mean anything to you?"

Guilt began to wedge itself into Jo's gut.

"*Please?*"

Jo almost had second thoughts—it wasn't every day Carrie used that word. "I don't have time to build a stupid dance floor, Carrie. In case you hadn't noticed, we're a little shorthanded right now."

"But it wouldn't take very long." The old thrill was back in Carrie's voice. "Anyone could do it. Perhaps one of the hired hands could help?"

"No." Jo refused to give in to Carrie. The rest of the world might, but she wouldn't.

"But I bet if you asked Levi or that new fellow— Mr. Brennan—they'd do it." An odd little twinkle danced in Carrie's eyes. A *very* odd little twinkle.

"Do what?" Levi asked as he and Will came through the door. They poured themselves what was left of the coffee, picked up the pie plate and some forks, and pulled up to the table as if they'd been doing it for twenty years instead of only a few weeks.

If Jo hadn't hated Travers so much, she might have found it comforting that he was so at ease in the house—almost like he was family—God forbid.

With her best pout yet, Carrie sighed. "I asked Joanna to do one little thing for the annual fund-raiser—an event that the town named after our own mother—and she won't do it."

Jo watched Levi's Adam's apple bob with each swallow of his coffee. Maybe if she was lucky, he'd choke on it. A single drop slid from his lips and hung on his stubbled chin. Why couldn't she look away? She tried, she really did, but there was some-thing about the way it clung to his sun-kissed skin, almost as though it didn't want to fall.

She knew the feeling.

Then Travers had to go and wipe it away with the back of his hand. Jo looked away as fast as she could, but not before their gazes met and held over a heartbeat. There, in the depths of his eyes, she saw it again—regret.

"What did you want her to do?" Will asked. Nei-ther he nor Travers bothered with plates, they simply used a fork to cut what was left of the pie in half and ate it directly from the pie pan. And even though Travers seemed intent on the pie itself, Will kept stabbing his fork on the empty part of the pan, as his gaze never left Carrie's face. "Could Travers and I help?"

"No." Jo and Travers answered at the same time.

Carrie's face lit up. "Why, yes, Mr. Brennan, I do be-lieve you might be able to." She flashed a "so there" look at Jo, then pulled her chair closer to Will's.

"Call me Will." A small smile lifted his mouth as color flooded up his neck.

"Thank you, Will." Carrie smiled back at him in what could have been her best performance of all time.

"All I want," she sniffed as she slid her sketch in front of him, "is a simple dance floor. But Joanna doesn't want to help. Would you build it for me?" She looked up at him from beneath her lashes. "I'd be most grateful."

Will's brow shot up to his hairline. "Grateful enough that you'd—"

Jo gasped at the same time that Travers yanked Will up by the collar.

"We've got a barn to clean out."

"B-but . . ."

"Now." He pushed his friend toward the door.

"What about the dance floor?" Carrie called sweetly.

"Yeah," Will called back to her. "Anything you want. Just tell me where and how big, and I'll—"

With a final shove, Levi pushed him out the door and let it slam behind them.

"See?" Carrie sneered. "Mr. Brennan will help me. Just because you're a big meanie, don't think I can't get it done one way or another."

Jo studied her sister with a new eye. She'd known for a while that Carrie wasn't a little girl anymore, but this was the first time she'd seen her for what she truly was; a conniving young woman who had only to crook her finger and any number of men would jump to her bidding.

The reality of it hadn't really hit Jo until then, until she'd seen Carrie flutter her lashes at Will. Will Brennan—a man they knew nothing about, save that he was a friend of Travers's and he seemed willing to lie at Carrie's feet and do whatever she bid him.

"Carrie, listen." She slumped into a chair, wondering how long until Ginny would be home to handle this. "You need to be a little more . . . prudent in how you do things. You're a very pretty girl and—"

"Thank you." Carrie smiled knowingly and fluffed her hair a little.

"*And,*" Jo continued, fighting not to roll her eyes, "if you're going to string men along, they're going to expect something from you that you aren't ready to give them."

"Good Lord, Joanna!" Carrie twirled one of her ringlets around her finger. "You make me sound like a common hussy."

"That's how you're acting."

"I most certainly am not." The hurt look she shot Jo was nowhere near her usual performance. "I'm being charming, something you never did learn. Men like that. They like to think they're big and strong and that we can't live a moment without them. So what's wrong with me letting them believe that?"

Jo groaned. "Because it's a load of . . ."

With a wave of dismissal, Carrie collected her lists and headed for the stairs.

"I'm just making sure I get what I want. If Levi won't take me to San Francisco with him, maybe Mr. Brennan will. They're going together, you know."

"You're going to ruin your reputation, Carrie." Or had that already happened? "Is that what you want? Do you think that's what Mama wanted for you?"

Carrie whirled around with a grand flourish. "Mama? What do you care about what Mama wanted? Look at you, for goodness sake! Do you really think

she'd be proud if she saw you dressed like . . . that."
She gestured toward Jo's clothes. "Never mind the
way you act."

Anger buried the ache in Jo's heart. "This isn't
about me, Carrie—I can look after myself. I'm not
interested in having any man do my bidding."

Carrie's pert little nose lifted. "You could have
fooled me."

Leave it alone. Jo inhaled a long breath, clenched
her teeth, and began to count. She made it to two.

"Watch your tongue, Carrie." She pushed away
from the table and loomed closer to her sister.

"Don't play coy with me, Joanna. We've all seen
the way you and Levi look at each other when you
think no one's watching." She rolled her eyes and
sneered. "You can't even seem to find your tongue
when he's around and we've all seen those cow eyes
he makes at you."

When Jo opened her mouth, Carrie cut her off.

"So don't you start preaching to me about repu-
tations, Joanna." Anger reddened Carrie's face. "I
know mine's intact. But it wouldn't surprise any of
us if you'd already tumbled with Levi out in the
barn."

Joanna's hand struck with such force it knocked
her sister back a step. Carrie steadied herself
against the wall, her fingers resting over the growing red stain on her cheek. After a moment, she
lifted her chin defiantly and glared back at Jo.

Bile filled Jo's stomach. What had she just done?

"Carrie, I'm sorry, I—" she stepped closer, but
Carrie moved away.

"I should have expected that from someone like
you, *Jo.*" She smoothed back her hair, then ran her

palms down her skirt. "You're jealous because men like me and I'm not afraid to let them. But you haven't got the first clue what to do with a man like Levi Travers. It's as simple as that." She glared hard before swooping out of the room and climbing the stairs as gracefully as ever.

"You're wrong, Carrie." Jo spoke to an empty room. "It's not simple at all."

Quiet consumed the room—and Jo. Mama certainly wouldn't be proud of the way either of her daughters was turning out, and it was all Jo's fault. She was supposed to be looking after Carrie, not fighting her at every turn.

There had to be something she could do, some way to keep Carrie's reputation intact. But how? She might be able to keep Travers and Will away from her while she was on the ranch, but if Carrie got her way and traveled west with them, there was nothing Jo could do for her.

And from the way Will had just looked at Carrie, he'd be more than happy to take her west. He'd be happy to take her a lot of places.

Jo grabbed her hat and raced out to the barn.

"Where's Brennan?" she bellowed. Several cows turned to stare at her, straw hanging from their mouths, their tails flicking in a steady rhythm. "Brennan!"

Travers stepped from a stall, hands out to block her path. "Calm down, Joanna."

She kept walking. "Get out of my way, Travers."

"Calm down," he repeated, his voice soft.

"I'm going to kill him. Where is he?" Her head moved from side to side, trying to see around Travers.

"It's not what you think."

"The hell it isn't! Where is he?" She tried to step around him, but he stopped her again. "Brennan!"

"He's not—"

"I'm right here." Will stepped through the door, pushing the wheelbarrow full of fresh straw. A huge grin covered his stupid face as though he had every right to be thinking what he was probably thinking.

Jo lunged at him, but Levi caught her around the middle and held her. Startled, Will jumped back, upsetting the wheelbarrow in the process. Straw scattered across the floor.

"What the hell? What'd I do?"

She tried to lunge again. "You sonuva—"

"Joanna!" Levi pulled her back. "He didn't do anything."

"How do you know? You saw the way they were carrying on in there—he would have done anything she asked."

"So?"

Jo wrenched free, a bit of the bluster sucked away with Levi's one word. "So . . . so then he'd want her to do whatever he asked, too. Unless they've already . . ."

Will's wide eyes stared back at her in disbelief. "Are you crazy? I said I'd build a dance floor, that's all. What's wrong with that?"

"Nothing," Levi interjected, his voice still calm and even.

"What's wrong," Jo snapped, "is what you were going to ask for in return—and the way you were ogling my sister!"

Will's lips twitched and his eyes crinkled, but he didn't smile. And he was damn lucky he didn't, too.

"Ogling?"

"Yes, Will—that's what it's called when your eyes

nearly fall out of their sockets." She pushed ahead, but Levi blocked her again.

"Listen, Jo." Will's smile broke free, followed by a short chuckle. "I was only going to ask her if she'd . . ."

A low growl began in Jo's throat.

"Uh, Will," Levi said, "I think you'd better leave. Now."

"But . . ."

"Go."

Will shrugged, gathered the empty wheelbarrow, and left the way he came in, muttering under his breath the whole while.

Jo paced the barn, her hands on her hips, her fingers itching to claw Will's ogling eyes right out of his face.

"Joanna." Travers's voice was gentle and soothing, but she didn't want to be soothed, damn it. She wanted to yell; she wanted to hit something—and if it meant him, that was fine with her.

"Don't 'Joanna' me, Travers." Her anger burned right through her skin. "You told me you trusted him—trusted him with your life, that's what you said. You told me he was the man for the job."

"He is the man for the job." He grinned slightly and stepped closer. "And I do trust him with my life." He stood right in front of her, his velvety brown eyes soothing her with each word. "I just wouldn't trust him with your sister." His cheeks dimpled with his smile and the rest of Jo's anger melted away. "Hell, I wouldn't trust any man with your sister."

"Dammit, Travers." She slammed her palm on the nearest rail.

"It's Levi. And you need to calm down."

"He's ogling my sister; he's probably been doing it since he got here but I've been too . . . distracted . . . to notice."

He pushed her braid back over her shoulder. "Your sister wants to be ogled."

How could she answer that? She couldn't deny it, but she couldn't very well agree that it made it okay for Will to do it.

She brushed away his hand and willed the shivers to stop tingling against her spine.

"You tell your friend to keep his eyes—and his hands—to himself. And you make damn sure he knows Carrie is *not* going to San Francisco with either one of you. Not now, not ever. I don't care what she says."

"Carrie's a grown woman. If she decides to go . . ." he didn't finish.

"Carrie doesn't understand what the hell she's doing. Will does. There's the difference."

"Maybe it's time she figured it out."

Jo heaved a huge sigh. "It's complicated." Why was she making excuses for Carrie?

"It always is, isn't it?" When his hand reached up to cup her cheek, it took every ounce of strength she had left not to lean into it. But Lord, how she wanted to.

She pulled back slowly, each step more of an effort than the last. "Don't."

His hand dropped, but he didn't move away from her. "Sorry. I can't help it." He paused, then almost whispered, "I like touching you."

A knot twisted in Jo's belly. She liked it, too; that was the problem.

"Look, Travers," she began, leaning against a stall door for support.

"Levi."

She ignored him. "You're very good at all this," she waved her hand between them and held her voice even. "But I'm not. And no matter what you say or how much I want you to say it, I won't be just another notch in your belt. And we both know that's all you're looking for."

His mouth opened, but closed again without uttering a word.

"We have to work together," she continued, amazed at the steadiness in her voice, "so we need to be civil with each other. But that's as far as it goes."

"What if I want it to go further?" Though barely a whisper, his words echoed through her head. Dammit, he was good. If she didn't get away from him pretty soon, there'd be no hope for her or her heart.

She took a moment to stare at the tip of his boot, swallowed, then looked back into his eyes. Those beautiful, soft eyes.

"You don't want to go further with someone like me, Travers, and we both know it." Her voice trembled, then cracked. "I'm just a distraction until you can skip town and head west. Or until some other girl comes along."

Silence was his only answer, and Jo didn't wait around for anything else. She brushed past him and ran back up to the house, leaving pieces of her heart scattered on the ground behind her.

His lack of response was exactly what she should have expected, but it didn't make it any easier.

Damn him. And damn herself for feeling this way.

Chapter 7

Day after day of stringing fence left Levi as tightly wound as the barbs themselves. Every day, his mood darkened like the weather, and the recent downpour had done little to cool his nerves. By the time the rain stopped yesterday, most of the smaller ponds had turned into thick mud bogs, much like Levi's mind.

He'd seen little of Jo, who avoided him at every turn and appeared only at mealtimes and whenever Will was near the house. She'd even gone so far as to build the dance floor herself.

"You comin' to town tonight?" Will tipped his hat back just enough to see out from under it. It was the first time he'd spoken a complete sentence all day.

Something akin to guilt raced through Levi's veins. In the weeks since Will arrived, they'd not once been to town.

"Come on, Travers," Will continued, with a look half-teasing, half-frustrated. "It's Saturday night, we don't have to work tomorrow, though God knows you'll make us work anyway, and if I don't get some whiskey into my gut pretty soon, I'm gonna bust wide open.

"Besides," he offered a short shrug, "she ain't said more than two words to you since that day in the barn. And you're not doing much talking to her either, so I reckon whatever you thought was gonna happen with her probably won't. So let's go find a girl we *can* make things happen with."

An objection jumped to Levi's lips, but he bit it back. Will was right. How many times had Joanna told him he was wasting his time? If the last couple of weeks hadn't proved that right, then he didn't know what would.

Truth be told, he could use a good long shot of Lefty's rotgut. And if Stella was available, well, he could use a good long shot of her, too.

He nodded at Will and forced a smile he didn't feel.

"Let's go."

They gathered their tools, righted the stack of posts, and secured the roll of wire with a few large boulders and some rope. By the time they'd saddled their horses and started back to the ranch, Levi had almost convinced himself that he wanted to go to town. Almost.

He rode a wide berth around the main house and the yards, and headed straight to his cabin. The thought of a quick bath in the creek crossed his mind, but quickly faded. Wasn't like he was going anywhere special, after all.

He pulled some money out of his old tobacco pouch and stuffed it in his pocket. Not enough to get him stupid drunk, but enough to straighten him out some, that was for sure.

Will was mounted and waiting when he stepped outside.

"Ready?" he asked. "I stopped at the house and told Miss Ginny where we'd be."

Levi fought back a wince and nodded as he swung up into his saddle. If Ginny knew where they were going, it was a safe bet Joanna would know soon, too. Not that it mattered, of course.

They rode out with Will in the lead and Levi plodding along behind. What was the big hurry?

The sun had just begun its descent when they left their horses with Big Bill at the livery. A few people lingered on the boardwalks, but for the most part, the stores were dark and the streets emptied.

Levi stepped through the saloon doors and grimaced. He shouldn't have come. There wasn't a thing in the place that held any interest for him anymore, and looking around, it was as though he'd never left.

Sal sat at the piano, screeching an unrecognizable, earsplitting "song"; Lefty leaned his round belly against the bar, his arms crossed over his chest; and every table was crowded over by drunks.

Wasn't so long ago he'd have joined right in on one of the card games or pulled up a chair and gotten sloppy drunk with the rest of them.

Today it didn't sound like near as much fun.

Will left him at the bar and went to find a game to join.

"Travers." Lefty eyed him carefully. "Whiskey?"

Levi nodded and slapped a handful of coins on the bar. "Leave the bottle."

Ignoring Lefty's annoyed look, he turned to survey the room. He'd played cards or gotten

drunk with most of the men there, but a few faces
he'd never seen before.

A head of hair the color of fire caught Levi's attention. Peter Carlson sat at the table under the
window with three of Pearson's men. Levi had
never liked Carlson; couldn't say why, exactly, just
rubbed him wrong. He'd do well to avoid Carlson's
table anyway. Though Pearson hadn't ordered his
men to shoot Levi yet, it wouldn't surprise him if
they did it anyway.

"How's Joey?" Lefty's hard, gravelly voice interrupted his thoughts.

Levi shrugged, but averted his gaze. "Joanna's
Joanna."

"And Mac?" He laughed—loud and crackly. "I'd
have given my other eye to see his face when you
walked up."

Levi couldn't help but laugh, too. "He's getting
used to me being there."

"An' you're full of shit, Travers," Lefty shook his
head, still grinning. "Mac don't get used to nothin'
too quickly, so he sure as hell won't be getting used
to you anytime soon."

"True enough, but at least he doesn't curse me
out every time he sees me now." Levi chuckled.
"That's more than I can say for Joanna."

Lefty's face sobered. "Don't you be messin' with
Joey." He poured himself a shot from Levi's bottle
and downed it. "Just do what you been hired to do
and leave it at that."

Even though he forced himself to keep the grin
on his face, Levi's blood began to boil. "I'm not
messing with Joanna."

Lefty raised a disbelieving brow. "Just figured

since you ain't been in here for a stretch that you must've found something—or someone—to keep you busy out there at the Double M."

"Well it ain't Joanna."

The bartender's eye grew wide. "You ain't carrying on with Carrie? Hell, Travers, she's just a little girl."

Levi didn't bother trying to smile anymore. He was getting damned tired of defending himself lately. In fact, it was taking every ounce of his concentration not to slam his fist into Lefty's chin.

"No," he ground out, "I'm not doing anything with Carrie, either."

Lefty didn't look the least bit convinced. "But you've seen Carrie, right?"

"Only at every single meal for the last month."

"And you haven't . . ."

Levi silenced him with a hard glare. "Stella around?"

"She's busy right now," Lefty answered. "Why don't you go find a game and I'll send her over when she comes down?"

Levi nodded, picked up his bottle and glass, and headed to the far corner of the saloon. He had no interest in cards tonight. Hell, he had no interest in anything tonight, least of all Stella, but maybe she'd work some of the tightness out of his shoulders. And everywhere else.

Will waved him over to his table, and more than a few others lifted their glasses in greeting, but Levi moved past all of them and hunkered down at a broken table in the darkened corner.

Carlson eyed him from across the room, said something to the other men at his table, then laughed. The other three men didn't laugh, just glared in Levi's direction. Levi returned their glare until they all looked away.

He leveled his gaze at the back of Will's head, silently cursing him out for suggesting this idea in the first place. He'd have been better off back at the ranch, alone on his cot, imagining all the things he'd like to do to Miss Joanna McCaine and all the things he'd like *her* to do to *him*.

Half a bottle of whiskey later, Levi's mood hadn't improved even the slightest.

"Was beginnin' to think I'd never see you again." Stella stood in front of him, her blond ringlets slightly askew, her dress more than a little wrinkled.

"Stella." He offered his glass, which she filled and downed—twice.

"Lefty said you might be lookin' for some company tonight." She ran a finger down his cheek, making him twitch. Had she always looked so tired? So empty?

Levi nodded and rose from his chair, lifting the bottle and his glass at the same time.

He followed her upstairs—the same stairs she'd just come down—and into the last room at the end of the hall. He'd never paid much mind to Stella's room before, but tonight he took a moment to look around.

Tattered white curtains hung from the dingy window and the rumpled sheets did little to hide the lumpy straw tick or the signs of the men who'd been there before him.

Stella's dress landed in a heap at his feet, leaving her completely naked, save for her boots. It was a sight that usually had Levi reaching for his own buttons, but tonight, it was Stella who reached for them.

"Come on, sugar, let's get you out of these clothes." Her grimy fingers fumbled with the top few buttons on his shirt before he stilled her hands with his own.

"That's it, lover," she cooed in a voice completely devoid of any feeling. She wound her fingers through his hair and pulled his face closer.

Levi dragged her up against him and kissed her hard. This is what he wanted, it's what he'd come to town for. So why wasn't he reacting the way he normally did to Stella?

She wiggled against him, moaning with his kisses and moving her hands down his back and over his backside. But her moan didn't sound anything like Joanna's did. Stella's was forced, a little too loud, and did absolutely nothing for him. Her hands didn't tremble when they touched him, either. Joanna's did.

"What's wrong, sugar?" she asked. "You're not yourself tonight."

Levi shrugged. "Too much whiskey, I guess."

Stella eyed the half-full bottle and flashed him a look of disbelief. "No amount of drink's ever stopped you before. Let's try something else."

Her hand moved over his thigh and up to his belt buckle. "First we need to get you out of these." She worked the buckle free, then set to releasing the buttons on his pants.

Levi kissed her again. He slid his hands over her body, feeling his way over her shoulders and breasts, down her belly, and over both hips.

Her hands groped against him, rubbing, touching, squeezing.

Nothing.

He might as well be kissing a tree for all the enjoyment he was getting out of it.

"Come on, sugar," she said, her voice losing much of its sweetness. "I'm ready any time you are."

"Sorry, Stella," he muttered, tugging her hands from behind his neck. "Just ain't gonna happen tonight."

She didn't even look disappointed; just lifted her dress from the floor and stepped back into it, her fingers working the buttons with quick precision.

"I still get paid for my time." She straightened the combs in her hair and fluffed out the fringe against her forehead.

"Yeah, of course." Levi pulled a few coins from his pocket and pressed them into her outstretched hand. Then he set about fastening his own buttons and buckle.

"Close the door on your way out," Stella said, then stopped as she pulled it open. Her pale eyes looked back at him, and she smiled. It was the first honest smile he'd ever seen cross her face. "I don't know who's got you all tied up in knots, Levi, but whoever she is, you either need to get *on* with her or get *over* her." Then Stella was gone.

Levi gaped after her for long minutes. What did she know, anyway? She was nothing but a two-bit whore working in a rundown saloon in the middle of cattle country. All he needed was some more whiskey. Then maybe he'd go sit in on a game or two downstairs. Winning someone else's money always made him feel better.

And if that didn't work, he'd find someone to plant his fist into. That'd do the trick.

"Jeez, you're fast." Will chuckled as Levi pulled up a chair. "D'you even give her time to drop her drawers?"

Levi put on his best game face and winked at Will. "If you knew Stella, you'd know she doesn't wear drawers."

Will and the other two men roared with laughter, forcing Levi to laugh too, though not near as loud.

As they all settled back down, Will shuffled the deck and began to deal. "You all know each other?" he asked.

"'Course," Levi answered, nodding at the other two men. Word was that Brooks Francis and Milt Mays had worked the Barnes's spread for more years than most could remember. And every Saturday night you'd find them at the same table, playing five-card draw and drinking Lefty's rotgut.

Brooks rearranged the cards in his hand. "Heard you two're working for them McCaine girls."

"Yup." Will fanned his cards, then slid them back together.

Milt shook his head and tossed a chip into the middle of the table. "Ain't right what they're doing over there."

Levi's skin prickled. "Yeah? What's that?"

"Fencing out their neighbors as though they was all criminals. Ain't right."

Brooks added his chips, then lay his cards face down on the table.

"Think so, do you?" Levi tried to sound disinterested as he added his chips and studied his cards.

"You think it's better for their neighbors to keep on stealing their cattle?"

Shock flashed across Milt's face. "Stealin'? Who's stealin'?"

Will cleared his throat. "I don't think Travers meant that the way it sounded." He shot Levi a warning look, but Levi just shrugged back. "He just meant that a lot of cattle go missing every year from the Double M, so Jo is just trying to keep them all contained now."

Milt slid two cards toward Will and clicked his tongue. "Jo. What kind of girl calls herself by a man's name, anyway?" His head shook slowly, but his eyes never lifted from his cards. "I hear her and her sister can't keep workers out there on that ranch."

Brooks called for two cards as well. "Could you abide workin' for a girl?" He shook his head in disgust. "Don't know how you two do it."

Levi's mouth opened, but Will beat him to the answer.

"Easy," he said. "We get paid on time, we get paid pretty well, and we get to eat Miss Ginny's cookin'."

Milt didn't look convinced. "We get paid on time, too, Brennan."

"Yeah, but have you ever had one of Miss Ginny's home-cooked meals?"

Both men shook their heads. "Can't say we have. I hear she's a helluva cook, though."

Will nodded. "You've got no idea."

"Are we playing cards or sharing recipes?" Levi pretended to focus on the game at hand. The other three hunkered down over their own hands and almost stopped talking altogether. Which was just fine with Levi.

After a couple hours, Will collected up his meager winnings and excused himself. "I see something that interests me more than these cards now, boys."

He adjusted his hat and strode over to the bar where Stella and one of the other girls, Crystal, stood talking to Lefty. In less than a minute, Will was following Crystal up the stairs.

Levi sat through another couple hands, even letting himself lose so the other two wouldn't think he was cheating. Then he made his excuses and headed for the door.

He tossed Lefty another coin. "Tell Brennan I've gone home, will ya?"

Lefty nodded and pocketed the coin, then turned back to wiping the bar with a dirty cloth.

"Travers."

Levi turned at the sound of his name and came face to face with Pearson's men who'd been sitting with Peter Carlson. He didn't answer them, simply stood with his hands stuffed in his pockets and waited.

"You no-good sonuvabitch." Frank Bellows stepped closer, the stench of cheap cigars wafting around him. "The boss is looking to tack your hide on his wall and I mean to help him do just that."

"Yeah?" Levi tried to sound indifferent. "Why's that?"

"You know damn well why." Bits of tobacco flew from Frank's black teeth with each word. "Stickin' his little girl the way you did and leavin' her ruined."

Carlson walked up behind Frank and smirked. "I can't believe Pearson ain't had you killed yet."

Levi shrugged as casually as he could. "Pearson

knows he can't prove anything. It's her word against mine."

"He'll have all the proof he needs in another month or so," Frank said. "Then we'll be coming for you, Travers."

Another shrug. "We'll see." He walked outside and down the boardwalk a few steps, thankful for a breath of fresh air. Carlson's voice trailed out after him.

"He's probably already stuck both them McCaine girls, too. Probably turned them both into his own whores out there." He laughed. "Hell, I bet he even had a go at Mac's old lady."

Levi had already turned back into the saloon the second he heard Carlson mention the McCaines. He grabbed Carlson by the shoulder, whipped him around, and slammed his fist into the other man's face. Carlson grunted, stumbled, then crashed against a table, sending cards, drinks, and men flying.

"Fight!" Several voices sent up the cheer as the tables around them emptied and were pulled out of the way so everyone could crowd around and get a better view.

Levi moved in again. He grabbed Carlson by the shirt, hauled him up, slammed another punch into his already bloody face, then let him fall again.

"Travers!" Lefty shuffled out from behind the bar, a thick board in his hand. "Get off him."

Levi made to reach for Carlson again, but Lefty pushed the board between them, his growl the only sound in the room. "I said get off." He didn't even flinch when Levi glowered at him. "You said you were on your way back to the ranch, so I suggest you get on your way."

"You sonuvabitch!" Carlson cried, his hands cupped over the blood gushing from his nose. "I think you broke it."

"You're lucky that's all he broke," Lefty growled. "Now get outta here. Both of you."

Levi straightened his shirt, jammed his hat back on, and pointed a finger at Carlson. "You even think about saying one more word about the McCaines, Carlson, and I swear to God—"

"Travers." Will slapped him on the back. "Looks like you've outstayed our welcome here," he said, smiling all around. "Let's go." As he pushed Levi toward the door, he called back over his shoulder. "Hey Lefty—tell Crystal thanks."

Levi pulled out of Will's grasp, cursing everyone around him—including Will. Especially Will.

Will raised both hands in surrender. "I was just trying to help you, friend. If you want to go back there and have the rest of them fellas beat you within an inch of your life, go ahead. But you're on your own."

Levi hesitated a moment before exhaling a loud, long breath and heading down the boardwalk. "Forget it. Let's just go home."

"Home?" Will muttered, falling in beside him. "Don't think I've ever heard you use that word before."

They paid Bill at the livery and rode for the ranch, each keeping whatever he was thinking to himself.

Jo lingered in the stable as long as she could. Every stall was clean; the gear was sorted, repaired, and put away; she'd even swept the floor. The crescent moon was high and the lamp oil low when she finally closed the door behind her and headed back to the house.

With each step, she gave herself a mental kick. What did she care that Travers had gone into town with Will? She'd been expecting him to do it every week since he'd arrived on the ranch, anyway. And who cared that it was well past midnight and he still wasn't back? Stella could keep a man busy for hours.

And she'd made it perfectly clear that he wasn't going to get anything from her, so why *wouldn't* he go see Stella?

The quiet of the house smothered her when she walked in. A small lamp burned in the kitchen, but that was the only light. The coffeepot was still hot to the touch, so she poured herself a cup, blew out the lamp, and went to sit on the porch where it wasn't so suffocating.

She sank down on the top step and leaned back against the post. Thin yellow moonlight filtered through the cottonwoods and somewhere high above, a lone meadowlark sang its mournful tune.

What was she going to do about Travers? Her brain and her heart seemed to be waging some kind of war she'd never known could be fought before now. He was smart, funny, and a strong worker. He made her think things she had no business thinking. And hell if he didn't have her feeling things she had no business feeling.

But he was Levi Travers. And right at that moment he was probably doing all sorts of unmentionable things with Stella—things he must have done with LeeAnna Pearson, too. Things he'd probably done with any number of women over the years.

And that was exactly why she couldn't let herself give in to his charm. She may be just plain old Joanna McCaine, but she'd rather die a virginal spinster than just be another woman Travers had his way with. Wouldn't she?

She used to think so. But knowing he was with Stella tonight was driving her mad. Was it jealousy or curiosity? Levi Travers must be some kind of man if women were willing to give up everything to be with him—even if it was only once. Maybe she should find out what was so great about him, then she could judge for herself.

Jo took a large mouthful of cold coffee and spat it on the next step before tossing the rest to the ground. Had she been sitting there that long?

She stood up, stretched, and took a final look around the yard. They really had done a lot of work since Travers signed on with them. Hard to believe, but he'd turned out to be exactly the kind of worker she needed. Of course, she'd rather die than admit that out loud, especially to him.

Hoofbeats sounded nearby, and they were getting closer, so Jo scurried back into the shadows of the porch. She couldn't have Travers thinking she'd waited up for him.

Travers and Will rode past, both silent, both looking ready to kill the first person who crossed their path.

Neither noticed her in the shadows, and she stayed right where she was until they were well past.

What would have caused them both to be so

angry? Probably fighting over Stella. Or Crystal. And if either was the case, then Lefty's girls were welcome to them both.

Will's voice carried over the still night air, but not quite loud enough for Jo to make out the words. Unable to stop herself, she hurried across the yard and hid behind the cottonwoods.

"All I'm saying is you ain't yourself these days, Travers. Maybe you need a few more nights with Stella to straighten yourself out."

"I'm the exact same person I was a year ago."

"No, you're not." Will sounded confused. "You even said it yourself—calling this place 'home'."

It sounded as though Travers cursed, but if he did, it was too low to hear. She leaned through the trees, keeping in the shadows.

"Look, Will. In a few weeks, that damned fence'll be finished. Then once we round up all Jo's cattle, we'll be outta here."

"You sure?"

"Of course I'm sure. I don't want to be here any longer than needs be. And she's made it pretty clear that she'll be more than happy to see my dust, too."

There was a long pause, some shuffling, and the sounds of leather slapping wood. They must have just hung their saddles.

Travers continued. "I mean it, Will. The sooner we're gone, the better."

"What about that Pearson girl?"

Travers cursed again. "What about her? She's no concern of mine."

A high squeak slipped through Jo's lips. If he didn't have a problem walking away from the woman who was carrying his child, he'd have no problem walking away from plain ol' Jo. She knew it—she'd *always* known it—but she'd also held on to a tiny shred of hope that she was wrong.

Now she knew she wasn't.

The stable door creaked open, then slammed shut. The two men muttered their good nights and stomped off in different directions.

Jo fell back against a thick tree, her breath coming in shallow gasps. In a few weeks, Travers would be gone. Gone. Forever.

She buried her face in her hands, but the tears squeezed out through her fingers. The knot in her stomach twisted so tight she thought she'd double over from the pain. Damn it, why did she care if he left?

A soft sob escaped her throat.

"Joanna?"

Jo nearly leapt from her skin at the sound of Travers's voice. She dashed her sleeve over her eyes and forced her tongue to work. It'd never taken so much effort before.

"I-I was just checking to make sure . . ." she paused, swallowed another small sob, then said, "that y-you two were still in one piece and able to work come Monday."

He stepped forward, his hand reaching toward her, but she ducked away.

"What's wrong?" Damn that voice of his! And double damn her weak heart.

"Nothing." She sniffed as quietly as she could and lifted her chin a notch.

"You've been crying."

She snorted. "I don't cry, Travers." At least she didn't use to. Not unless she was sitting at Mama's graveside.

When he took another step closer, she moved farther away and started heading back toward the house, but his hand closed around her arm, keeping her from escape.

"Joanna." His voice caressed her ears while his fingers did the same to her skin. "Tell me what's wrong—maybe I can help."

She laughed sadly and turned back to him, letting the tears fall freely now. "How can you help, Travers, when you're what's wrong with me?"

His mouth fell open, but no sound came out. He just stood staring at her as if she had two heads.

A gentle tug was all it took to free her from his grasp. Then she turned and ran all the way back to the house.

Chapter 8

Joanna wasn't anywhere around the house when Levi went up for breakfast the next morning. But Mac was.

And a more hostile man Levi'd never met.

"Joanna said to let him eat," Ginny murmured to her husband as she handed Levi a plate of food. "In peace."

No one else said a word throughout the meal, almost as though they all knew Mac was going to blast him, but they didn't want to be the ones to ignite the fuse.

The ham and eggs might well have been wood chips for all Levi could taste of them, and even though the coffee was scalding hot, he downed it in one long gulp, offered his thanks, and headed outside.

Though he'd questioned his own sanity more often than not lately, Levi wasn't completely stupid. He knew better than to make Mac come and find him—best to get it over with, and fast.

Thank God he didn't have to wait long.

Mac McCaine stomped out of the house, his hat low over his eyes, his jaw clenched tight, and his thick finger pointed right at Travers.

"You an' me are gonna have words."

Levi didn't answer, just followed Mac down to the far barn. The very empty, very quiet barn.

Mac stopped midway down the long, narrow aisle between stalls and turned to face Levi. It was more than clear he was fighting to control his rage. The vein in his forehead pulsed faster than was probably good for him and his fingers clenched and unclenched at his sides until it must have become too much.

Quick as lightening, he pulled back and smashed Levi in the nose with his left fist. Levi stumbled back, but kept to his feet. He made no attempt to swing back or even duck when Mac swung again, this time with his right fist.

The second punch connected with Levi's jaw and sent him into the wall, but again, he remained upright. Barely.

He tried to curb the blood that ran from his nose, but it wasn't much use. It trickled down his face and into his mouth, leaving a dirty iron taste. Damn, but his face hurt.

"I told you to leave Joey alone, Travers." Mac's voice, though low and even, was more threatening than a cocked .45. "I told you not to go toyin' with her."

"I didn't—"

Mac pulled himself back a few steps, but Levi didn't doubt for a second he was ready to throw a third punch if given half a chance. "Then why the hell was she up all last night crying herself sick?"

"I—" Levi steadied himself, rubbing his hand

across his jaw—damn, but that man could punch. Joanna cried all night? Over him?

"Don't tell me you didn't do anything, you sonuvabitch—I know all about you an' her carryin' on out at the fence."

Levi winced. It almost felt like Mac had slammed him again.

"Wipe that stupid look off your face, Travers. Clay told Newt everything." He paced the width of the aisle. "You're not stupid enough to think I wouldn't find out."

Levi couldn't answer, mainly because he had no defense. He'd kissed Joanna, kissed her good and well, too, without a single thought about the consequences. And Clay had seen everything. Of course the boy told Newt—the old codger was like a father to the kid—a rather sorry excuse for a father, but who was Levi to judge?

With a long exhale, he lifted his head so his gaze leveled with Mac's. "It didn't mean anything," he began, then snapped his mouth closed. Even if that hadn't been a lie, it wasn't the explanation Mac was looking for.

Mac lunged again, this time connecting with Levi's right eye. "Bastard."

Levi fell against the rail and took a long moment to find his balance before he turned again.

"Jesus, Mac," he groaned, "if you'd just give me a second—"

"What for? So you can tell me more about how you used my niece to relieve yourself when you got all horned up?"

"Wasn't like that."

"No?" Mac's snort would have done Jo proud. "You just told me it didn't mean nothin' to you."

"I—"

"It meant *everything* to her."

Dead silence filled the barn. No words had ever scared Levi more. He licked his suddenly parched lips, his gaze darting around the barn without seeing anything.

The kiss meant everything to Joanna.

"I didn't do anything about it then because I figured Joey knew what she was doing." Mac's eyes narrowed to mere slits. "If she'd wanted you dead, she'd have done it herself right then."

The fact that she hadn't killed him that day was still a bit of a shock to Levi. Mac tipped his head toward Levi's saddle.

"Pick up your gear and get your ass as far off this land as you can, you hear me?"

"Mac, listen—" Levi's head pounded with every breath. He wiggled his jaw a little, relieved to find it still able to move at all.

"You ain't got nothing to say I want to hear, Travers." The tight lines around Mac's mouth eased a little. Not much, but a little. "Can't believe I let you fool me, too. I almost believed you could be trusted."

"I didn't try to fool anyone, Mac. And you *can* trust me." Dammit, why did any of this even matter?

"Bullshit. You're nothing but a lying, no-good, yellow-bellied coward." The tightness returned to Mac's face—and his voice. "I don't know what you did to make Joey cry like that, and I don't care. All I know is I ain't never seen her like that. And you're the one who caused it."

He bobbed his head toward the gear again. "Now

get off this land before I do what Pearson should have done to you months ago."

"What about the fence?"

"That ain't none of your concern."

Levi inhaled a long breath, then risked his neck by taking a step toward Mac. "If you'd let me explain . . ."

But there'd be no explaining; the murderous look Mac gave him made that pretty clear.

"You've got ten minutes to get off this ranch. After that, I swear to God I'll shoot you myself."

With that, Mac walked out, leaving Levi alone in the barn.

The quiet surrounded him, the emptiness echoing back the sounds of his breathing. Still, it was nothing compared to the huge, gaping emptiness in his gut.

"You did *what?*" Jo's eyes nearly bugged from her skull. "Christ almighty, Mac—have you lost your mind?"

"Joanna!" Ginny gasped. "Such language."

But Jo didn't even pretend to pay her aunt any mind. "You can't just fire him like that—we need him!"

"The hell we do, Joey." She'd never seen, or heard, Mac so angry. "We'll do just fine without him—we've managed so far."

"Yeah," she snorted, "and look where that's gotten us. Half the goddamned herd's gone missing and with roundup coming up, we're sure as hell going to lose most of what's left."

"You don't know that." Mac sipped his coffee as though it was any other mealtime.

"Yes, I do, Mac, and so do you." Jo pushed her plate back and shoved herself out of her chair. "I'm going after him."

Mac jumped up, too, and blocked her path. "You'll do no such thing."

"Get out of my way, Mac. We need him to get the fence built."

"No, we don't. You an' me can build it." Doubt flicked over his eyes, but disappeared just as fast. "There's not that much left to go, anyway."

"And if you come in to work the fence, who's going to tend the herd?" Panic pooled in her veins. Levi couldn't be gone already. She wasn't ready for him to leave. Not even close to ready.

"We've still got Simon and Jimmy."

"Oh my God." Jo laughed in disbelief. "Those two couldn't herd themselves! And you're the one who's so worried about what goes on out there when you're not watching them."

Mac shrugged. "We'll make it work somehow. Maybe Will could take over either the fence or the herd." His old eyes looked so tired. "Anyone but Travers."

"Will's still here?" Carrie suddenly piped up, a slow smile curling her lips. Jo ignored her.

"Will's already running double duty between the fence and the herd," Jo said. "You know that."

"Maybe Newt—"

Jo threw her hands up. "Listen to what you're saying, Mac. You think Newt would be any use on the fence? He can't even hold the hammer, for Christ's sake."

"Then maybe with the herd."

"No," she cried. "Not with the herd, either. If he can't hold a hammer, Mac, how well do you think he'd do trying to rope a crazed bull? Hell—I could probably do a better job of roping than Newt."

"Are you sure Will didn't leave with Levi?" Carrie asked. "They're very close, you know."

Jo clicked her tongue at her sister, then made for the door again.

"Joanna," Mac began, but she moved past him. "He's only going to hurt you again."

Jo's feet froze beneath her. So that's what it came down to—Mac was trying to protect *her*, not the ranch. If only he knew the truth—that he couldn't protect her from herself.

"Mac, whatever happened between me and Travers"—she stopped Carrie's interruption with a raised hand—"which was nothing but a kiss, won't happen again. It was just as much my fault as it was his."

"No, Joey, it wasn't." Mac shook his head hard. "Travers is a no-good sonuvabitch who took advantage of you."

"No." Her laugh was dry and humorless. "He didn't. I could have stopped him whenever I wanted to." She paused, inhaled, and let the breath out slowly. "But I didn't want to. I let him kiss me, Mac."

Carrie's face broke out in a huge smile, as Ginny's gasp filled the room. "Joanna!"

"What?" she turned to face her aunt. "I'm supposed to pretend I don't want to be kissed? Sorry, Ginny, but I do." Mac's stare burned a hole through the back of her head, but she continued anyway. "I might not act much like a lady most of the time, but that doesn't mean I don't feel the same things you do."

Ginny's mouth opened, but she didn't make a sound. Carrie bounced up and down in her chair, clapping her hands. "Thank goodness," she squealed. "Now you can come with us to San Francisco."

"Doesn't mean I'm going to let it happen again," Jo continued, completely ignoring her sister. "I'm not stupid, and I know what kind of man he is."

She turned back to Mac and looked at him pointedly. "He was with Stella last night, that's part of the reason I was upset." Mac and Ginny didn't need to know that the very idea of Travers leaving the ranch made Jo want to cry all over again. "But that's only because I as much as told him to go. He's never promised me anything and I've no one to blame but myself for what I do or how I feel."

Mac's fingers tightened around the back of his chair, but he kept his mouth squeezed shut.

"I'm going to get him." Jo kept her voice even. "And he's going to stay here until the fence is finished. Then—and only then—will I let him, or anyone else, leave this ranch."

Ginny stepped toward her, taking her hand and sandwiching it between her own. "But you were so upset last night."

For someone who hated this kind of talk, Jo was sure bringing a lot of it down on herself this afternoon.

"Yes, I was. But it's not his fault I'm an idiot." She forced a small smile and kissed her aunt's cheek. "We need him here, and I'm going to bring him back."

"Joey—" Mac began, but she cut him off.

"I appreciate you looking out for me, but this fence is more important than me shedding a few tears." Mac didn't look the least bit convinced. "Besides, in a few weeks, Travers and Brennan will be long gone and then things can get back to normal. Whatever that means around here."

She smiled at Mac, but he didn't smile back. Fact was, he looked even more determined than ever to keep Travers off their land. But Jo needed that damned fence built. That, and she needed to see him again, to be near him again, even if she wouldn't let herself touch him. Just having him close by would be enough.

Or so she hoped.

"Jee-zuz, Travers—Joey finally put the boots to you, huh?" Lefty's roughened laughter turned to coughing, then choking, making him grip the bar for support.

Levi offered no help, just stood and watched until Lefty was able to breathe normally again. Well, watched might not be the best word, since his right eye had swelled almost shut. He and Lefty made a good pair.

"Whoo," Lefty exhaled loudly, wiping his eye. "She musta been some mad—what the hell d'you do?"

Levi slumped onto a stool and reached for the bottle of whiskey in the bartender's hand. Lefty held tight for a second, then laughed again and let Levi take it.

"Hell, anyone who can come in here lookin' like that deserves a good stiff one."

Levi took a long pull straight from the bottle, then swiped his sleeve roughly across his mouth.

New pain shot through his head; damn it—he shouldn't have done that. He took another swig to ease the new blast of pain, then a third for good measure.

"I knew Joey was tough," Left went on. "But I ain't never seen her hurt someone this bad."

"Wasn't Joanna," Levi mumbled, lifting the bottle again.

"Then who . . ." Lefty's eye widened. "Mac?"

Before Levi could even nod his head, Lefty was doubled over, choking through another fit of laughter.

"Glad you find this so amusing." Levi dared to look past the wheezing bartender to get a look at himself in the cracked mirror behind the bar. Wasn't much wonder Lefty was laughing so hard.

His right eye was not only swollen shut, but had turned a dark, garish purple and green. His nose, though not broken, had done some pretty good bleeding before he managed to stop it with a torn piece of blanket he'd found in the barn as he left the ranch. Dried blood caked around his mouth and over his nose, and even as he watched, more trickled down to his lip.

Just looking at the way his jaw puffed out to twice its normal size made Levi's head hurt even more. He'd been damned lucky to keep all his teeth.

Lefty's laughter died to a chuckle. "Well, hell, Travers, I bet even Carrie could whup Mac if she wanted to. Did you even try to defend yourself?"

Levi dropped his gaze to the bar. When he didn't answer, Lefty's voice got louder.

"You let an old man beat the crap outta you?" He choked. "What the hell's wrong with you?"

It was a question he'd been asking himself for days. Weeks.

"I couldn't hit Mac," he grumbled.

"Why not? You got no problem takin' a piece outta everyone else around here."

Levi shrugged. There was a time, not so long ago, when he had an answer for just about everything. Now, he was just a stupid fool.

"Musta been somethin' bad for him to lay a beatin' like that on you. What'd you do?"

Another shrug, this time with a slow shake of his head. "Doesn't matter now."

"Guess not." Lefty chuckled again. "Don't suppose you'd like to lie down for a while?"

"Oh, man, Lefty. I'd about kill for a soft bed right now." He half-grinned. "Hell, doesn't even have to be soft."

Lefty nodded and indicated his room behind the bar. "Go lie down. I'll bring you some coffee."

With mumbled thanks, Levi tripped into the tiny back room and tumbled onto the narrow cot. Wasn't soft or comfortable, but it was a bed and there wasn't anyone else in the room. Not that there was enough space for anyone else; the room was barely big enough for the cot and the small wood table that held nothing but an empty oil lamp.

He lay flat on his back, his hat still on, though the back was crushed behind his head, with his booted feet dangling off the end of the cot. His left eye drifted shut, the bottle of whiskey still clenched in his hands.

It was a while later when a waft of fresh coffee brought him around and forced his good eye open. He couldn't wait to—

Stella.

She sat on the edge of the cot, near his hip, holding a steaming cup of the mud Lefty called coffee. The feathers in her hair sat a little crooked and some of the paint had smudged under her eyes, but she still looked a little worried. Not a lot, mind you, but a little.

"Hello, sugar," she cooed. "Thought you was gonna sleep the night away, too."

She set his coffee cup on the small table, then lifted a bowl from the floor and rested it in her lap. When she rinsed a dirty rag in the water, Levi fought the urge to shudder.

With the cloth still dripping, she set to work on washing away the dried blood from his face.

"Lefty says you let Mac do this to you."

When he didn't answer, she smiled, her pale blue eyes blank and unfeeling.

"And though he didn't say why, I'm gonna guess it has something to do with that niece of his."

Again, he didn't answer.

"Shouldn't surprise me," she murmured as she smoothed the cloth down his cheek and over his blood-caked lips. "Carrie's a beautiful girl. I'm sure she was too much for you to resist."

"Carrie?" he croaked, then a second later wished he could take it back.

"Well, yes, she's certainly . . ." Stella stopped, the cloth hovering midway between the bowl and Levi's face. "You don't mean—"

Levi ground his teeth together then fought the urge to scream. Damn that Mac and his right hook.

"Joanna?" Stella whispered, her eyes huge. "You let Mac do this to you 'cuz of *Joanna*?"

Fighting back the searing pain, Levi managed to clench his jaw shut; he wasn't going to say another word about this. Not to Stella.

She dropped the cloth back in the bowl and laughed softly. "Never thought I'd lose a man to someone like Joanna McCaine." She set the bowl on the floor, then adjusted the neckline of her dress to show a bit more of her ample cleavage. "She's not near enough woman for you, Levi. But I am."

He shifted away from her, but she was quick. Damn quick. Her dry lips pressed lightly against his cheek, her fingers going to work on his belt buckle.

"Stop it, Stella." He gripped her hands with his own and moved back another inch until he hit the wall.

"Come on, sugar," she purred. "Just once more for old time's sake." She leaned in and kissed his chest through the opening at his collar.

Levi released her hands to push her away, but in that split instant his gaze flicked over Stella's head and stopped at the person standing in the doorway.

Joanna.

"Shit." Forgetting his attempts to be gentle, he shoved Stella off the cot, sending her stumbling to the floor. But Joanna was already gone.

"Ow." Stella's whine didn't even slow him down. He half-ran, half-stumbled after Joanna and only caught up with her as she untied her horse from the rail outside.

"Joanna, wait," he panted, tripping down the two steps to the ground.

Fire flashed in her green eyes; her back was stiff as a rod and her throat bobbed against a hard swallow.

"Don't let me interrupt," she said stiffly.

"You weren't interrupting anything." He took a step closer and walked straight into her horse as it turned its muzzle toward him. Pain blasted through his face, sending him staggering backward into the steps.

"Argh!" Blood began pouring from his nose again. He should have just stayed where he was, just kept his ass planted on that step, and let Joanna go. But since he didn't seem to be on speaking terms with common sense lately, he pushed himself up and moved toward her again.

Jo had straddled her horse and was glaring down at him, her voice icy. "I just came to tell you if you still want the job, it's yours. Otherwise, come and collect the wages we owe you and be on your way."

She kneed her horse, but Levi lunged forward and grabbed the loose reins in his hand.

"Wait." If he lived through the day, through the pain that shot through him with every move he made, he'd die of shock.

Though she didn't say anything, and she didn't bother to even look at him, he could see her pulse pounding in her neck—that beautiful, soft neck.

"I don't know what Mac told you," he said, "and I don't know what you're thinking right now, but if you'd let me explain—"

With a hard yank, she pulled the reins from his grip and shook her head. "No need to explain anything to me, Travers. Do you want your job or not?"

He nodded slowly.

"Then I'll expect you back at the ranch first thing in the morning. That should leave you plenty of time to finish up with Stella."

Levi dropped his hands to his sides, silently cursing

every breath he took. Damn, but Joanna was ornery. And why was he even bothering to explain himself? He hadn't done anything wrong!

He should find his horse and ride out of this sorry town once and for all. Forget his owed wages, cut his losses, and head to San Francisco like he'd planned—with or without Will.

But he knew he wouldn't. If there was one thing he needed to do before he left, it was to prove to Joanna—and Mac—that he wasn't the sonuvabitch they both thought he was. And the only way to do that was to prove he wasn't the one who got that Pearson girl in trouble.

And the only way to do *that* was to wait it out until the baby was born. If his suspicions were right, and luck was on his side, one look at the baby would answer everyone's questions.

Chapter 9

"Is he back?" Mac hadn't touched his breakfast and his coffee mug was in jeopardy of being smashed between his hands.

"Haven't seen him," Jo answered, then forced one last forkful of ham into her mouth. "He said he'd be here, though."

"I don't give a damn what he *said*."

"Mac." Ginny scolded. "Enough with that kind of language. You're not out with the herd, you know."

"Joanna says worse," Carrie chimed in.

"That doesn't make it right." Ginny looked pointedly at both Mac and Jo before starting to clear the table. "What would you like me to do with his breakfast?"

Mac's face turned even redder.

"I'll take it to him," Jo answered. The thought of having to face Travers made her want to bring her breakfast right back up, but a deal was a deal; if he was going to hold up his end of it, so was she. And that included three squares a day.

Ginny handed her a full plate and a steaming

mug of coffee, then held the door open for her. Mac didn't so much as look up when she walked by.

The usual noises greeted her in the yard, but this morning they seemed louder and sharper and all seemed to clamor as one great, deafening blare inside Jo's head. The chickens clucked and squawked continually, puppies ran around the grass yapping and nipping at Clay's ankles and each other's tails, and the barn cows bawled for their udders to be relieved.

Will met her as she walked past the corral.

"That for Travers?" he nodded toward the plate. "I can take it to him for you."

"Thank you, but I'll do it." She kept walking. "I want to make sure he's here and able to work."

"He's here," Will sighed. "But . . ."

Jo climbed the cabin steps and rapped on the door. "Travers—you in there?"

Will's voice followed her. "It might be better if I take that in, Jo."

She kept her back to him. "I said I'd do it."

"But—"

"Don't you have work to do?"

Will didn't answer, and a moment later, the sound of boots pounding the dirt receded across the yard.

"Travers!" She banged again, louder.

Through the door, she could hear him moving around, almost like he was crashing into things. She waited another few seconds, then opened the door herself.

"Travers?" she stepped closer. "Oh my God."

The plate shook in her hand and half the coffee splashed onto the floor before she could set them on the table. She moved toward the seated man whose only resemblance to Levi Travers was the length and color of his hair.

He'd looked bad when she saw him at Lefty's yesterday, but today was a hundred times worse. His right eye, covered by a dark purple bruise, had swelled to about the size of a small apple. His other eye bore the same color bruises, but at least it was open. Sort of.

A long, thin cut ran the length of his nose and there was still blood caked around both his nose and mouth.

"Did Mac . . ?" Guilt washed over her in currents.

"That man's got a helluva right hook," he mumbled.

"Didn't know it was that good." She reached her fingers out to touch the purple bruise on his cheek, but he gripped her hand and pulled away.

"Don't," he begged. "For God's sake, don't touch it."

"Sorry." Jo yanked her fingers back and stuffed her hands in her front pockets. Damn, he looked bad. For half a second, she was glad—glad he'd felt some of the pain she'd felt and glad he'd have something to remind him of it.

But those feelings were quickly washed away by stronger waves of guilt. Sure, Mac had done the damage, but she'd done her part, too, by carrying on like such a ninny. His face—his gorgeous, smiling face—looked like something the stage had run over—twice.

"I brought you some breakfast," she said. Anything to keep him from feeling her guilt.

"I can't chew." Then, to her complete shock, he grinned. It wasn't the usual sexy grin he flashed at her, but still—it was something to see beneath all the blood and swelling.

"How about the coffee, then?" she asked. "No chewing involved. Just sipping."

"Is there any left?" his lips barely moved. "Or do I need to sip it off the floor?"

Jo looked back at the small puddle she'd left behind her. "I'll get that. Any rags?"

She handed him the coffee cup and set to cleaning up the mess while guilt gnawed at her gut. Mama would be horrified to see what she'd done to Travers—whether he deserved it or not.

She knew he had a fondness for Stella, knew he'd eventually go in to see her, and she'd damn well known right from the get-go that Travers would leave once the fence was done. But she'd gone and let herself soften to him until just the thought of Stella—or of him leaving—made her do things she couldn't even begin to explain.

Like the way she carried on the other night. It was because of her that Travers had gotten beaten to a pulp. She couldn't have felt worse if she'd done the beating herself.

When she'd spent as long as she possibly could wiping up the coffee, she inhaled a long breath and turned to face him. But before her words could come out, a thought struck her and changed the direction of her tongue.

"You didn't fight back."

Travers didn't answer, just sat sipping his coffee. Very slowly.

"Why not?"

No response.

"Travers . . ."

"I got no cause to hit Mac," he mumbled. "He's never done anything to me."

"Except beat your face in."

Another shrug. "Guess he thought he had cause to."

"Yeah," she whispered, her face flaming under his gaze. "About that—"

He stopped her with a raised hand and turned her words back on her. "No need to explain anything to me."

The knot in her stomach twisted even tighter. She deserved that.

"I think I do need to explain," she said, lowering herself to the edge of his bed. "And to apologize."

He shook his head slowly, then winced. "As much as I'd love to hear you admit you were wrong," he winced again, "can we do it later? My head's killing me."

Relief flooded through her. The last thing she wanted to do was admit to Travers that she'd been jealous of Stella. "Of course. Sorry." She pushed back to her feet. "Why don't you lie down?"

A soft chuckle escaped his swollen lip. "'Cuz my boss expects me at work this morning. And believe me, you don't want to make her mad. She's got a temper like—"

"Okay, Travers," she said, rolling her eyes. "You've made your point."

Jo pulled the blankets back and patted the pillow. "I'll talk to your boss and make her see reason. Might even convince her not to dock your pay for today."

His lip curled upward slightly. "I wouldn't count on it. But I'm happy to lose a day's pay if it means I can go back to bed."

Jo's heart tripped over its next beat as Travers slid

onto the bed, boots and all. He'd always seemed . . . well, almost indestructible. And now even the slightest movement obviously pained him. She had to fight back the urge to curl up beside him and do whatever he asked to ease his pain.

She ached just looking at him. But this ache was more than just guilt; this wasn't like anything she'd ever felt before. None of the stories about Travers mattered anymore. Stella didn't matter anymore. And not even the thought of LeeAnna Pearson and her baby mattered anymore.

Travers had let Mac beat on him because of Jo. Did he think he deserved it? That was nonsense, of course. He'd never promised her anything; he'd never even hinted at a promise.

Something akin to nausea flooded Jo. Why did she suddenly feel like laughing and crying all at the same time? And what were all these strange feelings battling for attention? Watching him settle against his pillow nearly ripped her heart in two; she couldn't do this anymore.

If Travers wanted her, then he could have her. If he didn't, then she'd have to learn to live with that. And the more she thought about it, the more she knew she'd have to learn quickly.

She tugged his boots off and set them beside the bed. Both socks were worse than threadbare, and the big toe on his right foot stuck through a huge hole. Several other holes had been darned—not well, but darned nonetheless.

The man needed a woman in his life. One who would tend to these things for him. Jo frowned. She'd never threaded a needle in her life. But Carrie had.

Travers sighed and reached for the blanket just as Jo pulled it up over his chest. Almost instantly, his breathing fell into the soft, steady rhythm of sleep.

Even all swollen and purple, he was a fine looking man. Knowing he'd taken the beating for her made him even more attractive to her and, though she knew that was the stupidest thought she'd had in a long time, it somehow made sense to her.

She brushed a lock of hair from his forehead, then leaned over and pressed a soft kiss in the same spot—the only part of his face not swollen.

She backed up a step, then stopped. She shouldn't do it; she wouldn't do it. So why was she leaning back toward him?

Jo touched her lips to his, wincing at the way his upper lip had swelled like a giant sausage.

"Feel better, Travers."

He mumbled softly, but she couldn't make out what he said. She was tempted to touch his bruises, to somehow try to make them go away, but that was more nonsense. Best to let him rest; she'd check on him later.

Clay was in the yard playing with the puppies when she stepped out of the cabin and closed the door.

"I've got a job for you," she said.

The boy looked as eager as ever. "Yes, ma'am."

"I'm going to go work on the fence in the east corner. When Travers wakes up, you come and get me."

Clay nodded solemnly. "Is M-Mr. Travers okay?"

Jo rumpled his already mussed hair and smiled. "He'll be fine. Just needs some rest is all."

"Good."

Jo watched the relief wash over Clay's face. The poor kid had been honestly worried. She knew he'd spent a lot of time with Travers, but didn't know what they did or what they talked about.

"You like Travers, huh?" she asked, squatting down to eye level with him.

"Yes, ma'am," Clay nodded. "M-Mr. Travers talks to me. An' he lets me talk back."

Jo fought back a chuckle. "Yeah? What kinds of things do you talk about?"

A shrug. "Stuff. Like how him an' me ain't got no folks."

That's right—Travers had told her his mother was dead. "What about his father? Brothers or sisters?"

Clay shook his head. "Tol' me his ma was a . . . th-that she worked in a saloon. They lived there, t-too."

"In the saloon?" Jo gaped. "Are you sure?"

He nodded. "Uh-huh. Says they moved into a house with a bunch of other women when he w-was 'bout my age."

Travers grew up in a whorehouse? It was no wonder he'd turned out the way he did—with no respect for himself or anyone else.

"I tol' Mr. Travers he should s-stay here an' we'd be his folks. Jus' like you're my folks now."

A small lump crept up Jo's throat. "That'd be nice, Clay, but I think Travers is keen to move on. Once we're done with the fence, he'll be heading to California."

The boy shrugged again, then sniffed. "I know. I was jus' kinda hopin' is all."

Swallowing hard, she pushed to her feet and

smiled down at Clay. "Hope is a good thing, Clay, as long as you don't let yourself believe in something that's just not going to happen. Do you understand?"

He nodded, but she knew he didn't understand one bit. Hell, *she* didn't understand it. And once Travers left, the poor kid would lose the closest thing he'd had to an older brother. And she'd lose the closest thing she'd ever had to a . . .

To a what? What was Travers to her? And what was she to him? Too many questions. Her brain swam in them, begging for some kind of answer. Any answer.

"I gotta go," she said, "but you'll come get me, right?"

Clay nodded again, then shuffled off after one of the puppies. If Jo thought she had half a chance of making it work, she'd adopt that kid on the spot and give him a real family. But boys needed fathers, and that was the one thing she couldn't give him.

Levi opened his eyes to find the sun had begun its slow descent in the western sky. His jaw still ached, and his eye still wouldn't open all the way, but at least he could see a little better than he could earlier.

It'd been a long time since he'd slept the day away. And even longer since someone had tucked him in the way Joanna had, with a soft caress and a kiss. Two kisses, actually. He'd felt her staring at him, felt a growing tension coming from her, and then she'd kissed him . . .

Levi groaned.

If he hadn't been so tired, or so sore, God only knows how he'd have responded to her.

He pulled on his boots, grabbed his hat, and stepped out into the yard. Clay scampered out of the barn, eyeing him carefully.

"How you feelin', Mr. Travers?"

Levi chuckled. "Probably better than I look. D'you know where Joanna is?"

"Yup. I'm 'posed to go get her from the east corner as soon as you woke up."

When he turned back to the barn, Levi stopped him. "Hold on, Clay. I'll just ride out there myself."

"B-but she said—"

"It's okay," he said. "I promise. But I'd sure appreciate it if you'd saddle my horse for me. Can you do that?"

"Yes, sir!" Clay disappeared inside the stable while Levi walked around the corral, trying to ease some of the stiffness from his back.

Mac rounded the corner and stopped dead. For long seconds, they stood staring at each other, neither one moving. Then Mac broke the silence.

"Joey tells me I done wrong by layin' that on you." He kept his glare steady. "I ain't gonna apologize, though, because I still think you deserved it."

Levi didn't answer.

"Says you never promised her anything, so she got no right to be upset like she was." He stepped closer and Levi braced for another blow. "I don't care about any of that, Travers. All I care about is seeing her cry. Make her cry again, and I swear—"

"Here you go, Mr. Travers." Clay led Levi's mare from the stable, then came up short when he saw Mac.

"Thanks, Clay." Levi took the reins and returned

his gaze to Mac. "I've got no plan to hurt Joanna. And I've got no desire to meet you in the barn again."

"Then we're clear."

Levi nodded. "Clear as can be. Now, if you don't mind, I've got work to do." He swung up into the saddle, careful not to wince in front of Mac.

"You're going to work like that?" Mac barked. "You can hardly see."

"I can see just fine." Yup, he saw plenty fine now. Joanna'd been jealous the other night—that's what got her so upset. And though her being upset shouldn't make him smile, he couldn't seem to help himself. She'd been jealous of Stella. How stupid was that?

The late day sun warmed his back as he rode slowly east, thinking on what he'd just learned. If Joanna was jealous, did that mean she was feeling the same way he was? And what the hell was that anyway? It sure couldn't be what Will had called it—love—because Levi didn't have the first idea what that meant. Or how it felt.

Lust was a part of it, no question, but there was something else, too. Something stronger, something that made his heart beat too hard and too fast, and something that made him want to run in the other direction, yet at the same time, it made him want to run straight to Joanna and spend the rest of his days listening to her snort.

He must be losing his mind. That was the only explanation he could come up with for why he was still grinning like a fool, ignoring the pain throbbing in his head, and riding toward a woman who'd probably tell him to go straight to hell if he told her any of this.

But he had to tell her. Even if it meant another beating from Mac.

Joanna looked up as he rode closer, her arm shielding her eyes from the sun.

"You should be in bed," she said.

Levi bit back the response that jumped to his tongue. He'd like to go back to bed, but only if she went with him. And she'd be doing more than just tucking him in and kissing his damn-fool forehead this time. And there sure as hell wouldn't be any more of those chaste kisses she'd touched his mouth with, either.

Pain or no pain, he needed her to kiss him good and proper again.

"I've slept enough." He cleared his throat. "Time to get back to work." He eased from his saddle and tossed the reins over a nearby branch.

"Sure you're up to it?" She gave him a doubtful look.

"'Course." He grinned. "Just so long as I don't have to swing a hammer or make any sudden movements."

She smiled back, then paled, the hammer twisting in her hands. She almost looked like she was going to be sick. Or, God help him, cry.

"Look, Travers, I gotta say something to you."

He lowered himself to a chunk of cut-up log and tipped his head up to see her face.

Joanna cleared her throat. "It's my fault Mac did this to you and I'm sorry. He was just looking out for me because I was being an idiot. You didn't deserve this."

He hesitated a minute, then shrugged. "Well, see, I don't agree."

A flash of shock crossed her face before she rolled her eyes. "You think Mac was right to take a piece out of you the way he did?"

"Well, no, but he had his reasons. And you didn't make him do it."

Her chin fell against her chest. "Yes, I did. I knew you'd been with Stella that night and . . ." The hammer flipped in circle after circle in her hands.

"And what?" he prodded, loving the way her face flushed so many different shades of pink.

"And it made me mad." Up came her chin again, challenging him.

Levi couldn't help but grin. "Mad? Or *jealous*?"

"Jealous?" she cried, but averted her gaze. "I . . . I was n—"

"Joanna." He pushed off the log and moved in front of her, easing the hammer from her fingers. He tried not to smile at her, but she was so gorgeous standing there lying through her teeth.

"What?" She crossed her arms over her chest, but she couldn't hide from him anymore. She was only trying to hide the way her hands trembled.

"You're a lousy liar," he said.

If her cheeks went any redder, they'd probably burst into flames.

"Were you jealous?" he asked again.

She flicked her braid over her shoulder and shrugged. "I've got no reason to be jealous. It's not like we . . . like you and I . . . oooh!"

Even though it sent pain spiraling through his head, Levi couldn't help but laugh. "You're right.

You've got no reason to be jealous, because nothing happened between me and Stella."

Her mouth opened, closed, then opened again, but no sound came out. Piercing green eyes narrowed at him while her teeth worried her bottom lip. If his mouth weren't so sore, he'd just lean over and kiss that lip of hers. In fact, he might have to do it anyway—damn the pain.

She blinked hard and stepped back. "But you and Will went to Lefty's. And yesterday, I saw you—"

Damn. Missed his chance.

"Look," he sighed. "I went to Lefty's on Saturday night to get with Stella." When Joanna's eyes widened and shimmered, he hurried on. "But I swear nothing happened. And yesterday, what you saw was Stella trying to *make* something happen."

Confusion mingled with her wariness. "W-why didn't anything happen? I thought you and Stella . . ."

Levi blew a long breath between his lips. "D'you really want to know?"

Her head shook, then stilled. "Yes."

"Okay, but just remember—you asked."

Joanna slumped onto the log he'd recently occupied. Her hands twisted around the cuff of her shirt and her eyes looked everywhere but at him. For some Godforsaken reason, Levi needed her to look at him. He needed to see her eyes when these strange, and probably stupid, words came tumbling out of his mouth. Then he'd know how much time he had to get off the Double M alive.

"Look at me."

Her eyes flitted upward, then darted away again.

"Joanna. Look at me." He upended another log and positioned it so they sat knee to knee. Slowly, she looked back at him, almost as though she was searching his face for something. Not that she'd find anything with all the bruises.

Levi took a deep breath. He could do this. He *had* to do this.

"Nothing happened with Stella because I . . . I kept thinking about someone else."

She looked away again, but he turned her face until she looked back at him.

"You, Joanna." There, he'd said it. "I kept thinking about you. About how you felt in my arms that day, about how I'd never known a woman could feel so . . . hell, I don't even know what word to use."

Why didn't she say something? Anything?

He swallowed and went on. "And I couldn't stop wondering what the hell I was doing *there* when you were *here*."

Her head started to shake, so he nodded. "Yes. It's true, Joanna. All I wanted to do was come home—I mean, to the ranch—and find you."

Two tears tipped out of her eyes and slid down her cheeks. Levi frowned as he wiped them away with his thumb.

"Seems I keep having this effect on you."

Her bottom lip trembled and her voice crackled. "Why me, Travers? I'm nothing—just plain old Jo."

Levi let out a snort that made them both laugh. "You're not 'just' anything, Joanna. Sure, you're as ornery as any bull on this ranch, and sure, you're bossier than anyone I've ever met." He smoothed away more tears. "But you're also smart, funny, and a damn sight sexier than any woman I've ever clapped eyes on."

"Don't say that." Her voice was barely more than a whisper.

"Why not?" He pushed her hat back and reached for her braid. "It's true, Joanna, whether you want to believe it or not."

With the string tossed aside, he fanned her hair out, loving its silkiness as it tickled through his fingers. She closed her eyes and leaned into his hands, letting the rest of her tears dry on her cheeks.

"God, you're beautiful." The temptation was too great, her lips too close. He leaned in and touched his mouth to hers, soft at first, testing her reaction. Her bottom lip trembled slightly, but she didn't pull away, and that's all the encouragement he needed.

He kissed her again, longer, deeper, until she sighed and parted her lips for him. He traced the edge of her mouth with his tongue, tasting her tears, her skin, her whole being. And damn, if she didn't respond. Her fingers, shaking slightly, crept around his neck and up into his hair, working their way through the too-long mess, but it felt too good to stop.

She whimpered softly against his lips, drawing him closer. But he couldn't get close enough—not when they were sitting the way they were. Without releasing her lips, he used his hands to shift her body until they were both on their knees, then he hauled her up against his chest and kissed her hard. Long and hard. It still wasn't enough.

Shoots of pain radiated through his head, but it didn't matter; he had Joanna in his arms again and he wasn't about to let her go this time.

Her fingers found his shirt collar and followed it

down to the first button. Levi stiffened all over. He had to stop this—it was crazy. The feather-light touch of her fingers against his skin was pushing him closer to the edge of reason, but he was helpless to stop it.

This is what he'd wanted from the first minute he'd met her. This is what he'd *needed* since that first day.

His mouth left hers to travel the length of her jaw, then down her long, silky neck. He couldn't get enough of her neck. It was long, silky soft, and it led right down to that V in her shirt. He kissed the hollow of her throat, then moved lower. Still she fought with the buttons on his shirt. He couldn't stand it anymore. With a quick rip, he sent his buttons flying in every direction. It didn't matter. All that mattered was feeling her hands against his skin.

Joanna chuckled, then pressed her palms flat against his chest, sliding them over each nipple and down his belly. God help them both if she touched his belt. Just the thought made him harder than he'd ever been.

Her hands were like silk against his skin, her nails scraping gently over his ribs.

He tugged her shirt from the waistband of her pants and slid his hands inside. Damn. He should have known she'd be soft. She might not look it in those clothes, but Joanna McCaine was all woman. Soft, silky, and full of curves.

His hands eased over her breasts, pulling a quick gasp from her throat. Then she arched into his palms while her own hands gripped his shoulders tight. Levi left a trail of hot wet kisses at the V in her shirt, then pushed beneath it to reach the silky mound he needed.

Joanna seemed to open herself up completely to him. She melted into his arms, silently giving him everything he wanted. And he wanted it all—every inch of her, every breath of hers, and every last one of those soft little whimpers.

He wanted to give her everything, too. Every inch of him, every breath of his, and every last moan she could pull from him.

His heart nearly burst from his chest at the sudden realization. He loved Joanna, loved her more than he *ever* would have believed possible, loved everything about her—even the way she snorted.

He loved her.

Dammit.

He really and truly loved this woman.

Double dammit.

And because of that, he couldn't do this. Not there in the middle of the east pasture. And not now, knowing she deserved so much better than him, so much better than he'd ever be able to give her.

Dammit dammit *dammit*.

"H-hold on," he stammered, pulling back just enough to separate them, but not an inch farther.

Joanna's eyelids fluttered open. "Wh-what's wrong?"

He swallowed back huge gulps of air and still didn't fill his lungs. "This. This is wrong."

She reached for his chest again. "No, Travers. This is very right."

"No." In his haste to back away and stand up, he lost his balance and landed on his backside. Joanna followed.

"Yes, Travers. Don't tell me you don't want this."
She kissed him this time, nipping at his lip, pulling
it into her mouth and teasing it—and him—mer-
cilessly with her tongue.

Levi groaned and pulled her onto his lap so she
straddled him. There was no denying how much he
wanted her now. Her fiery green eyes widened in
shock, then smoldered, their heat boring straight
through him.

She slipped her fingers through his hair, lowered
her mouth to his, and wiggled her bottom against
him.

"Joanna," he groaned again and felt her smile
against his mouth. "You're killing me here."

"Now you know how I've felt all this time."

"Wha . . ?" He pulled back again, shocked to see
the love shining in her eyes. Everything he felt for
her, everything he wanted for her, was reflected
there in the depths of her eyes. *Dammit!*

"We can't do this." He lifted her off his lap and
deposited her in a heap next to him. Then, before
she could move again, he leapt to his feet and
paced the ground beside her.

"Look, Travers," she began, her voice losing the
velvety softness it'd had a moment ago, "I don't
know what kind of game you're playing here, but
one thing's for certain. We both want this." She
waved her hand between them, as she'd done so
many times before.

He couldn't stop his head from nodding.

"And from what I've heard, you've never been one
to refuse a woman before, so what's the problem?"

God, where did he start? *He* was the problem. For
the first time in his life, he didn't want a quick roll

with a woman. He didn't want to have sex with her and then move on. He wanted to make love to her and spend the rest of his Godforsaken life with her. He wanted her to depend on him, to love him, and to give him children. Lots of children.

The pain that shot through his heart made his head seem like little more than a splinter. LeeAnna Pearson was still claiming that child was his. He knew it wasn't, but no one else believed it. And if the baby's looks didn't prove who the real father was, Levi would be in a heap-load of trouble. He couldn't put Joanna through that.

"I'm sorry." He stepped back, adjusted his shirt the best he could without any buttons, and reached for his horse's reins. "I know you think I'm an idiot, and you're probably right. But when we do this," it was his turn to wave a hand between them, "and we *will* do this—it's not going to happen on the hard ground where anyone could walk up on us.

"When it happens, it's going to happen somewhere private, where I can take my time over every inch of you and you won't have to worry about anything."

"I'm not worried." She stepped forward and he let her. He had to be the weakest man in the world.

"Joanna." He kissed the frown across her forehead. "You're the one who made me respect you. You're the one who made me want to be a better man."

"Me?" She snorted. "I didn't have anything to do with that."

"Yes, you did." He tipped her chin up so she had to look him in the eye. "I want you more than I've ever wanted anything in my life."

Tears glistened in her eyes.

"And because of that," he went on, kissing away the tears as they tripped over her lashes. "I don't want this to be like anything else ever was. I want you to be in my arms, and in my bed . . ." he hesitated, swallowed, and kissed her as softly as he could, "for the rest of my life."

Joanna's eyes shot open, her jaw dropped. For a long minute—too long—she said nothing, did nothing. Then more tears flowed down her cheeks, faster than Levi could wipe them away.

"Y-you—" she shook her head, licked her lips. "What?"

"You heard me." He wiped her cheeks again, then cupped her face between his hands. "I love you, Miss Joanna. And I want you to marry me."

She slumped against him. "You what?"

"Stop saying that." He chuckled as he tucked her head under his chin. "You heard me. And it's not like you to be speechless about anything, so what d'you have to say about that?"

"I . . . I . . ." she snorted against his chest, then wiped her nose on his shirt. "Mac's gonna kill both of us."

"I really don't give a shit about your uncle right now, Joanna." He held her shoulders and eased her back so he could see her face. "Tell me."

She swallowed hard, but said nothing.

"Just say it, Joanna." He grinned. "You'd be amazed how much better you feel once it's out."

"I, um, I . . ." she lowered her head, but he tipped it back up again. It was a motion he seemed to do a lot with her.

"Tell me," he murmured. "Or tell me to leave. But for God's sake, say something."

Panic shot through her eyes. "Don't leave me, Travers." She wound her fingers around the front of his shirt and pulled him closer until their noses touched. Her voice was barely a whisper. "I love you. Are you happy now? God, but I love you." She shoved him back a bit, but kept her fingers clenched in his shirt. "And if I even think you've gone near Stella again, the beating you took from Mac'll be nothing next to what I do to you."

Laughter exploded from Levi. He should have known she'd come out with something like that. But he didn't care. She loved him. Him, of all people. There couldn't be a happier man in the world.

Now if he could only prove to her and her damned uncle that he was worthy of her love, then everything else could go to hell.

Joanna loved him. Knowing that made the love he felt for her explode inside him. He might never stop grinning.

Chapter 10

"Have you asked anyone to the dance, Mr. Travers?" Carrie's voice dripped with its usual sweetness.

Levi finished his coffee and shook his head. "Don't imagine I'll be attending your shindig, Miss Carrie, even if Will and I are still here."

A brief look of shock crossed her face, then irritation. "You and Joanna—I swear the two of you are trying to drive me mad."

He sat a little taller. "Joanna's not going?"

"She never does," she answered almost indifferently. "Aunt Ginny, have you heard from the Harveys yet?" Carrie ran her finger down the list in front of her on the table, carefully crossing off several things.

"No," Ginny collected the dirty dishes as she spoke.

Levi looked from one woman to the other. "Why?"

Carrie glanced up. "Because they're supposed to be bringing chairs and we're going to need all we can get."

"No." Levi frowned. "I mean why doesn't Joanna go to the dance?"

Carrie opened her mouth to answer, but Ginny stepped in. "She doesn't like them."

"That's not it," Carrie piped up. "It's all P—"

"Carrie." Ginny's tone was soft but firm. "It's Joanna's business, no one else's." She turned back to Levi. "She's not fond of all the fuss and dancing. She'd rather be on her own."

"Really?" Levi shook his head. It was the only reason he'd even considered going to the fund-raiser—just to see Joanna in something other than her dead father's clothes.

In the days since they'd confessed their love to each other, they'd both agreed it probably wasn't a good time to let anyone else know. Especially Mac.

But this—this was a perfect opportunity to touch her again. And it'd be in front of the whole town, so he'd have to behave himself. The temptation might kill him, but at least he'd get to hold her.

He smiled. Maybe this was the year she'd learn to like the fuss and dancing. He suddenly needed to talk to her, to hear her whiskey-smooth voice—even if it was yelling and telling him he was an idiot for even considering this whole idea. But hell, he'd missed her so much over the last few days, he'd be happy to sit and listen to her yell.

It was a risk. If anyone at the dance thought for one second there was more to Joanna and Levi than work at the ranch, her reputation would be ruined forever. And he'd be run out of town quicker than he could take a breath.

But the memory of their kisses, the taste of her

sweet lips against his, and the way her fingers twisted through his hair . . .

Levi blew out a long breath and leaned back in his chair, hands clasped behind his head. Carrie's voice prattled on about what needed to be done for the dance, but Levi ignored her; Ginny could deal with her. He had other things to think about.

Joanna. This whole love business was complicated. Why the hell couldn't he stop thinking about her? He'd never spent so much time wondering about one woman; hell, he probably hadn't spent so much time thinking about anything. She'd crept under his skin, into his brain, and lodged herself deep in his chest—at least that's where it hurt the most. It was a good hurt, though. Most of the time.

What amazed him the most was that she'd done it without even trying, and without even realizing it. Just by being Jo, she'd done something he'd never believed could be done; she made him want to be a better man. She demanded so much from him on the ranch, expected to be treated with respect, and took nothing less.

And God help him, but he found himself wanting to give her more than she asked. If only she'd ask for something other than his ability to string a fence or tend the ranch. But she hadn't. Even after she'd said she loved him, she didn't ask anything of him. She never even said she'd marry him.

Deep in his brain, he knew what that meant. She might love him, might enjoy his kisses, but she wouldn't marry him. Mac had been right. Levi wasn't near good enough for Joanna, but he couldn't help himself. The memory of their kisses haunted his every breath. He needed one more—

just one—and then, if she wasn't going to marry him, he could leave the Double M a happy man.

There was little doubt that no matter how he felt, or how much he wanted to make Joanna his for the rest of his life, Mac would kill him before he'd let that happen.

And with the way things were, there wasn't a hope in hell of kissing Joanna again anytime soon. Not unless he got himself some kind of miracle. And it'd have to be a quick miracle, too, because the fence would be done sooner than he expected and after that, he'd be run off the Double M. If only he could prove to Mac he wasn't the lying cur-dog he thought Levi to be.

In the meantime, he had to see Joanna, had to touch her. And if no one else was around, he'd have to kiss her good and hard, too.

He left the house and rode for almost an hour before he found her, up to her knees in a thick mud bog, with her arms wrapped around the horns of a frantic, bawling steer.

Here was Levi's miracle.

"Need some help?" he asked innocently from atop his mare.

"Get me out of here, Travers, before this animal gores me." She almost sounded scared. Almost.

"Calm down." He slid off his horse and dropped the reins to the ground.

"Don't tell me to calm down," she grimaced. "I've been standing here for . . . well, I don't know how long, but this young fella isn't looking nearly as friendly as he did when I first found him."

Levi tipped his head to the side and frowned. "Why didn't you just rope him?"

Jo's face flushed a deep pink. "Would you shut up and just get me out of here?"

He pulled a rope from his saddle and stepped as close to the mud as he dared, eyeing the steer's position. They stood about six feet apart, with nothing but mud between them. He climbed back on his horse and nodded toward Jo. "Let him go."

"What?" Jo's green eyes flew wide. Damn, but she had pretty eyes. "Are you crazy?"

"Probably," he shrugged. "But you're going to have to trust me on this one."

"I swear, Travers—."

"It's Levi. And I've heard you swear before, so you don't scare me." *This better work.* "Let go."

With a long, doubtful look, she released the steer and promptly fell backward. The animal bawled, pushed its horns toward her, and tried to lift its front foot.

"Travers!"

Levi whirled his lasso over his head and tossed it around the animal's horns. With a quick yank, he pulled the rope tight and looped it around the pommel on his saddle. He urged his horse around the edge of the bog until the steer had no choice but to turn in the same direction, the rope forcing him around.

Joanna tried to push herself out of the mud, but slipped back onto her rump. Levi kept the rope taut, despite the animal's determination to get free. He kneed his mount on further until the steer pulled its legs from the muck and stepped up onto dryer land.

"Ya!" With a quick flick of his wrist, Levi released the loop from the frightened animal and chased it off in the other direction. Then he turned back to the next problem. Joanna.

The mud, which had been almost to her knees, now covered her to the waist as she struggled helplessly to stand. He slid from his saddle and stood smiling down at her. How could he not?

"Are you going to help me or what?" A great blob of mud flew from her hand and landed just under her eye. She tried to wipe it off, but only managed to smear it down her cheek.

"That depends on two things."

"What?" she cried.

"First, stop yelling."

"I'm not yelling!"

Levi crossed his arms and looked at her, his brow raised, his head tipped to the side.

"Okay," she breathed. "I'm not yelling anymore."

"And . . ."

"And what?" She pushed up again and landed on her left side.

"No yelling," he repeated with a grin. This was going better than he'd even hoped. He'd missed being this close to her, missed their fights. And Lordy, she was sexy when she was mad. Even covered in mud.

She closed her eyes and took a few deep breaths. "No yelling. No yelling."

"Good," he said. "The other thing is easier. You have to go to the fund-raiser with me."

Jo's eyes sprang open. "Not a chance."

"Okay." He picked up his horse's reins and gripped the pommel.

"Wait," she yelled. "You can't just leave me here."

"Then you'll go to the dance with me?"

"No."

Levi slipped his foot into his stirrup.

"Travers!"

"It's Levi. And don't worry, I'll send Clay back to help you. With his skill and sense of direction, he should have you out of there by Thursday. Friday at the latest."

"Please."

Had she ever said please to him before? Not that he could remember, that was for damned sure.

Levi pulled his foot out of the stirrup and turned. "Then you'll go?"

Her chin trembled slightly. "Why that?"

He cleared his throat and crouched as close as he dared. "First you tell me why you won't go."

She sat in the mud for a full minute before she answered. Her brow wrinkled and her mud-speckled mouth turned down in a small frown.

"I went to the first one. Papa and Ginny spent months organizing the whole thing; there was music and flowers and more food than could feed a whole army." Jo's gaze seemed to drift off to another place and time. Levi sat back and watched the storm build in her eyes.

"Ginny even made me a new dress." A smile touched her lips. "Pink—just like Carrie's. Had lace around the collar, too." Her finger traced where the collar would have been on the dress, leaving a streak of mud across her chest.

"I bet it was real pretty."

"Prettiest dress I'd ever seen," she breathed.

"So what happened?"

Jo's smile vanished as the clouds washed over her expression. "Me, that's what happened."

"What d'you mean?"

"Look at me, Travers." She waved her hand in front of herself, indicating the mud, the tattered blue shirt, and her old, weathered hat. "Do I look like someone who should be wearing pink silk?"

He did his best imitation of her snort. "Now's probably not the best time to ask me that." With a quick dodge, he just missed getting hit with the handful of mud she threw at him.

"It was awful," she said. "I tripped over everything and everyone. Stepped on everyone's toes when we danced and then . . ." she stopped and wiped her muddy arm under her nose.

The thought of lassoing her, too, danced through his mind, but only for a second. Instead, he tossed her the rope, waited until she had a good grip on it, then tugged her from the mud. She landed on the ground beside him and sat there, covered in mud, looking better than any woman ever had.

"And then what?" he asked, lowering himself down beside her.

"And then," she sniffed, "Peter Carlson told everyone that no amount of silk or lace would ever turn an ugly goat like me into a princess like Carrie."

Fury gnawed at his gut. He should have killed Carlson when he had the chance. If anyone was an ugly goat, it was Carlson himself. So why would Jo let a fool like him scare her off?

"That's it?" he said. "That's why you've never been to another one?"

Jo shoved him hard and stood up. "I always knew you were a skunk, Levi Travers. You're no better than Peter Carlson and I wouldn't go to that stupid dance if you were the last idiot on earth."

She headed for her horse, hobbled in the shade of a tall cottonwood.

"I didn't mean . . ." He pushed himself to his feet and strode after her. "You let someone like Peter Carlson—*Peter Carlson*—scare you off that easy? He's about the biggest idiot I've ever met."

"He didn't scare me off." She whirled around. "I just realized he was right, is all. I don't belong there."

"Yes, you do. And I want you to go with me."

"No."

"Why?"

A moment's hesitation, then a shrug. "I have nothing to wear."

"I'll take care of that."

"You most certainly will not." She hooked her foot into the stirrup, but with the mud quickly caking on her pants, getting up into the saddle was proving a little difficult. "Can you imagine the talk if people knew you'd bought me a fancy dress?"

"Come on, Joanna. It'll be fun."

She stopped and turned to face him. "I can't dance."

"Who cares?"

She snorted. "I'm sure the men I dance with will have a few concerns about it."

"Ah," Levi nodded, then tipped her face up to his, wiping away some of the mud as he did. "Well, see, there's the thing. I'm not about to let any other man get his grubby hands on you. If you go with me, you dance with me and no one else. And I don't give a hot damn if you step on my toes all night."

Her eyes narrowed. "You're the one who insisted

we keep all this quiet for a while. And now you want to parade me in front of the whole town?"

"I'm not going to *parade* you," he chuckled, then moved against her. "But if I don't get to touch you soon, I'm going to bust."

"Travers—" she tipped her head back so he could nuzzle her just below the ear.

"It's Levi."

"Levi." Her voice rasped between her lips—lips he quickly covered with his own, urging a long and passionate response from her. She shifted her stance so his thigh pressed between her legs, then wrapped her arms around his neck.

"Say it again," he begged.

"Levi."

"Say you'll go with me."

She stiffened in his arms.

"I swear I'll keep my hands to myself. I won't do anything that'll make anyone—least of all, Mac—suspect a thing."

She blushed—right through the mud. That had to be a good sign, didn't it? "Wish I could make you the same promise."

Levi groaned loud and long. "Dammit, woman, don't say things like that to me."

"Why not? You said it to me." She kissed his chin, then his mouth, the taste of her filling him completely.

"That's different," he whispered.

"No it's not." She kissed his Adam's apple as it bobbed. "I want exactly what you want and if you're allowed to say it out loud, then so am I."

"Sweet Jesus." He tugged her arms from his neck and held her hands between his. "Just say you'll go with me to this stupid dance."

For a long moment, she worried her bottom lip. Man, what he wouldn't give to be the one chewing that lip. But if he went near her again, they'd both be in a lot of trouble.

"But what if Peter's there?"

Levi lifted his hat, scratched his head, then jammed it back on. "Well, the last time I saw Carlson, he had my fist attached to his face. I'm pretty sure he won't be a problem."

Jo's eyes widened. "You had a fight with Peter? When? Why?"

Damn. "Doesn't matter. My point is Carlson will keep his distance, and if he doesn't, I'll sick Mac on him."

They both snorted over that. Then Jo sniffed and shrugged, but it didn't look the least bit convincing.

"You'll never find a dress on such short notice."

He waggled his eyebrows at her and grinned. "You'd be amazed at what I can do in a short amount of time."

Joanna's brow shot up at his insinuation, then she eyed him with frank disbelief. "You think you're going to be able to find me a dress—that fits—in a week?"

"Eleven days, actually, and yes." God, but he hoped so.

She aimed her finger at him. "It has to be a pretty one."

"Prettiest one this side of the Mississippi."

She still didn't look convinced. "And nothing your friend Stella would wear to work."

Levi roared with laughter. She *would* think of something like that. "It'll be respectable *and* pretty."

"And you swear I won't have to dance with anyone else?"

He tapped her on the nose, then tucked a wayward strand of hair behind her ear. He just couldn't keep his hands off her. "I'll shoot the first man who tries to cut in."

A soft giggle escaped her lips. He'd never heard her giggle before. Laugh, yes. Snort, several times. But this giggle was a first. Who knew one little sound could shoot a man straight through the heart?

"Is that a yes?" he asked, his throat suddenly very dry.

"You'll never find something on such short notice."

"But what if I do?"

Her eyes almost sparkled, then dimmed. "You won't. So unless you can rope yourself a miracle, it looks like you'll be dancing with yourself and I'll be sitting up in the barn loft counting the minutes until everyone leaves again."

"I won't be dancing by myself." He gave her his best smile, but it didn't seem to sway her. "And you definitely won't be sitting in a smelly old barn by yourself."

"No," she said, turning away from him. "I don't imagine you'd be dancing by yourself. I'm sure there's more than a few girls—Carrie, for starters—who'd be more than happy to fill your dance card."

Could she be any more infuriating? With as much restraint as he could muster, he turned her back to him.

"Men don't have dance cards," he said. "And even if I did, you'd be the only one on it."

Uncertainty streaked across her face. "It's easy to say that now, Travers, when it's just you and me standing here. But once everyone arrives and you see all those other girls in their fancy dresses and—"

He silenced her with a long, slow kiss. "I don't give a hot damn about any other girl in any other dress."

Joanna took a long time to catch her breath. "Okay, so even if you do somehow pull off a miracle and find me a dress, why is this so important to you?"

"Because."

Jo shook her head and stared him in the eye. "I told you why I wouldn't go, now you tell me why it's so important to you that we do go."

If only he had a good reason—one that sounded more respectable.

"We could sit up in the loft together instead," she suggested, a longing look in her eyes. "No one else goes in there."

A long groan escaped his throat as his chin fell to his chest.

How could she be so infuriatingly tempting? And how much longer was he going to be able to resist her?

"I'm not going, Travers, if you won't tell me why you want to." She put her foot in the stirrup, but couldn't bend her knees enough to lift herself up into the saddle.

After the third try, fighting a losing battle against the caked mud on her pants, Levi wrapped his hands around her waist and lifted her into the saddle.

Ideas began to form in the back of his brain. It would take some work, but with what he'd been imagining the last few weeks, and a little help from Ginny, he could do it.

He took hold of the bridle and squinted up at her. Now that she was safely out of his reach, he could tell her. Then she could ride off and leave him to battle his own private torture.

"I just want to dance with you, Joanna. I want to hold you in my arms and dance with you on that stupid floor you built. I want to see you all prettied up—*for me*—and I want you to have fun for a change." When she didn't say anything, he shrugged, feeling the heat rush over his face. "Stupid, huh?"

"N-no," she stammered out through a choked, strained voice. "I, um, well . . ."

Silence fell between them for a moment before Joanna shook her head.

"Damn it, Travers. Don't start being nice to me now—I can't stand people being nice to me."

He shrugged again and grinned up at her. "I promise not to make a habit of it."

"Good." She worried her lip again, and Levi thanked his lucky stars she was already in the saddle, out of reach, or he'd be sorely tempted to take her right there.

"So what d'you say, Joanna? Will you go with me?"

She inhaled a long breath. "A pretty dress?"

He nodded.

"Shoes, too?"

"Of course," he laughed.

"I'll only have to dance with you? No one else—especially not Peter Carlson?"

"Only me. And if he even glances your way, he's a dead man."

"And you swear you won't be nice to me all night? I don't like to be coddled."

"Yeah, I've gathered that." He couldn't help but laugh. "But can I be a little bit nice to you? Just a little—nothing so anyone would notice, mind you."

She seemed to consider that for a moment. "Okay," she relented. "But just a little bit. Wouldn't be good for Mac to be getting any ideas about us."

"No, of course not." Levi tried to sound serious, but he couldn't stop from grinning a huge, stupid grin. Joanna was going to dance with him. And he didn't care how much she hated it, he was planning on doing a lot more than coddling.

If she was going to torment him with her touches, her kisses, and the things she said to him, then he was damn well going to do his best to drive her crazy, too.

"Fine." Jo straightened in her saddle and lifted her chin a bit. "You get me a dress and some shoes and we'll talk. No dress, no dance. Deal?"

"Deal." Holy mother of God, where was he going to find a dress on such short notice? Even if he could persuade Ginny to help, it was going to take more than a small miracle to make this work. It was going to take the help of every angel in heaven.

And God knew, Levi hadn't done anything to deserve their help.

"Fine," she said again, keeping herself rigid, while Levi kept grinning his stupid grin. After a moment, she kicked her horse into motion and they sprinted off toward the house, leaving Levi to stand and stare.

Well, he'd roped himself one miracle today, maybe he could rope another. All he had to do was convince Mac's wife to help him find the prettiest dress in the world and somehow not go crazy in the next eleven days. Shouldn't be too hard, should it?

Chapter 11

Two days before the fund-raiser, they finished the fence with wire to spare.

They celebrated at supper with one of Ginny's best meals—a huge roast with boiled potatoes, carrots, and rhubarb pie for dessert—made by Ginny, not Carrie. She even allowed the men a drink at the table.

Mac eyed both Travers and Will with the same venom he had for the last few weeks. "You two'll be moving on now, I suppose."

Levi's gaze flicked from Joanna to Mac and back again. But before he could answer, she pushed back from the table and kissed Ginny quickly on the cheek.

"You outdid yourself tonight, Ginny," she said through a smile. "But the barn's not going to clean itself."

She didn't even glance Levi's way as she walked out. Was that because she was afraid of Mac or afraid of what she thought Levi's answer would be?

"So will you?" Carrie asked, leaning closer to Will.

"Will we what?" With a grin that big, he'd be doing whatever Carrie wanted him to do.

"Be moving on, silly." Carrie slapped his arm playfully. "To San Francisco."

"Uh, yeah," he answered, then shot Levi a questioning look. "I think so."

Mac's glare scorched Levi. He'd been dreading this conversation more and more every day, especially since he and Joanna hadn't made any plans. But now he was going to be forced to take on Mac again, with or without her.

After a long, low exhale, he turned to Mac. "Can I have a word with you?"

"What for?" Mac snarled. "In a few days you'll be nothing but a bad memory. No need for words now."

"Oh, but you won't leave before the fund-raiser dance," Carrie almost pleaded. "You must stay for that."

"We'll be here for a while yet," Will nodded. "Still need to round up the herd and get them inside the fence."

"That won't take long," Mac stated. "What d'you think I've had Simon and Jimmy doing for the last few weeks?"

"Oh." Will's gaze darted around the room before settling on Levi, silently pleading with him to say something. Anything.

Carrie looked to be on the verge of tears and Levi wanted nothing more than to throw up.

"Mac?" he said. "This'll just take a minute." He pushed away from the table, but Mac remained where he was until Ginny poked him.

"Go with the boy," she whispered. "Just hear him out."

"Waste of both our times since he ain't got nothing to say that I want to hear."

Levi put his back to Carrie and Will so he couldn't see their reaction to his next words, and so they couldn't see his, either.

"It concerns Joanna." He offered a brief nod to Ginny and walked out of the kitchen onto the porch where he had more hope of breathing normally. Didn't work. In fact, it got worse the second Mac stepped outside.

"What is it?" he asked, his arms crossed over his chest.

Levi wet his lips and swallowed hard. Before he spoke, though, he offered up a quick prayer Mac wouldn't take another swing at him because, by God, he'd be swinging back this time.

"Well, the thing is," he began, twisting his hat between his hands. "It's that, well, I uh—" He blew out a long breath. "I love her, Mac."

All color drained from the other man's face. His jaw twitched and his lips tightened into a thin line. But he didn't make any moves toward Levi.

"I do," he continued. "I love her. And I mean to make her my wife."

"You what?" Mac roared, moving faster than a speeding locomotive until he was toe to toe with Levi. Chairs scraped the floor inside the house. "Don't think for one goddam second I'm going to give you my blessing, Travers."

Shit. So much for this going well.

"I'm not looking for or expecting it." With every word, he felt the strength return to his voice. "I'm simply telling you as a courtesy. I love her and she loves me. That's all that matters."

"Bull-bloody-shit!"

Levi took a few steps back as mockingbirds scattered from the trees around the house, and though he couldn't actually see them, he could sense Ginny and Carrie at the doorway.

"You are *not* going to marry my niece!"

"Yes, sir, I am." He forced breath in and out. "If she'll have me."

"She won't." The vein in Mac's neck bulged. "You're the bastard son of a whore, Travers. You don't know the first thing about being in love. And you sure as hell don't know what it's like to be loved."

"Yes, I do." Levi swallowed back the bile that rose in his throat. "Joanna's shown me what it's like."

"Why you sonuva—" Mac made to move toward him, but Ginny's voice cut through the air.

"Samuel Arthur McCaine! Don't you even think about it." She stepped out into the moonlight, with Carrie at her heels.

"Get back in the house, Ginny," Mac snarled, his fist lowering, but still clenched. "This ain't got nothing to do with you."

"It most certainly does." She moved between the two men, her gray eyes snapping like lightening. "Joanna is just as much my niece as she is yours. Do you think I like to see her upset? No, I don't. But she loves Levi—that much I can see. It's just a pity you can't."

"Joey's too smart to fall for a bastard like Travers."

"No, Mac." Ginny laid her hands on his arms.

"Joanna's too smart *not* to fall in love with a man like Levi."

"What?" For the first time, Mac tore his glare from Levi and focused on his wife. "What the hell does that mean?"

"It means she was raised by good people who taught her right from wrong. She's a strong woman with a good, sensible head on her shoulders." Ginny squeezed his arms, but Mac didn't look the least bit convinced. "She's not going to do anything stupid."

Mac snorted. "What do you call *him*?"

Fury blasted Levi in the heart. "You listen to me, you miserable old man," he closed the short distance between them, but stopped at Ginny's outstretched hand. "Joanna's not done anything she should be ashamed of—you hear me? She's not nearly as stupid as you must think she is, and I'm not about to do anything to compromise her that way."

Another snort. "You, Travers? Since when have *you* ever been concerned about a woman's virtue?"

"My only concern is Joanna." He leaned closer as Ginny pressed one hand against each of them and tried to force them apart.

"That's right," Mac seethed. "You've got no concern for the Pearson girl at all, do you?"

"No," he snapped back, "I don't. I've never touched that girl."

"That's not what she says."

"I don't give a hot damn what a spoiled brat like LeeAnna Pearson says." Levi leaned over Ginny until his nose nearly touched Mac's. "I know what I did and *didn't* do."

"You want me to believe that while you were out

working for Pearson, you suddenly got particular about the girls you poked, is that it?"

"Mac!" Ginny's cry went ignored by both.

"Believe whatever the hell you like," Levi ground out. "Seems you had your mind made up long before I set foot out here."

"Damn right I did." Mac's face bordered on purple. "No one earns a reputation like yours without some of the stories being true. And with your upbringing—"

"Stop it," Ginny pleaded. "Just stop it."

For a long moment, neither man moved or blinked, they just pressed against Ginny's hands as she kept herself wedged between them. But for the first time in his life, Levi was not going to let his past dictate his future.

Finally, with another small roar, Mac jerked away and took a couple steps back.

"Damn you, Travers." He swiped his huge palm over his face. "Why our Joey? Of all the girls in the county, why her?"

"Why *not* her?" Levi forced his breathing to return to normal, inhaling long, slow breaths and releasing them in the same way. "I've never met anyone like her."

"She'll boss you around your whole life." Mac paced the short width of the porch.

"She's even more beautiful when she's bossy."

Ginny's weary face broke out into a smile at his words.

"She's mean," Mac continued.

"No, she's not." Levi shot Ginny a quick wink when he was sure Mac wasn't looking. "She just doesn't take shit from anyone."

"She dresses like a man, for God's sake."

"And works twice as hard."

Tears began to roll down Ginny's cheeks.

"Goddamn it." Mac slapped both palms against the side of the house. "If you hurt her again . . ."

"Won't happen." Levi still didn't step back, even when Ginny patted his shirt and offered him a small smile.

"If it does—"

"She'll shoot me long before you even have your gun loaded."

"My gun's always loaded."

"Does this mean you won't be going to San Francisco after all?" Carrie asked, her perfectly made-up face tilted to the side.

"For Christ's sake, Carrie." Mac rounded on his niece, but was again held back by a now beaming Ginny.

"Language, Mac."

"I'm just asking," Carrie snipped.

Ginny ushered the two of them back into the house, leaving Levi on the porch to catch his breath. It wasn't long, though, before Will stepped out.

"Hiding, were you?" Levi asked, gripping the porch rail and leaning his backside against it.

"Damn right," Will chuckled. "Didn't want to be anywhere near him if he was gonna start swinging again. And for a minute there—"

Levi laughed, too, but nothing felt funny to him. "You heard?"

"Hell, Travers. There's a dead man in New York who musta heard."

"Yeah." He sighed. "You're probably right. Joanna's gonna skin me alive."

"Why d'you say that?"

"She loves that old bastard," he grumbled. "Last thing she'll want is me making him go off like that again." He leaned closer and lowered his voice. "Did you see his face? For a minute there, I thought he was going to burst open."

Will offered him a grin and a shrug. "At least there's no question about where you stand with him."

"That's supposed to make me feel better?"

"Sure."

A soft breeze cooled the sweat on the back of Levi's neck, but did little to ease the tension in his gut.

"Some of the things he said, though—"

"Like what?" Will adjusted his hat. "You mean the parts about you being a bastard? And your ma being a whore?"

He couldn't help but roll his eyes at Will.

"Nothing you can do about those two facts, Travers," his friend said. "You were born a bastard. Not your fault, just bad luck, I guess. But that old man in there is a bastard by choice."

"I'm doubting Joanna's going to see it that way."

"Oh, hell, Travers," Will chuckled, "I've seen the way she looks at you, and no matter what he said, or where you come from, that girl's stupid in love with you."

Levi wished he felt as sure as Will sounded.

"Besides, unless I'm off my mark," Will went on, a mocking grin splitting his face, "don't matter how mad you make her, she ain't gonna skin you. There's a few other things she probably wants to do to you, but skinnin' you ain't one of them."

Levi couldn't help but grin through the heat rushing up his neck. God, he hoped Will was right, because he had plenty of things he wanted to do to her, too.

Will moved in beside him. "Guess this means you're staying here, then?"

"I sure hope so."

"What about all that talk of seeing the ocean?"

He hadn't thought about that in a long time. "Seen one ocean, you've seen them all, right?"

With another shrug and grin, Will turned to face the yard. "Never thought I'd see you like this— giving up everything for a woman."

"I'm not giving up anything," he said. "I'm getting everything."

"Jee-zuz, Travers. She's really done a number on you, hasn't she?"

"Yup." Levi answered, completely unashamed.

"And you're really going to be fine living here for the rest of your life?"

"Yup." He nodded toward the kitchen door. "Though I don't imagine it'll be much fun for the first while."

"Ah, he'll get over it. Just so long as you don't go and do something stupid. Like you usually do."

"Thanks, Will," Levi chuckled.

They stood in silence for a while, watching the night close in around them. A lightening bug flitted by and landed on one of Ginny's rose bushes.

"What are your plans?" Levi asked. "Will you stay on here?"

"Nah." Will shook his head. "I'm not the ranching kind, you know that. I reckon I'll head west when we're done here."

"What about Carrie?"

The question hung like a fog between them.

"I don't rightly know," Will finally answered. "She's pretty set on going."

"I know, but—"

Will slapped Levi on the shoulder and made his way down the steps. "We'll see what happens, my friend. In the meantime, you might want to go see if your young Miss Joanna loves you enough to spite her uncle and marry your sorry hide." He nodded toward the barns. "No time like the present."

Levi couldn't stop the huge grin. Or the quake that rocked him in his boots. How would she feel when she found out the truth about him—that he really was the bastard son of a whore? It had been one thing to let Mac throw it back in his face, but the thought of Joanna doing the same scared the bejeebers out of him.

Jo lingered by the barn door, the pitchfork in one hand, her dirty old bandana crunched in the other. She strained to see the house through the stand of cottonwoods, but could only make out shadows.

No shots had been fired, so that was a good thing, wasn't it? Unless, of course, Mac had beat Travers to death this time.

A shadowy figure moved through the trees toward the barns. Travers? No, whoever it was swaggered too much. Had to be Will.

"You heard?" he asked, a strange smile lifting his lip.

She shrugged. "Some." In truth, all she'd heard was Mac roaring.

He wrapped his hand around the handle of the

pitchfork and gently tugged it from her grip. "Travers needs to see a friendly face when he gets down here, not someone brandishing anything that could be used as a weapon."

"I . . ." she grinned guiltily. Surely Travers hadn't told Will about the first time in the barn. When she spoke next, it was barely a whisper. "Is he okay?"

Will laughed. "I think he's more scared of you than that uncle of yours." He made to walk past, then stopped and turned back. "He ain't never been this way with a woman before, so he's more 'n likely gonna do some stupid fool things that'll make you want to kill him yourself."

A small lump crept up Jo's throat. This was the most Will had spoken to her in all the time he'd been at the ranch.

"I'm only telling you that so you'll go easy on him. He's pretty unsure of himself right now."

She couldn't hold back the snort. "Travers? Are you sure we're talking about the same man?"

Will didn't even crack a smile. "That's what has me worried." He lifted his left shoulder in an almost shrug. "I'll be seeing you in the morning."

"Yes," she hurried to answer. "Good night, Will."

When his cabin door closed behind him, silence surrounded Jo. Not a single sound broke the air—not a mockingbird's call, not a coyote's howl, not even a peep from the chickens.

Her heart pounded in her chest, her breaths came short and ragged.

"Good grief," she muttered to herself. "It's bad enough you left him alone with Mac. The least you can do is go to him now."

Even if it meant he and Will were leaving. Even if

it meant her time with him was almost up. She had to go to him.

With heavy feet and a quaking heart, she walked toward the house, step by painfully slow step. She kept her eyes cast down, hoping if she didn't see how close the house was, it somehow wouldn't be.

As she stepped through the stand of cottonwoods, he was there. She sensed it before she saw him, but his scent filled every part of her, warming her, yet scaring her half to death.

"Joanna." That voice. That face. Those hands.

He stepped up next to her and wound his fingers through hers.

She forced a smile she didn't feel and lifted her face to him. "It was getting a little loud up there. Probably gave Lefty something to talk about."

"We need to talk."

Oh God. She couldn't do this—she couldn't have him walk out of her life now. Not now. Not when he'd given her the one thing she'd always wanted— love. Not when he'd taught her what it meant to be valued, to be treasured, and to be loved even though someone much prettier was right there.

"No." She tried to pull free, but he held her hand tighter.

"There's things you need to know, Joanna." His voice was so impossibly gentle.

"No." A sob caught in her throat. Why did she cry so often around this man? "Don't do this, Travers."

"Do what?" He pulled her closer, then wrapped his hands around her upper arms.

"D-don't leave me." Another sob broke free. "I don't care what M—"

He cut her off with a kiss, a soft, delicious kiss

that tasted of want, need, and a heady dose of all that was Levi Travers.

"Will you shut up for a minute?" he murmured against her lips. "Let me talk for a change."

Don't let that be our last kiss. She followed him over to a grassy spot under one of the trees, the only spot bathed in moonlight. He sat back against the trunk and tugged her down sideways on his lap.

"No matter what, keep quiet until I'm done." He smiled gently and kissed the tip of her nose.

"But—"

"Joanna." He pressed his finger against her lips. "Shut up."

For a moment, she considered taking that finger into her mouth. How would he react to that? Would they still have to talk then or could they forget about talking and get back to kissing?

Before she could find out, he lowered his hand and wrapped it around her, tucking her head under his chin. His pulse beat out a strange rhythm in his neck, but holy hell, he smelled good. She snuggled closer and smiled when he let out a low moan.

"Joanna," he began, his voice soft in the night air, "there's some things you need to know about me before you make any decisions about what you want."

"I know everything I need to know."

He tightened his hold around her and growled. "You're talking again."

"Sorry."

They both knew she wasn't.

"I'm sure you've heard most of the stories about me, about where I came from and who I've been with."

She opened her mouth to speak, but he clamped a hand over it.

"Quiet. Listen." He moved his hand away and let it rest on her hip. The simple touch began a reaction inside Jo she'd never felt before. Heat coiled deep within her, her pulse quickened, and she had to fight the urge to wiggle against him again.

"I wasn't exactly born Lord of the manor," he went on. "Truth is, my mother was a—" He stopped, took in a few breaths.

Jo wanted to tell him to stop—she knew all this. But for some reason, Travers needed to tell her. Besides, the longer he talked, the longer his hand kept moving over her hip and across her belly.

"I'm the bastard son of a whore. Don't have a clue who my father is. Could be any one of a thousand men."

Joanna watched his Adam's apple bob, then she traced its path with the tip of her finger. Late day stubble covered his chin and neck; it felt so itchy against her fingers, she couldn't help but scratch it for him.

"Joanna!" He stilled her hands with his and rested them in her lap. "Don't you have anything to say?"

Jo raised her brow in mock innocence. "You told me to shut up and let you talk." With her hands being held down in her lap, she leaned closer to him and kissed his neck softly, once, then again. And again.

"Joanna," he groaned, louder this time. "Stop that."

"What? You don't like it?" She kissed him again, this time on the chin, then higher until she reached his bottom lip. She flicked her tongue against his lip but eased back when he tried to take control. "Keep talking," she murmured. "I'm listening."

Before she could taste his lip again, Travers lifted her unceremoniously from her position and turned her so she faced him.

Much better angle this way. But he held her at arm's length. His face was bathed in the pale moonlight so that Jo could barely make out the faded bruises. Her fingers twitched to touch them, but Travers seemed intent on keeping her at a distance. *Coward.*

"Don't you have anything to say about what I just told you?" Frustration flared in his eyes—those beautiful, soft brown eyes—and in the tenseness of his shoulders.

"About what?" she asked. "About you being born a bastard? Or about your mother being a whore?"

The color drained from his face. "Well, both."

She leaned closer, but not to kiss him this time, only to force him to look at her, right in the eye.

"Did you have any say in who your mother would be?" She cocked her brow again, but didn't let him answer. "No more than I did. Did you ask to be raised in a whorehouse? I'm guessing no to that one, too."

His head lowered, but she cupped his stubbly cheeks in her hands and lifted it again.

"But if you'd been born to anyone else, or raised any other way, do you think we would have ever met?" She smiled, letting another course of tears trickle down her cheeks. "Do you think you'd be the man you are today if you'd been born and raised any other way?"

He didn't look the least bit convinced.

"I'm not saying it's a good thing you grew up without a father and that the only women you saw in your childhood were whores, but it made you who you are."

He snorted and rolled his eyes. "Yeah, well, according to your uncle—"

"I don't care about Mac." She looked deep into his eyes, willing him to see the truth. "I only care about *you*. I love you, Travers, and everyone else can go to hell."

A wave of relief washed over his face. "Ah, Joanna." He pulled her against his chest until their hearts beat in rhythm. "Are you sure?"

"Do I ever do anything unless I'm sure?" She laughed, her fingers toying with the top button on his shirt.

"There's one other thing."

"Jeez, Travers," she whined, giving him a soft slap on the chest, "are you ever going to stop talking?"

"I thought most women liked to talk."

"I'm not most women."

He laughed, a low choking sound that reverberated through his chest. "I've noticed."

"Okay," she sighed dramatically. "What is it now? You can't read or write? Ginny can teach you. You can't cook? Neither can I."

"Joanna."

"Okay, fine." She sat up straighter so she could see him clearly. "I'm shutting up."

"It's about LeeAnna."

Fear gripped Jo's heart. She'd known they'd have to face this sooner or later, but she wasn't nearly ready for it.

"If you chew that lip any harder, you won't have

anything left." Travers wiped his thumb over her bottom lip, easing it out from beneath her top teeth.

"Just say it, then." Jo closed her eyes and inhaled deeply.

"Look at me, first."

She'd rather face down Mac right about then, but Travers didn't say another word until she pried her eyes open, one at a time.

"I want you to see I'm telling you the truth, okay?" he asked, then waited for her to nod. "I'm not that child's father. I never touched LeeAnna, though God knows she wanted me to."

Jo went back to work on her lip until Travers wiped his thumb over it again.

"I swear to you, Joanna, it's not mine." He held her gaze, but it was clear to Jo that he'd rather look anywhere else. "You know I've been with some of the girls in town—"

"*Some?*"

"Okay," he relented, his eyes swimming in guilt, "more than just some. But she wasn't one of them."

"Why would she say it was yours, then?" It wasn't that Jo didn't believe Travers, because she did, but she didn't understand why LeeAnna would pick Travers of all people. It wasn't like he had near the kind of money she was used to or anything.

His cheeks flushed a little beneath the stubble. "Seems she fancied she was in love with me and when I didn't return the feelings, I guess she got desperate."

"But whoever the father is, he must know it's his child."

"That's what I figure, too."

She eyed him suspiciously. He knew something else, but what? Then it hit her.

"You know who the father *really* is, don't you?"

Travers's lips pinched together before he finally nodded. "I have an idea, yeah."

"Who?"

He shook his head. "No point dragging him into this if I'm wrong."

"But—"

"No, Joanna," he murmured, his hands brushing the skin beneath her sleeves. "Once the child's born, it should be clear enough, but in the meantime, I'm not going to ruin someone else by starting rumors."

"So what are we going to do until then?" Jo asked, finally releasing the top button, then going to work on the next one.

"We?"

"Yes, *we*, Travers." She leaned in and kissed his neck. "Unless it was someone else yelling up at the house a while ago, I'm pretty sure it was you telling Mac that you were going to make me your wife." She kissed him again, loving the salty masculine taste of his skin. "So that makes you and me a 'we'."

He swallowed hard—again. "Does that mean . . ."

Jo shrugged and forced back a grin. "Well, you've mentioned marriage twice now and even though you've yet to actually ask me proper-like, I guess—"

Travers stood up so fast, she was thrown from his lap and landed on her backside in the grass. He yanked her to her feet, taking a moment to steady her.

"What the . . ." Her throat dried up almost completely, leaving her to squeak out, "I was only kidding, Travers. For God's sake, stand up."

"No." Down on one knee, with his hat in his hand, he'd never looked more handsome. And she'd never been more terrified or excited.

"I love you, Joanna McCaine. I love you more than anything else in the whole world. More than I ever imagined a man could love a woman."

He looked so serious, she couldn't help herself. "Even more than the Pacific Ocean?"

"Will you shut up and let me do this?"

She laughed out loud, then bit the inside of her cheek when he glared at her.

"You make me want to be a better man." He inhaled what must have been four lungfuls. "You make me want to be more than who I am."

Jo's smile died completely away, leaving her lips to tremble uncontrollably. He really *was* serious!

"You make me want to be a husband—a good husband—*your* husband. And more than that, you make me want to be a father."

"A fa . . . you mean . . ." she gaped.

"Yup." Now he grinned. Waits until he's scared the life half out of her, and then he grins. She could have smacked him. "Kids, Joanna. Lots of them, too."

"Not lots."

"Oh yeah," he chuckled. "Lots."

"I can't have lots of kids," she gasped. "I don't know how."

He laughed. "You can do anything, Joanna. Besides, I want to see your belly all big and beautiful and know it's my baby growing inside you."

She couldn't stand it any longer. She threw herself

at him, wrapping her arms around his neck and sobbing against his shoulder.

"I'm not done," he mumbled. "Stand up and let me finish."

"No," she cried, then, "Yes."

"What?"

"Yes."

"What d'you mean 'yes'? I haven't asked you anything yet." He tried to pry her arms away, but she clung tighter.

"Then ask, for God's sake!"

"Joanna," he began, giving up on trying to pull her off. Instead, he smoothed his hands up and down her back and pressed his face into her neck, his voice a husky whisper against her neck. "Will you marry me?"

"Yes, you idiot." She wiped her nose and eyes against his shirt, then snorted. "Took you long enough."

Travers's laughter echoed through the still night air as he held her tighter against his chest.

"Um, Travers?" she whispered. "There's something you need to know about me, too."

"Don't tell me," he chuckled softly. "You really want to sit in the house and plan tea parties."

"Lord no." She pinched his arm hard.

"What is it, then?"

"Well, you're going to find out sooner or later, so I might as well be the one to tell you." Without releasing him, she eased back just far enough that she could look up into the growing worry clouding his eyes. For a smart man, he could sure be gullible. "The thing is . . . and I hope this doesn't change your mind about me."

"What?" His eyes flicked over her face, as though he could find the answer there somewhere.

"There's something I can't do, no matter how much I want to. No matter how much *you* want me to." Jo swallowed the laughter rising in her throat and nodded as stone-faced as she could. She slipped her fingers beneath his shirt and slid them over the hard planes of his belly and chest. "God knows I wish I could, because I've heard others get a lot of enjoyment doing it."

Another low groan. "Joanna." He grabbed her hands through the material of his shirt and held them still. "If it's what I think it is, we can practice until you're an expert."

She pressed closer to him, until her hip was pressed against his hardness.

"It scares me," she whispered, barely able to contain her laughter now.

"What is it?" his voice came out low and raspy. "I swear, woman, if you don't say it right now—"

"I can't rope."

Silence.

She looked up into his face, giving him her best Carrie imitation, with the fluttering lashes and everything. A low growl began deep in his throat and grew louder the more she smiled at him.

"Rope?" he ground out through gritted teeth. "You can't rope? That's your big secret?"

She shrugged through her laughter. "Hardly a secret, Travers. Even Lefty knows. But since you didn't know, I thought I should tell you." She backed up a step, then two.

"And you—" he narrowed his eyes at her, but

light twinkled in them as he lunged, caught her in his arms, and rolled her to the ground.

Jo struggled to get away, but was laughing too hard to get very far.

Travers pressed her down onto the grass, holding her hands above her head and then straddling her hips, but he kept his weight from crushing her. He lowered his face closer to hers, breathing kisses over her eyes, then around to her ears.

All laughter died from Jo's lips. God, he smelled good. And those lips . . .

He nibbled her earlobe, then moved down her neck, nuzzling, nipping, and tasting. She arched into him, offering everything she had, if only he'd take it.

But dammit if he hadn't gone and turned respectable on her.

"Joanna," he said on a sigh. "You gotta know I want to make love with you right here."

"And you gotta know I wish you would." Her whole body ached for his touch, his smell, and his taste.

"Not here, Joanna. I told you before, when we make love, it'll be in my bed where I can take my time with you. Not out here in the middle of the yard."

"You're just afraid Mac'll find us," she teased.

"No," he answered, with a hint of laughter in his voice. "When I think about making love to you, Joanna—and believe me, I've thought about it plenty—Mac doesn't factor into the picture at all."

He pulled her into his arms and rolled over so she lay on top of him, with her head resting against his chest and his rock-hard desire pressing against her thigh.

They lay in each other's embrace, hearts slamming against each other, and both trembling slightly. Travers pressed kisses against her hair while his hands moved slowly up and down her back, drawing small circles as they moved. Jo toyed with his buttons—she just couldn't get them undone fast enough—until she could finally slide her hand beneath the fabric and feel his skin against hers again.

"Ah, Joanna," he sighed. "You might not be able to rope cattle, but you sure as hell roped me in good and proper."

"Yeah?" she whispered against his chest. "Does that mean I can brand you, too?"

"Hell, darlin', I was branded the first time I clapped eyes on you."

"Good answer, Travers." She wiggled against him just to torture them both a little more. "Now, answer me this. How much longer am I going to have to wait?"

"For what?" he pressed up against her, sucking in a deep breath at the same time.

"For that," she smiled, knowing he ached as badly as she did.

"Depends," he rasped. "How soon can we be married?"

"Sooner the better, I say." She pressed her lips against his, loving the way he tasted against her mouth.

"That's what I'm thinkin', too." He smiled against her mouth.

"You know Mac's gonna kill both of us," she laughed, settling back on his chest. Nothing in the world had ever felt better than lying under the stars wrapped in his arms.

"Not before I get you married and in my bed."
He kissed her hair again. "You can mark my words
on that, sweetheart."

"Oh, I will," she laughed. "I will."

Chapter 12

The day of the fund-raiser dawned clear and beautiful, just as Carrie said it would. Jo had been up since dawn and was doing her best to think of anything *but* the dance that night. She had other things to do besides wonder what her dress might have looked like, whether it would have had lace and ruffles or intricate beadwork on the bodice. And she certainly didn't have time to wonder about the color.

It was nonsense anyway, because in the last ten days, Travers hadn't mentioned one more word about it and a dress had never arrived. Not for her, anyway.

Carrie's dress had been hanging in her room for almost a week—pale pink silk with two lavender silk orchids pinned at the waist, and yards of lace. No doubt she would be the belle of the ball. Again. Men would be lined up from the front door to the next county waiting for a dance with her.

Jo was glad she didn't have to worry about that problem. Glad she didn't have to wonder anymore what it would feel like to have Travers's arms around her all night while they danced under a blanket of stars, glad she could watch it all from the quiet comfort of the loft like she did every year.

She and Travers had their entire lives to dance, one night wouldn't make much difference.

Maybe Travers would join her in the loft this year—that'd make it all worthwhile.

She collected the last of the eggs from under the hens and left the basket in the kitchen. The sweet aromas of fresh baking lingered throughout the house. Cakes, breads, and pies covered every inch of table space in the kitchen and parlor, and a huge pot of stew simmered on the stove.

Thanks to Ginny and the other ladies in town, there would be more than enough food, and then some. Flowers from every garden in the county adorned the yard and not a speck of dust could be found anywhere in the house.

Yes, if there was one thing Carrie was good at, it was organizing people. Maybe she'd be willing to organize someone else to do the milking.

Jo turned an empty pail upside down and perched on it, holding a second one beneath a very full udder. There was work to be done—dance or no dance—and she'd just as soon be out in the barn than in the house surrounded by all that party excitement.

By midday, with only a quick stop to eat the jerky and bread from her saddlebag, she was out at the corral, mending the broken slats and readying it for the branding and castrating they'd do next week.

Thanks to Mac's direction, Simon and Jimmy had

managed to round up most of the herd while Jo and Travers strung the fence, so it was quick work to get them all accounted for and inside the fence.

If she'd had time to think on it, and if she didn't love the idiot so much, she probably would have cursed Travers for being such a skunk. A real man would have at least told her he'd been unable to find a dress, or come up with some other excuse to weasel out of taking her to the dance—especially since he claimed to love her. But he'd done neither. He'd gotten her hopes up and then left her to wonder. So it was a good thing she was too busy to think about it.

The sound of feet pounding the dirt pulled her attention away from the plank she'd just split in half by pounding the nail in too far. Clay raced toward her, a look of fierce determination on his grubby face.

"Miss Ginny sent me to fetch you and she tol' me I wasn't t'come back without you."

Jo pushed her hat back and swiped her arm across her forehead. "What's wrong?"

"Dunno, Miss Joanna. But she made me promise."

Ginny never sent for her unless it was something important. Something bad. Was someone hurt? Mac? *Travers*?

She dropped the hammer and nails, clambered over the rails, and sprinted across the yard, leaving Clay to catch up.

Ginny stood on the front porch, one hand fisted on her hip, the other shielding her eyes from the bright afternoon sun.

Jo took the steps two at a time. "What's wrong?"

Ginny clicked her tongue and waved Jo through the open door.

"What?" Jo repeated. "Who's hurt?" Did she really want to know?

"Hurt?" Ginny's brow puckered. "No one's hurt, for goodness sake. Now come along, we have a lot of work to do."

"Work?" Jo released the breath she hadn't known she was holding. "For the love of God, Ginny, I thought someone was dying."

Ginny half-pushed Jo up the stairs toward her bedroom.

"Stop pushing me, Ginny. What do you need? And can I at least have some water first?"

"Nothing and no." Ginny opened the bedroom door and stood back, giving Jo a clear view of the room.

A deep green taffeta gown, with a matching ribbon sash and tiny shoulder bows, shimmered on her bed. No silk, no lace, no pearls; just a simple gown made of the most beautiful fabric Jo had ever seen.

It was nothing like Carrie's gown.

It was perfect.

"Oh my," she breathed, taking a hesitant step toward the bed. "It's better than I ever imagined."

"And there's more." Ginny ducked into the hall for a moment, then hurried back in, carrying a pile of crinolines and other underthings.

Heat raced up Jo's neck. "He didn't . . ."

"No," Ginny smiled. "I picked these out. But he did choose these." From beneath the heap of crinolines, she pulled out two mother-of-pearl hair combs. She handed them to Jo and fished out a pair of emerald satin evening shoes. "And these."

"Oh my," Jo repeated. "But I thought . . ."

"Wait," Ginny said. "One more thing." She reached into her skirt pocket and pulled out a bar of soap.

Jo's heart sank. "Soap? He thinks I stink?"

Her aunt's face split into a sympathetic smile. "Oh, Joanna. You poor dear." She patted Jo on the cheek and set the armload down on the bed. "He doesn't think you stink. I do."

They laughed together, but a lump began to form in Jo's throat. She'd cried more in the last two months than she'd cried in ten years.

"It's not often you get dressed up," Ginny said, "so when you do, I want you to feel—and smell—as pretty as you'll look."

"Oh, Ginny." Tears choked Jo's words. "You don't think I'll make a fool of myself again?"

Ginny's smile faded. She took Jo's hands in hers and looked straight into her eyes. "Now you listen to me, Joanna McCaine. That Peter Carlson has been an imbecile since the day God set him on this earth. No one else paid him any mind that day, so you shouldn't have, either."

"But . . ."

"No buts. I can't believe you let a ninny like him scare you off."

Why did people keep saying that?

"I wasn't scared off." The lie fell flat. "I prefer the word humiliated."

Ginny sniffed. "Choose whichever word you like. The fact of the matter is you are a beautiful, strong woman who has more sense than to let one person's opinion scare—sorry, humiliate—you like that."

"I don't know, Ginny."

"Well I do." She squeezed Jo's fingers. "It's time you realized how very precious you are. And it's long past time you let other people see it too."

"I'm not precious," she snorted. "I'm crankier than Mac most days."

Ginny shrugged, her eyes crinkling against her smile. "I wouldn't suggest you let on to your uncle about any of this," she said. "He assumes I picked it all out for you and I haven't felt the need to tell him differently."

Ginny was lying to Mac? Holy Lord, she must really like Travers.

"I'd hate to get Mac all riled up again." Jo grinned. A tiny light sparked deep in her heart. "Especially since Travers went through so much trouble."

"Oy." Ginny's eyes rolled heavenward. "You don't know the half of it, young lady. That there's a man in love."

The light in Jo's heart grew brighter. He loved her, he really did. And as soon as LeeAnna's baby was born, they'd get married. But until then, they had to pretend nothing was going on, even if it killed them. If LeeAnna's father thought for one second that Travers was messing with another girl, he'd for sure hunt Travers down and start shooting.

"Oh, Ginny—this is all wrong." Jo slumped against the wall and covered her face with her hands.

"What do you mean? He thought you'd love this."

"I do." She reached for the silk stockings and rubbed them between her fingers. "But how will it look when people find out Travers bought all of it for me? They'll think—well, you know exactly what they'll think."

"Does it matter?" Ginny's voice was soft, soothing, but questioning.

"Yes, it matters," Jo cried. "He's done nothing wrong, Ginny—not with me, anyway."

Her aunt's smile pushed Jo on.

"Believe me, Ginny, I've been the one pushing for more, but Travers won't let . . . anything happen. Not until we're married."

Ginny pressed her hands against her heart and sighed. "It's been a long time since there's been any romance in this house," she sighed. "He's a good man, Joanna, no matter what Mac thinks. He might have had some troubles in the past, but now . . ."

They both smiled. Now was a whole different story. Still, unease nibbled at Jo's conscience.

"But once people find out that he went to all this trouble for me, they're going to think he's still the same old Travers."

"And who's going to tell them?" Ginny stood with her small hands bunched on her hips, her brow arched in a challenge. "The only ones who know are you, me, and Levi. We both know you and I won't say anything, and I certainly don't believe he'll tell, either. After all, he has enough to worry about, doesn't he, without starting any more rumors."

"But he picked it all out," Jo said. "Surely that must have caused a few raised eyebrows in Mrs. Lloyd's shop."

Ginny's smile returned. "I'm not supposed to tell you this, because he wants you to think he did it all himself, but . . ." she paused.

"What?" Jo reached for her aunt's hands and stared into her twinkling eyes. "Tell me."

"He knew there'd be talk if he went into the store himself, so I went with him on the premise that I was doing some shopping and he had the bad luck of having to drive me into town."

"You didn't!"

"We did." Her aunt's eyes gleamed. "So while he went about gathering supplies, I looked through the catalogue, turning pages whenever he walked by. Then, when no one was looking, he flipped to the page he liked. Didn't even have to think about it, either. He told me as soon as he saw it, he knew it was the one for you."

Panic slid through Jo's veins. "But Mrs. Lloyd is going to be here tonight—she'll see me in it."

"You didn't let me finish." Ginny sighed through a smile. "He took the catalogue numbers, wired a store in Humbolt, and had them send it straight to him."

So much trouble—just for her. Surely this must be wrong. Nothing that felt this sinful could be right.

"What would Mama think about all this?" She hadn't meant to say it out loud and started when Ginny answered her.

"Your Mama was a smart woman, Joanna. She'd want you to be able to enjoy tonight as much as anyone else." She squeezed Jo's hand. "You're a smart woman, too. You're not about to do anything you aren't comfortable with, nor are you about to let anyone tell you what you should or shouldn't be doing."

Jo chewed her lip. Why was she suddenly struck with such uncertainty? Travers loved her and she loved him. That's all that should matter. Yet she couldn't stop the doubts creeping through her mind.

She didn't want anyone thinking any less of Travers, but oh, how she wanted to wear that dress. And more than that, how she wanted to dance all night with him. The last two days had been nothing less than torture knowing they were finally going to be together, but not knowing when.

Still, Jo couldn't help but smile. "I haven't worn a dress in years—not since the pink one you made me. How did you know what size to order? And there's no corset, either." She winked at her aunt. "Not that I'm complaining, mind you."

A deep blush flooded Ginny's cheeks. "Levi told me what to buy—and what *not* to buy—and he knew the sizes, too."

"But how . . .?"

"You'll have to ask him, dear."

Jo's mouth snapped shut. Of course Travers would know how big she was—he'd had his amazing hands on her enough times to at least make a guess. "But what if it doesn't fit? There's no time to make alterations."

Ginny laughed softly. "We'll worry about that later. In the meantime," she pointed to the other side of the bed where the tub had been set under the window, steam rising from its depths, "I want you to scrub every last inch of your body—do you understand me? *You're* going to be the belle of the ball tonight."

"Let's not get carried away, Ginny." Jo hugged her aunt close. "I'll leave all that nonsense to

Carrie. I'd be happy to make it through the evening without spilling punch on that dress."

"You'll be fine," Ginny assured her with a teasing smile. "Just don't go near the drink table." She turned to go, then stopped.

"Oh, there's one more thing," she said. From beneath the pile of crinolines, she pulled an old brown leather belt. "He told me to give you this. Said you'd know what it meant."

Jo looked at it for a minute, then once again found herself laughing and crying at the same time. Ginny finally gave up trying to understand, and left Jo to stare at the belt in disbelief.

After Ginny left, Jo spent a long time doing things she hadn't done in too many years to count. She took her time brushing out her hair, one hundred strokes, just like Mama used to do. She played with the length—up, down, twists, ringlets. No, she wouldn't wear it in twists *or* ringlets. No doubt Carrie would, and the last thing Jo wanted was Peter Carlson accusing her of trying to be like her sister again.

She took her sweet time in the bath, watching through the window as the sun began its slow descent in the west. People would be arriving soon, but Jo didn't care. The soap Ginny gave her left a delicate strawberry scent on her skin and in her hair. It was no wonder Carrie loved to be pampered—it was glorious! Of course, tomorrow it'd be nothing but a memory. But for as long as it lasted today, Jo would savor every last second of it.

Levi looped the string tie around his collar and tightened it just enough to be respectable. Damn, but he hated those things. In fact, he'd sworn them off years back, but he'd bought one for tonight. He wanted to look his best for her tonight, so she'd be as proud to be seen with him as he was with her.

He'd even gone so far as to shave a second time today and, with the help of a smug Will, he'd cut his hair. No matter how respectable he looked, it was sure to be a hard lesson in self-control with Miss Joanna McCaine on his arm all night, wearing that dress.

And what a dress. The minute he'd seen it, he knew it was the one for her. The color was the exact same as her eyes when she was yelling. There wasn't anything frilly about it, either. There was a time when he'd liked all the frills and frippery some women wore, but not on Joanna.

She was simply the most beautiful woman in the world and she sure as hell didn't need any frills or other crap to make her more so.

Though, knowing Jo, she'd probably strangle him with his damned string tie for not buying her ruffles, but that was one risk he was just gonna have to take.

Guests had started arriving almost an hour ago, but Levi hung back until Will was ready to go, too. Couldn't let anyone think he was too anxious, even if his heart was hammering inside his chest and his throat was dryer than the Mojave.

They made their way toward the house and the crowd milling around it—women in fancy silk dresses with bustles and bows, men in expensive-looking suits and hats, and cowhands, dressed in their cleanest denim and leather, ready to dance the night away. Or drink the night away, whichever seemed more promising.

Good thing Carrie and Ginny had stocked plenty of whiskey.

The yard had been raked and swept until every last leaf and twig was in place. And God help the first breath of wind that dared blow any of it back. Tables and chairs had been set up in long lines beside the porch, each table decked out with flowers of every color and shape, while huge pink ribbons hung on the back of each chair and from the porch.

Joanna's dance floor sat smack in the middle of the yard, a giant wooden platform, raised about two inches off the ground and sanded smooth of every last splinter.

Levi left Will to talk to Jimmy while he made his way through the crowd, stopping along the way to speak with friends or taking the time to introduce himself to strangers. Seemed most folks were amazed by his transformation and wanted to find out what had caused it, because for every step forward he took, he was pulled back two, until the house looked farther away than when he'd started out.

Levi cast a glance up at the top floor windows just in time to see the curtains flutter closed. Anticipation riddled his veins. He couldn't wait to see her—couldn't wait to dance with her, to touch her again.

God help him if the dress didn't fit.

He nodded politely to Big Bill and his wife and excused himself. If he didn't get to that house soon, he was going to explode right there in front of everyone.

"Watch where you're going there, Travers." Mac's warning came just in time to stop Levi from falling up the porch stairs. A frown tugged at the corner of Mac's mouth as he leaned over the railing. "Little distracted, are you?"

Levi straightened his tie, then loosened it a bit. He couldn't stop from chuckling nervously. "Little. Is Joanna ready?"

Mac's lips tightened into a thin white line. His nod was barely discernable.

Levi swallowed hard. Of all people, Mac was the last person he should be asking, but he couldn't stop himself. "How does she look?"

A faint smile lit Mac's tired eyes. "You wouldn't believe me if I told you," he mumbled. "Just remember what I said—the first hint that you're messing with her or you've upset her in any way . . ."

Levi nodded and gave Mac a pat on the shoulder. Before he pushed through the door, though, he reached over the porch railing and plucked a single red rose from one of the bushes. He'd never been one to bring flowers before, but it seemed the thing to do.

Carrie was just coming through the parlor when he walked in. As usual, she looked like something right off the candy counter—pink and fluffy and sweet enough to make a belly ache.

"Hello, Mr. Travers," she sang. "You look very handsome."

"Thank you, Carrie. You look fine yourself."

Her lip came out in its usual pout. "Fine? I look *fine*?"

"Well, yes, ma'am. You sure do." It took some doing not to laugh at her, but he managed.

"Is Will with you?" There was a strange look in those blue eyes, but Levi couldn't be bothered to try and figure it out.

"No, he's talking to some of the boys outside."

"Oh good, he hasn't left then."

Unease settled in Levi's belly. "No, I don't reckon he'll head out until tomorrow sometime."

She smiled, but that look lingered until her little button nose scrunched. "Has that horrible Milly Jean Carlson arrived? I can't bear to see her yet."

"Wouldn't know. I've never seen the girl before."

"Believe me, you'll know her." Carrie leaned closer. "She's quite a . . . sizeable . . . girl who will, no doubt, be dressed in a white silk dress that's three sizes too small."

That must be a huge blunder in the fashion circles, but he couldn't have cared less about Milly Jean Carlson, her dress, or her size. The only girl he cared to see was certainly not sizeable and she wouldn't be wearing white. In fact, of all the fancy dresses out in the yard, not one came even close to the color of Jo's.

Was that a good thing? If pink was the popular color, maybe he should have gone with that instead. Damn, but he was losing his mind. Since when did he care about dress colors? He couldn't help but smile. Ever since he met Miss Joanna, that's when.

"Joanna will be down in a moment." Carrie sashayed closer. "Shall I save you a dance, Mr. Travers?"

He smiled as charmingly as he could. "Sorry, Miss Carrie. I'm spoken for all evening. Maybe next time."

"All evening? My goodness, Mr. Travers, after that

big speech you gave Uncle Mac, you still have an eye for the ladies, don't you?"

"Nope," he felt his smile turn into a big dopey grin. "Just one."

Her blue eyes opened in disbelief, glanced up the stairs, then looked back at him. With a loud humph, she lifted her chin and flounced past him.

Levi paced the parlor, twisting the rose between his fingers. What if she hated the dress? What if she'd changed her mind? She hadn't actually spoken to him about the dance since the day in the mud, so maybe she'd had second thoughts. Maybe . . .

A sharp gasp made him turn. "You cut your hair."

Beautiful didn't do Joanna McCaine a bit of justice. The deep green of the dress—Ginny told him it was taffeta—made the emerald fire in Joanna's eyes blaze. And it fit even better than he'd hoped. The neckline swooped low enough to let him admire her bare shoulders, but was still modest enough to not cause any raised eyebrows. A matching ribbon sash and tiny shoulder bows were the only adornments on the bodice that molded against her like a second skin.

No silk, no lace, no pearls; just a simple gown that seemed to be made just for her.

It was nothing like Carrie's.

It was perfect.

Levi's throat burned, but try as he might, he just couldn't swallow.

Joanna's hair, rich and glossy, sat in a loose pile on the crown of her head, with the two combs he'd sent tucked neatly along the sides. A soft fringe covered her forehead, but there wasn't a ringlet or a twist in sight. It was almost as if she'd read his mind.

"Your hair," she repeated, with what he could only call a look of horror.

"Y-yeah," he stammered, fingering the edges. "It's not that bad, is it?"

"Why did you do it?" There she went, chewing that lip again.

"I-I wanted to . . ." He stopped. Had he ever felt more the fool?

"You wanted to what?" she stepped closer, edging his fingers out of the way and replacing them with her own. The cool softness of them made his breath catch.

"I, uh," he swallowed, "wanted to look good for you."

"Oh, Travers," she purred. "You always look good to me. And tonight you look even better. But you'll let it grow back, right?"

When he caught his breath, he stepped toward her, slowly. He knew his mouth was hanging open, but he didn't care.

"You look . . ." What was the word?

"*Fine?*" she teased.

"No." He blinked. "I mean yes, but that's not it."

"Nice?"

"Nope."

"Handsome?"

"Definitely not." He tapped a finger over his mouth as he continued to stare. Okay, he wasn't staring, he was ogling, but since she hadn't belted him yet, he'd just keep on doing it.

"What's wrong with handsome?" She began to fidget with the sash. "Everyone said my mother was a very handsome woman."

"I'm sure she was," he answered as matter-of-factly as he could, "but that's not you."

Jo's brow lifted. "Pretty?"

"Sorry."

A tiny frown pulled her mouth down. That delicious soft mouth. He took her fingers in his and lifted them to his lips. A tiny flame smoldered in her eyes.

"Unbelievable," he murmured.

"W-what?"

"You. You're unbelievably beautiful." When she blushed and moved away, he turned her face back with the tip of his finger. "I knew you'd be more beautiful than usual, but this . . ." He whistled. "You're unbelievable."

She began to shake her head, but he nodded.

"Yes." He hadn't released her fingers. Didn't want to. In fact, if she'd let him, he'd touch her all night long—and it would include more than just her fingers.

"Thank you." She seemed to have a difficult time with that word. "If I am pretty . . ."

"Not pretty," he interrupted. "Unbelievable."

Her color deepened. "If I am what you say, it's all your doing. You shouldn't have gone to all the trouble."

"Believe me," he smiled, "it was well worth it."

"Thank you, Levi." Even her voice was softer. "It's the most beautiful dress I've ever seen." Her eyes glistened behind unshed tears.

"No." He shook his head. "Thank you. I'm going to be the envy of every man out there."

She rolled her eyes. "I doubt that very much, but it's nice of you to say."

"I, uh, I . . ." he exhaled a long breath, then grinned back at her. "Wow."

"You look pretty 'wow' yourself, Travers." A sparkle danced in her smile.

"Call me Levi." He stepped closer until only their joined hands separated them. The pulse in her neck quickened and her tongue darted out to moisten her bottom lip.

"Nice tie, *Levi.*"

"I think it's choking me."

"I like it."

"Then I'll never take it off."

Her soft giggle tickled his ears. And damn it all if she didn't smell good, too—just like strawberries.

"Is that for me?" She glanced down at the rose he'd practically crushed in his fingers.

"Uh, yeah. Sorry." It was beyond repair, but he had to try. Much as he hated to, he released her fingers and tried to straighten the petals. "It looked a lot better when I picked it a minute ago."

"You picked one of Aunt Ginny's roses?" Her eyes widened in feigned shock. "She'll have your hide tacked to the barn wall."

Levi held the bud toward her and winked. "For you, I'd pick every last one of them."

"My, but you're laying it on awfully thick, aren't you?" She accepted the withered offering and held it beneath her nose. "Between the rose and the belt . . ."

Levi's eyes crinkled at the corners. "Ginny thought I was crazy when I told her to give it to you. But I knew you'd understand."

"Oh yes, Travers. I understood perfectly."

They stared into each other's eyes for a long moment, then whispered at the same time, "No more notches."

"Best gift anyone's ever given me." Joanna's smile lit the room. "But I think I should warn you."

"Warn me?"

She nodded. "You may have plied me with more gifts tonight than I've had in my whole life, and I might even look a little different tonight, Travers . . ."

"A little?"

She ignored him. "And we might even have agreed to get married." Her eyes teased him beneath her lashes. "But no matter what, I'm not about to let you wrinkle this dress."

"Is that so?" He offered up his brightest smile and for a second there, he thought he'd almost won her over. Almost.

"Yes, that's so." With her head tipped slightly to the right, there was something strange in her voice; she was still teasing him, but there was something else there, too. "It wasn't my idea for you to buy me all these fancy things. I was happy to go sit in the loft, remember?"

"Yeah, I remember." Then it hit him—she liked being all dressed up! Despite all her bluster, she truly enjoyed the fuss and fanciness. He ran his finger down the length of her jaw.

She shivered. "But now that you've gone to all this trouble and spent all your hard-earned money—"

"Hard-earned doesn't even begin to describe it."

She swatted him softly. "You won't be getting any . . ."

Levi's grin widened. "Any what, Miss Joanna?"

"It's Jo." She lifted her chin, but a smile still tugged at her beautiful lips. "And as I was saying, you won't be getting anything from me tonight, in this dress, that you wouldn't give to me when I was wearing my pants and hat."

He pushed his smile away, but couldn't help winking at her. She was so cute when she acted tough. "First of all, you are anything but a Jo tonight. You're very much a Miss Joanna."

She chewed her bottom lip, but gave no other outward sign of what she was thinking. He couldn't wait to taste that lip again.

"And secondly," he raked his gaze over the length of her, "after seeing you dressed like this, I don't think I can ever allow you to put that thing you call a hat back on your head."

Just as he'd hoped, that got her going. Fire sparked behind her eyes; her hands balled into tight fists.

"You can never allow me? And who are you to decide what I can and cannot do—my father?"

"No, thank God."

"What's that supposed to mean?"

He traced the line of her lips with his finger, feeling her tremble. Just once, and only slightly, but it was something. "It means if I were your father, I'd burn in hell for the things I'm thinking about you right now."

Her skin flamed, her eyes widened. Then she tipped her head to the side and smiled coyly.

"Really?" she asked. "And what is it that you're thinking right now?"

"Oh, no, Miss Joanna," he laughed. "You're not going to get me started and then make me stop when it gets too hot for you in that dress."

"I'm already hot, Travers," she answered in a low, sexy voice. "And I'm not the one who keeps stopping things, remember?"

God, how he wanted to haul her upstairs and

wipe that teasing little smile off her lips, those lips she could drive him crazy with just by pressing them against his neck.

"Besides," Joanna shot him a wink. "I will not be charmed out of this dress, Travers. In fact, I may never take it off."

"Oh, you'll take it off all right. And you'll take it off tonight. For me." He slipped her hand beneath his elbow and guided her toward the parlor door.

She pulled back, a tiny flicker of panic crossing her face. "But you said we'd wait until after we were married. Until after LeeAnna's baby was born." Her lip began to tremble. "You said—"

"Will you shut up and let me finish?"

She pressed her lips together, her fingers fidgeting at her waist until he stilled them in his own hands.

"One of Pearson's men rode over this morning; seems she had the baby yesterday. A boy."

Joanna blanched.

"And now we have proof he's not my son." He lifted her chin and placed a soft kiss on her trembling lips. "Apparently, the kid's got a head full of fire-red curls."

Joanna gasped. "You mean . . ."

Levi nodded. "Always knew Carlson was a lying bastard. And now everyone else knows, too."

It was a rare moment that caught Joanna speechless, but this was one.

"So that's behind us," Levi continued. "Now we just need to focus on the other problem."

"W-what other problem?" Her eyes shimmered, but she blinked back the tears.

"The problem," he whispered against her cheek, "of us getting married. Quick. Tonight."

"T-tonight?"

"God yes. Surely there's a preacher somewhere out there among all those people."

"Well, yes, there should be, but—"

"But nothing, Miss Joanna." He brought her fingers up to his mouth and kissed each one. Slowly. "After seeing you in that dress, the only other thing I want to see is you *out* of that dress."

"Oh Lord," she whimpered. "You're killing me, Travers."

"Levi."

"Fine, *Levi*. Let's go find us a preacher."

He must have looked like some kind of fool with a grin that big on his face, but what did he care? He held the door open for her, then repositioned her hand beneath his elbow.

Mac and Ginny met them on the porch, Ginny's eyes brimming.

"You look wonderful," she whispered.

Levi puffed his chest out. "Thank you, Ginny. Wasn't sure if I should wear the tie or not, but Joanna seems to like it, so what the hell."

Even Mac smiled as he rolled his eyes. "I believe she was talking to her niece, Travers."

"Oh *her*. Right, of course." He shot Joanna a wink. "Yeah, I guess she looks pretty good, too."

The color flooding Joanna's face only made her more beautiful, but true to form, she retaliated with a pinch to the inside of his arm.

Her grip loosened and a teasing glint shone in her eyes. "You'd best behave yourself, Mr. Travers. I'd hate to have to hurt you in front of the whole town."

He met her challenging gaze. "Behave myself? With you in that dress? I don't think so, sweetheart."

She laughed at him, but her whole face flushed again. He led her down the stairs toward the overburdened tables.

"Would you like a drink?" he asked. He could use a whole bottle of Jack Daniels himself.

"Yes, please." As they neared the crowded tables, her fingers tightened slightly on his arm. The laughter that had danced in her eyes just moments ago vanished, replaced with guarded apprehension.

"It's okay," he whispered behind his smile. Damn, he'd like to do something for her to ease her nerves. But what?

"There's so many people here." Her voice trembled slightly.

Levi moved so he stood directly in front of her. Her gaze darted around the crowds, never settling on one person for more than a second or two.

"Look at me," he said. Of course, she didn't, so he repeated it a bit louder. "Look at me, Joanna."

Reluctantly, she met his gaze. For a moment he thought she was going to turn and run back into the house. He couldn't let that happen.

He itched to take her hand, but God only knew what kind of stir that would cause. It was one thing to do it when they were alone, but out among the crowds was a completely different game. Until that preacher showed up, anyway.

"You're Joanna McCaine," he began. "You're intelligent, strong, and once in a while you're actually funny." He winked. "But without question, you are the most beautiful woman here."

When she made to interrupt, he held up a hand to stop her.

"And that includes your sister." He lowered his voice. "You should see yourself, Miss Joanna. You take a man's breath away."

"You're just saying that so I'll stay and dance with you." Her eyes narrowed suspiciously, but at least she was smiling again. "And so you can peel this dress off me later."

"Wrong." He wished he could kiss her—right there for everyone to see. "You clear knock the air from my lungs every time I look at you."

Green eyes, as big as dishplates, stared back in shock.

"It's true," he continued. "Even up to your elbows in mud, you were the most beautiful creature I'd ever seen."

"I . . ."

"Don't say it." He smiled, mostly to ease the frightened look from her face. "We've got the rest of the night for you to tell me how handsome I am."

Her laughter sang into the air. "Charming and modest. You're quite the man, aren't you?"

"Yes," he nodded through his grin, "I am. Good of you to finally notice."

"Joanna McCaine—is that you?" An older woman with a face full of wrinkles and eyes the color of moss stared openmouthed at Jo.

"Hello, Mrs. Burke." Joanna's smile never reached her eyes. "It's so good to see you."

"I . . . I don't think I've ever seen you like this." The woman's face clouded, almost as though she didn't believe what she was seeing.

"It's been a while," Jo agreed. The look she shot

Levi made him want to gag the old woman, but before he could move, Mrs. Burke made it worse.

"Audrey," she called over her shoulder. "Come and look at this—it's Joanna! In a dress!"

Levi cringed, but could do little more than offer a supportive smile. Color crept up Joanna's neck and over her face.

Audrey Brooks walked over, dragging Big Bill behind her. "Joanna McCaine?" she repeated. "In a dress?"

"Yes," Mrs. Burke nodded. "Look!"

And look they did. First it was Audrey and Big Bill, then Maggie from the restaurant in town, and then Jimmy and Simon, who nearly tripped over their own jaws.

Joanna's cheeks pinched inward, her smile a mere grimace.

"Oh, look," Levi sputtered. "There's Will. Excuse us, won't you?" He took her arm and hurried away across the yard, over the dance floor, and toward another table loaded down with a huge punch bowl and dozens of mismatched glasses.

"Well, that was fun." Joanna downed a glass of punch in one gulp, then reached for another.

"Sorry," Levi said. "I had no idea."

She inhaled a long breath, took another drink, and frowned. "I did."

"Maybe I should have gone with the brown potato sack like I wanted to in the first place."

A small smile lifted her lips. "Or maybe we should have just forgotten this whole thing."

"Not a chance, sweetheart. Look at you!"

"I don't have to," she grimaced. "Everyone else is doing enough of that for me."

"Well," he said with a low chuckle. "What did you expect? I don't think any of them ever stopped to notice how beautiful you are—you shocked the hell out of them."

"I hardly think . . ."

"Stop thinking." He stared into her eyes, which were now filled with uncertainty. "Trust me. You're the most beautiful thing this town's ever seen, and you're all mine."

"I can hear the talk already . . ."

He cut her off with a raised hand. "The only talk will be about how you took a perfectly worthless man and turned him respectable." When Joanna continued to look doubtful, he continued. "Hell, Miss Joanna, everyone in this town will think you're some kind of miracle worker."

"But I haven't done anything."

"You've done everything."

They finished their drinks slowly, glancing over their glasses at each other. Heat began to coil in his belly. He needed a distraction, something to make him stop staring into those eyes, something to make him stop wanting to kiss the breath out of her, and something to make him stop wanting to pull that dress off of her.

"Ready?" he asked. He pried the glass from her fingers and set it back on the table.

"No."

"Come on, Joanna. The worst is over."

She snorted. Even all dressed up and looking like an angel, she could still snort.

"I'll stay right beside you all night. If someone even thinks of upsetting you, I'll have you out of there in a heartbeat."

With a short nod, her lips curled up into something that resembled more of a snarl than a smile.

"Good."

Levi tucked her hand under his arm again and strolled out through the crowd.

"First things first," he said, "I'm supposed to warn Carrie when we see—what's her name? Big girl in a white dress—the Carlson girl she talks about all the time."

"Milly Jean."

He snapped his fingers. "That's it. Milly Jean Carlson. Might have to track down her brother, too. There's a few words I'd like to share with him."

Truth be told, he'd like to plant his fist into Peter Carlson's face again and finish what he started back at Lefty's.

Chapter 13

Jo marveled at the way Levi moved her through the crowd—always time for polite conversation, but never staying a second longer than necessary. Friendly, attentive, and courteous, he seemed to ignore the stares and whispers that followed his every move. Or was it *her* every move?

Newt limped toward them, his arthritic fingers curled around the top of a makeshift cane. Even though he lived in the bunkhouse, Jo hadn't seen him in more days than she should admit. In his condition, she should have checked on him more often.

"Joey." His pale blue eyes disappeared behind a row of wrinkles. "You look good 'nuff to eat."

"And you're full of malarkey." She took his free hand in hers and leaned in to kiss his cheek. "How are you feeling?"

"Like hell," he muttered. "First time I been outta bed in a week."

"I'm sorry, Newt," she said. "I had no idea."

"What're you sorry for?" he shrugged. "Not your fault I'm old. 'Sides, Clay kept me company." His gaze shifted to Levi, then back to Jo. "Kept me in-formed, too."

Even though Travers stood there grinning like an idiot, Jo felt the flush wash over her.

"Yes," she said, then cleared her throat. "I'm sure he did. Can I get you a chair?"

"You'll do no such thing." His smile faded, but the affection shining in his face did not. "Don't need no dame cluckin' over me like an old mother hen."

Jo laughed at his protest. No one loved to be clucked over more than Newt. And no one liked to stick their nose into her business more than Newt, either.

"You be nice to our Joey," he said to Levi, his creaky voice steady. "Got that?"

"Got it."

"Won't have her being treated like any of your other girls."

"Wouldn't do that, Newt." Levi's expression never flinched—he neither smiled nor frowned, but held Newt's gaze when he spoke. "Joanna's different."

"Damn right she's diff'rent. Ain't no one like our Joey." Newt crooked a finger at Levi, his voice a low warning. "If I hear you've been messin' with her, you'll be sorry you was ever born, got that, junior?"

If Jo didn't know better, she'd have thought Levi almost looked humbled. But Levi Travers had never been humbled in his life. Had he?

"Newt." She put her hand on his arm, but Levi interrupted.

"Got it." He offered a slight nod and a grin. "But I appreciate the warning."

"Good." Newt glanced around the milling crowd. "Now you listen to me. If Peter Carlson so much as looks at her sideways, I'm holdin' you personally responsible. I won't have our Joey bein' upset by that little weasel again."

"Oh, Newt." Jo put her arms around his shoulders and hugged him tight. "You're such a sweetheart."

"Now cut that out." He struggled out of her embrace and pretended to adjust his vest. Behind his wiry gray beard, his cheeks turned decidedly pink. Levi looked on with a strange, warm, faraway look in his eyes.

"Can I get you a drink?" Jo asked. "Or something to eat, maybe?"

"Dames," Newt muttered. "I telled you before—I don't need to be clucked over. 'Sides, I hear the Widow Burke is here." He waggled his straggly brows at her and limped off toward the tables.

Jo watched after him for as long as she could before the heat from Levi's gaze forced her to turn and face him.

"I'm sorry about Newt," she said. "He gets a little protective sometimes."

Levi shook his head slowly, his eyes never leaving hers. "Don't be sorry. He's a good man and there aren't many of us left."

Jo opened her mouth to reply, then saw the twinkle in his eye and snapped it shut.

Good man, her big toe. Newt might be one, but Travers? He was only after one thing—and she was it.

"Come on," Levi laughed, taking her by the arm. "Let's eat or something. When does the music start, anyway?"

"I don't know." Jo took three steps and stopped. About a hundred feet in front of them stood Peter and Milly Jean Carlson.

Levi turned, a questioning look on his face.

Jo indicated the Carlsons with a short nod. "They're here."

Levi shifted his gaze to where she had indicated. His eyes widened, then he shook his head.

"Carrie was right—that girl needs a bigger dress." He spoke only loud enough for her to hear. "And him—he still looks like a weasel. But what d'you expect with hair like that? That poor kid of his doesn't stand a chance."

Jo snorted back a laugh. There had been a time when she thought Peter's chaotic red curls were the cutest things she'd ever seen. Of course, she'd been ten years old at the time and had long since outgrown that notion.

Too bad he hadn't outgrown the curls.

"Come on." With his hand on her back, Levi pushed her toward the Carlsons. "Let's go say hello."

"No." She fought back, tried to drag her feet, then remembered her pretty new shoes and stopped.

Besides, Levi was very determined. He kept pushing her toward them, slowly but steadily.

"Oh yes," he whispered. "Just remember, I've been threatened with my life if I let Carlson say anything to upset you. And since I rather enjoy my life, I'm not about to do anything that would put it—or you—in jeopardy."

All too soon, they stood face to face with the only two people in the county Jo despised.

Milly Jean, in her trademark white, offered a look of false shock as she looked Jo over.

"Joanna Belle McCaine—is that really you?" Her white-blond hair was tied back in a severe knot and

her chubby face had been painted with far too
much of her mother's rouge.

The white dress was worse than any she'd worn
before. Fitted through the bodice, she'd obviously
gone without a corset again. Jo had never been one
to wear the tortuous garment herself, but then she
didn't carry half the weight Milly Jean did. Lace
and frills covered the too-low neckline and ran in
strips down the length of the skirt. What on earth
had she been thinking when she picked it out?

With a forced grin, Jo nodded. "It's me all right,
Milly Jean. Don't you look . . . what I mean is . . .
your dress. I've never seen anything like it before."

Levi poked her discreetly in the ribs, but she
didn't flinch, just bit the inside of her cheek.

"Yes." Milly Jean smiled in conceited agreement.
"As soon as I saw it, I told Papa I had to have it. It's
from New York." She twirled in a circle, then leaned
closer to Jo. "Your dress is an *interesting* choice. The
color is a little too bold, but perhaps once you get
used to dressing like a girl again, you'll have a better
idea of which shades and styles look best with your
coloring and shape."

If Levi hadn't stepped between them, Jo would
have told Milly Jean exactly what she could do with
her shapes and styles.

"Name's Levi Travers." He didn't offer his hand
or even a bow. He just looked Milly Jean over with
an unsatisfied eye.

"Travers," Peter said coolly. "You'll be keeping
your distance from my sister."

"Believe me, Carlson, your sister is perfectly safe."

"You mean—" Milly Jean gasped. "Levi Travers!
Oh my Lord—and Joanna's here with *you?*"

A ball of knots twisted in Jo's stomach.

"Peter," Milly Jean went on, "surely you're not acquainted with this . . . man."

When Peter squirmed, Levi snorted and answered for him. "Met your brother when I was working out at the Pearson place."

Milly Jean gasped again, louder.

"I was working," he clarified, "but your brother, it would seem, was playing."

Peter's cheeks reddened until they almost matched his hair.

"Travers," he growled, but Levi cut him off.

"How is the baby, Carlson? What did you name him?" He lifted his brow as though truly interested. "And should we expect a wedding anytime soon?"

"Peter," Milly Jean squeaked. "What is he talking about?"

Almost everything in Jo made her want to laugh at Milly Jean's expression, but she didn't, only because there was one tiny part of her that actually felt pity for the girl. And for that poor baby who was now part of the Carlson family, whether he wanted to be or not.

Peter crossed his arms over his chest and shrugged. "Don't think that's any of your concern, Travers."

"No, it's not," Levi agreed. "But since you let everyone believe it *was* my concern all these months, I can't help but ask."

A slow sneer crossed Peter's weasley face. "And once you figured it all out, you moved right on to Joey."

"Is it a problem that I'm here with her?" Levi's voice held calm. Cold, but calm.

"Not for you," Peter scoffed, "but I don't imagine it'll do much for her reputation."

"My reputation is none of your business," Jo snapped. "You stupid sonuva—"

"Joanna." One word from Levi froze her tongue in mid-sentence. "Don't."

"But . . ."

He shook his head slowly, then glared at Peter again. "I'm not done with you yet, Carlson, but let me deal with your sister first."

Peter shrugged, but Levi didn't seem to notice. He'd already turned his attention to Milly Jean.

"Given the dress you're wearing, Miss Carlson, you obviously don't have enough fashion sense to be commenting on what Joanna—or anyone else—is wearing."

Milly Jean produced a tiny, lace-covered fan and began flapping it in front of her face.

"How's that, Mr. Travers?"

"Miss McCaine's dress is the most beautiful one here." He nodded toward Jo, then continued. "Just look at the way the color matches her eyes. Makes them absolutely sparkle."

And to Jo's surprise, Levi's sparkled when he raked his gaze over her.

"There's nothing worse than a pretty girl in a colorless dress."

If only the ground would have opened up and swallowed Jo whole, she'd have felt so much better. Peter and Milly Jean stood staring at her in complete disbelief.

Levi pressed on. "Those light colors make a woman look all washed out—almost sickly."

Milly Jean's mouth opened, then snapped shut. Peter just blinked.

"And the style of the dress," Levi continued, then let out a low whistle. "I'm no fashion expert, but look at her—that dress is a perfect fit, not too tight, or too revealing. And best of all, it's not covered in all that lace and frilly crap. Some women need all that to make them look pretty, but not Joanna." He turned, winked at Jo and smiled. "It's simply beautiful."

A lump formed in the back of Jo's throat. No one had ever defended her like that before. She'd never wanted anyone to; it would only make her look weak, and she'd spent far too many years proving she was strong enough to handle anything. Yet hearing Levi stand up for her, feeling his love shining at her through his smile, caused her bottom lip to quiver and her eyes to burn.

"Despite your words to the contrary, you certainly seem knowledgeable about women's fashions, Mr. Travers." Milly Jean's lips curled into an evil grin. "I guess with all the practice you've had removing Stella's clothing, you've learned a great deal."

"You listen here." Jo tried to push past Levi, but he held her back.

"Anyone with half a mind knows what's pretty— and what isn't." He raked her with a sneer. "But I guess you're too busy flapping your gums with the rest of your cronies to have a mind of your own."

Milly Jean's mouth fell open.

"And maybe," Levi continued, leaning closer, "given what we've all learned about your brother, your time would be better spent trying to pull your family's name back out of the mud instead of standing here dragging down everyone else around you."

"Peter," she huffed. "Are you going to let him speak to me that way?"

Peter's ice-blue eyes moved from Milly Jean to Levi and then back again as he seemed to weigh his options.

A new strength filled Jo. How had she ever let a spineless weasel like him make her feel so worthless? And the look Levi was giving them only made her stronger.

"Say what you like about me," Levi said, turning back to Milly Jean. "I couldn't care less. But if I hear you so much as whisper one more thing about Joanna—or Carrie, for that matter—I swear you'll live to regret it."

Milly Jean swallowed hard, but didn't answer. Her cheeks blanched beneath the rouge and her eyes nearly bulged from their sockets. In one stride, Levi stood toe to toe with Peter. Peter's pasty complexion turned almost gray with fear, but Levi's expression remained cold.

"And you," he seethed. "You worthless bastard. How dare you even show your face here when you've got a child waiting for you to give him and his mama your name?"

Peter and Milly Jean both gaped openly.

"That child didn't ask to be born to parents who didn't want him, Carlson. But for once in your sorry life, be a man and take responsibility for what you've done."

Jo had to swallow back a huge wave of tears.

"Might not be the life you planned," Levi said, the fury fading from his voice—and his expression, "but just because you made a mistake doesn't mean that boy should grow up thinking he was it. The mistake was yours and LeeAnna's, not his."

Silence surrounded the four of them—Milly Jean and Peter still gaping in shock, Levi still glaring at the two of them, and Jo falling in love with him all over again.

After a painfully long moment, Levi straightened and jabbed his finger into Peter's chest.

"As for tonight," he said, lowering his voice again so the rest of the town didn't hear, "you don't even so much as look the wrong way at Joanna. In fact, don't look at her at all. Don't talk *to* her, don't talk *about* her. Am I clear?"

The briefest nod was Peter's only answer.

"Fine, then." Levi stepped back and nodded. "So long as we all understand each other."

He tucked Jo's hand under his arm and offered the Carlsons a final glare. "Have a good time tonight. And then go out to the Pearson place and do what needs doing."

Giggles bubbled up through Jo's throat, but she held them back until they were a safe distance away.

"Oh my," she said. "I think you about scared them half to death."

He didn't laugh with her; he didn't even smile. In fact, the cold, hard, expression on his face was beginning to scare the life out of her, too.

"What is it?" she whispered, barely able to smile at the Widow Burke, still staring in disbelief at Jo, when she passed by.

Levi's lips thinned for a moment. He led her away from the crowd, far enough to be out of earshot but close enough to not cause any talk.

He seemed to study the toe of his boot, then the

milling crowd behind her. Why wasn't he looking at her? Jo folded her hands together and forced her tongue to work.

"Just say it, Travers. Whatever it is, it can't be that bad."

He licked his lips and finally met her gaze. "Carlson's right. This was a bad idea."

Jo snorted. "Peter's an imbecile."

"True," he agreed. "But he's still right. You're not going to be able to lift your head in this town after tonight. People keep staring at us and there's not a hope in hell they're going to be saying anything good about me and you being here together."

Dread settled over Jo. So this was it—he was going to humiliate her in front of the whole town and leave her standing there by herself.

The hell with that!

"Forget it, Travers. You're not going to back out on me now."

"It's not that, Joanna."

"No?" She spoke through gritted teeth, her hands twisting at her waist. "Then what is it?" Oh, how she wanted to yell at him. But that would never do—not in front of everyone like this. It would be bad enough to be humiliated by someone else, but to do it to herself . . .

He took forever to answer her. When he finally began to speak, his voice was as taut as a bow, ready to snap.

"There's so many things I've done that I'm not very proud of."

"So what? So have I."

"Not like this." His fingers curled around the bottom button of his vest. "People have opinions about me and, for the most part, they're right. I don't want them to think that way about you."

She swallowed hard. He'd picked a hell of a bad time to turn honorable.

"Listen, Travers," she ground out, "if you think for one second that I'm going to let you leave me standing here in this getup, you're even more of an idiot than I thought."

"You don't understand." He reached for her hand, but she stepped back.

"No, Travers. I do understand." She bit her lip, then continued. "You're scared."

It was his turn to step back. "I'm what?"

"You're scared," she repeated, lifting her chin a notch. If only she could stop her fingers from twitching. "You're scared that people might actually think you're not the lying, cheating sonuva . . . gun they've always taken you for. You're afraid you can't live up to their expectations. To my expectations."

All light drained from his eyes. His lips tightened into a thin line. Jo pressed her hands over his, which were still gripping the bottom of his vest.

"You don't understand," he said, shaking his head. "If we get married now, people are going to think it's because we *have* to."

"We do have to," she answered, forcing a laugh. "Remember, it's the only way you're going to get me out of this dress."

"That's not what I mean." He didn't show the least bit of a smile at her pathetic attempt at humor.

"I know." She sighed. "But I don't care, Levi. I really and truly don't care."

"I do."

"That's just too damned bad." She was giving all

she had to keep her voice strong, but it didn't keep her hands from trembling against his, or her heart from slamming against her ribs.

Levi gazed at her hands, resting over his, then covered them with his own and squeezed.

"Look, Travers," she lifted her chin and challenged him with a long, hard stare, "you can either stop talking this complete bulls . . . nonsense, or I'm going to mess this dress up enough that everyone'll be talking about us anyway. Either way, we will be married tonight."

When he looked up, a tiny sparkle had returned to his eyes.

"You would, too, wouldn't you?" His lips curled into a slow grin.

With a long breath, she blinked back the burning in her eyes and smiled. "Yes, I would. So I guess the question now is, are you going to get over this obsession you have with what people think about us? Or are you going to turn tail and hide out in the loft, watching everyone else dance the night away on that stupid floor I built?"

The warmth of his fingers ceased her trembling; his thumb moved in slow circles over her palm.

"I'd hate to see you on that dance floor with someone else," he said. "Especially in that dress. Besides, I don't even want to think about what Newt'll do to me if I upset you. Never mind what your uncle will do."

What was that feeling jumping around in her belly? Relief, fear, or a combination of the two?

The sound of fiddles started behind them. Big Bill and Mac squared off from the far side of the dance floor, both men sending their bows flying across the strings. Simon moved in between them, a harmonica sliding across his mouth in a tune that had people's toes tapping and hands clapping.

"Come on, everyone," Big Bill hollered. "Let's put this floor to use!"

Levi tucked Jo's hand under his elbow and motioned toward the dance floor. "Shall we?"

Jo froze. Any bravado she'd felt a moment ago now lay in a pool of dread at the pit of her stomach.

"I . . . um . . ."

"Oh no you don't." Levi tugged her forward. "A promise is a promise. I got you that dress, now you're going to dance in it. With me." He tugged harder. "Let's go."

"But . . ."

"No buts, Miss Joanna. Let's give Milly Jean something good to talk about tomorrow, shall we?" A wicked grin covered his face and Jo couldn't help but smile back.

Levi should have believed her when she said she couldn't dance. With every second step, she tripped over either her own feet or his, and once she nearly crashed right into him.

It shouldn't have surprised him that she was obviously not used to being led. But he'd be damned if he was going to let go of her. Not now that he finally had her back in his arms.

"Joanna," he whispered. "Stand on my feet."

Her head whipped up. "What?"

"Shh." He smiled over at Jimmy, who was holding Milly Jean a little closer than he should be. "No one's looking, just step up on them."

"Why?"

"Trust me."

And she did. She stepped up on his boots, her hands tightening around his for balance.

"Good," he murmured. "Now hold on." And he twirled her around the dance floor, moving in and out of the other couples as though everything was completely normal. He caught Ginny's eye, who looked quizzically at them before she noticed the gap of air between Joanna's hem and the floor; then she smiled brightly and mouthed a thank you to him.

He grinned back and whirled Joanna around again, savoring the scent of strawberries that floated around her, the way her hands held his without question, and how she squealed softly, then giggled every time they turned.

When the song ended, he forced himself to release her, but kept her hand tucked under his elbow. Her eyes sparkled in the twilight, like two dancing stars in the night sky.

"Have you seen Carrie?" she asked, glancing around the yard.

Levi shook his head. "Not since we were up at the house."

That uneasy feeling crept back over him. Something wasn't right, but hell if he knew what. He led Joanna back to the tables and filled two clean glasses with punch.

"Thank you," she murmured, her cheeks flushed.

"You're welcome. Cheers."

But Joanna didn't drink. "I don't mean for the punch."

"I know." He winked over the rim of his glass.

"But drink up anyway. The night is young and there's a whole lot more dancing we need to do."

He loved it when she blushed like that. Tough ol' Joey McCaine wasn't so tough after all, was she? They sipped their punch in silence, their gazes locked on each other. A mournful tune sounded from Big Bill's fiddle and the floor began to fill up again.

"Come on." Levi lifted her glass from her fingers and set it on the table next to his.

"But I'm not finished."

"You can drink anytime you want," he grinned, pulling her toward the music, "but how often do you get to waltz all over my feet?"

She hurried after him, giggling the whole way. Would he ever get tired of that sound?

As soon as they reached the floor, she put her hand in his and stepped up onto his boots again. He held her as tightly as he dared, though it wasn't near as tightly as he'd like. He couldn't remember anything feeling as good as she did—and he was barely touching her.

"Have I mentioned how beautiful you are?" he whispered, loving the way her hands trembled at his words.

"I think you might have mentioned it once or twice."

"Only once or twice?" He chuckled. "Better correct that." He lowered his voice even more until it was little more than a murmur. "You're the most beautiful creature I've ever seen, Miss Joanna. And though I have no idea why the prettiest girl in town would want to dance with a skunk like me, I'm sure happy she does."

"Travers," she began, but he cut her off.

"Levi."

A self-conscious smile flickered on her lips. "Levi. I'm sorry I called you that. I didn't mean it."

"Yes, you did."

"Okay," she laughed. "I did. But I don't think you're a skunk anymore."

"You don't?" He forced a look of shock, then sniffed the air.

Joanna's foot began to slide off his boot, but with a quick shift in balance, he had her back in position without missing a step.

"No," she admitted, her gaze skitting nervously over his. "In fact, you're a very handsome man, Levi, and you . . ."

"I what?" he was whispering again—mainly because he could barely find his voice.

"You smell wonderful tonight."

He puffed his chest out in false bravado and grinned. "Do I now?"

She nodded. "You always do. Even when you stink from working all day, there's something about you . . ." She leaned closer, shut her eyes, and inhaled deeply.

"Stop it," he winced.

"What?" Joanna pulled back and glanced down at their feet, her eyes wide. "Did I hurt you?"

He groaned. "No, you didn't hurt me, but you're sure as hell killing me."

The music stopped and the crowd wandered off the floor, leaving Levi and Joanna standing there by themselves. Before they could move, the fiddles began again and Levi swept Joanna around the floor, but this time his attention wasn't completely on her.

"Where *is* Carrie?" he asked. "You'd think she'd be right in the middle of all this, wouldn't you?"

"She must be here somewhere," Joanna said, sounding a little unnerved. "Believe me, she'll turn up. Probably just waiting to make her grand entrance."

No, he thought, that's not it. Something's wrong.

Halfway through the song, Levi caught sight of Jimmy making his way toward them, a smile on his face, his brow raised in silent question as he nodded toward Joanna. Levi answered with a hard glare that sent Jimmy heading back to his crowd of half-drunk cowboys.

Levi'd promised Joanna she wouldn't have to dance with anyone else and that was one promise he intended to keep—even if it was for purely selfish reasons. The music played on for another half an hour and neither Levi nor Joanna made any attempt to leave the dance floor.

When Big Bill announced a short break, the disappointment Levi felt was mirrored back in Joanna's eyes.

Boy, was he in trouble. Joanna had no idea how vulnerable she looked just then, how everything she was feeling shone clear from her face. It was one thing for him to be able to see it, but they didn't need the rest of the town seeing it, too.

He cleared his throat and nodded toward the yard. "Shall we?"

She blinked hard, as though suddenly remembering where she was. "Oh, y-yes," she stammered. "Let's walk."

They moved across the grass, his hands clasped behind him, hers twisting at her waist.

"Carrie still hasn't shown her face." He instantly regretted saying it out loud.

"So what?" Joanna eyed him carefully. "Why's it so important to see her?"

"It's not that . . ." he stopped. No need to ruin Joanna's one night of fun by sharing his worries about her sister. "Sorry," he muttered. "I just think it's odd, that's all."

"No, I'm sorry," she said, only loud enough for him to hear. "I shouldn't be so prickly. And I'm sorry about that dance, too."

Levi frowned. "What are you talking about?"

"You know." Her face flushed. "Back when I . . . and then you groaned. I didn't mean to make you uncomfortable like that."

Levi stopped in mid-stride. "Uncomfortable?"

She had stopped, too, but kept her gaze on the ground. "Yes. It's not fair of me to get you so . . . upset . . . like that."

Levi released a tight laugh. "You didn't upset me," he said, shaking his head.

"But you hardly spoke to me after that." She looked up quickly, then away again. "I just thought . . ."

She really didn't understand, did she? Levi raked his fingers through his hair and looked around, trying to find a way to explain it.

Milly Jean Carlson and another girl about the same age stood a ways off—but not far enough for Levi's liking. He started walking again, nudging Joanna along beside him, yet keeping a safe distance. Where the hell was Carrie?

"Joanna," he said. "The things you say and do to me don't make me uncomfortable."

"They don't?" she almost looked disappointed.

"No. I didn't say anything because the things I wanted to say would have gotten us both into a lot of trouble."

"What . . .?" There was a brief look of confusion in her eyes before understanding finally dawned. "Oh."

"Yeah," he sighed. "Oh."

They stopped under a giant cottonwood, Joanna leaning back against it and Levi standing with his back to the yard. The constant chatter of the crowd filled the air around them, but neither paid it any mind.

He shouldn't do it, but she'd tortured him so badly the other night that he couldn't help but retaliate. Especially with so many people moving around—it was too good a chance to make her crazy. Sure, he'd be ready to burst, too, but watching her reach that point would be well worth it.

He tipped her chin up so she had to look at him. "There are things I want to say to you, Joanna, things I want to do to you. But I made you a promise and I mean to keep it, even if it kills me." He offered her a wry grin.

Her face flamed scarlet. She looked away, her fingers twisting feverishly at her sash. "I'd like to, um, well, I mean . . ."

"What?" he whispered. "What would you like?"

In typical Jo fashion, she lifted her chin and looked at him defiantly. She hated to appear weak—especially in front of him— and he knew it.

She took a breath and let the words fall from her lips. "I'd like to hear what you have to say."

He smiled—slowly and wickedly. He'd hoped she'd say that. "Would you now?"

"Y-yes."

"Good, because I really want to say it."

She clenched her hands in front of herself and tipped her head to the side as though bracing herself. Levi chuckled softly. She'd need a lot more than clenched hands by the time he was done with her.

"Do you know why I chose that dress?" he asked, keeping his voice low.

She shook her head slowly.

"Because it was one of a kind—just like you. I knew no other woman would dare wear such a bold color; no other woman would be able to wear such a color. No silk for Miss Joanna McCaine, either— silk is too common at dances like this. You needed something totally unique, but nothing with ruffles, because you're not a ruffles kind of girl."

She laughed lightly and seemed to relax against the tree. He'd have to fix that.

"Wanna know how I knew the size?"

She nodded—barely.

Levi took his time in answering. As he spoke, he moved slowly around the tree until he stood on her left.

"I closed my eyes and pictured you in my arms, with my hands on you, under your shirt, sliding over your silky skin."

A soft moan slipped from her lips.

"Your waist was this big." He held up his hands as though he were spanning her waist again. "Under all that heavy denim and cotton, you have this tiny little waist. And the way my hands rested on your hips . . ."

"Oh God," she half-choked, her eyes slipping shut.

"Open your eyes, Joanna," he murmured, stepping closer and waiting until she did. Her neck and chest had turned the sexiest shade of pink. He lowered his voice even more, knowing she'd have to strain to hear more if she wanted. "I remembered the way your breasts felt in my hands. The way they filled them perfectly, as though they were meant for my hands. And I remembered how they tasted, too."

Joanna's chest heaved with each intake of breath.

"The rest," he said, "I've been imagining since the day I first met you at Lefty's."

He moved to face her again, loving the way her cheeks looked almost aflame. "I've spent every night dreaming about what was under your daddy's clothes and every day wondering how I would ever find out."

Joanna opened her mouth, but he silenced her. "Shh, I'm not done yet."

He glanced around to make sure no one was nearby. "Then you gave me the chance I needed. You put me in charge of finding your dress, Miss Joanna. And I've got to admit," he raked her head to foot with an appreciative gaze, "you're even more unbelievable than I'd imagined. There's only one problem."

"W-what?" she squeaked.

"You make it impossible for me to keep my hands to myself." He moved around the tree again, whispering into the still night air. "I want to touch every inch of you, Joanna. I want to taste every inch of you, to feel your bare skin against mine, and to let you feel me against you." He paused, swallowed hard, and forced back his own groan of anticipation. "To let you feel me inside you."

Another whimper slipped from her lips. Levi faced her again, but her eyes were closed, her mouth open the tiniest of slits.

"Would you like that, Miss Joanna?" he murmured. If he didn't stop soon, he was going to need a good long soak in the creek, but he couldn't help himself.

Her head moved in the briefest of nods.

"Remember how good it feels when we kiss?" he asked, and smiled when her fingers moved over her lips at the memory. "How we fit together—that's what I want to feel again. I want to taste your sweet mouth against mine; I want to feel you shiver at my touch." He took a moment to catch his own breath. "And then I want to slide my . . ."

"Let's dance!" Big Bill's voice shattered the moment.

Joanna's eyes flew open; her breathing labored and choppy.

"Tell me," Levi said, grinning down at her. "Would you rather I said all that on the dance floor?"

"N-no," she stammered through a short laugh. "I, um . . . wow."

"Yeah, that's one word for it." He straightened his already straight tie. "Shall we dance?"

She scanned the area. "I don't know. Should we? I mean . . . after this . . . I don't know if I can."

"Well I can." He grabbed her hand and almost ran back to the dance floor. He'd be damned if she was going to slip away that easily. Not when they had each other to hold on to.

Chapter 14

Jo held on to Levi as tightly as she dared, but not nearly as tightly as she wanted to. Whenever she thought of what he'd just said to her, her whole body trembled again. She shouldn't have let him say those things to her; but worse than that, she shouldn't have been thinking the exact same things he was.

Every step they made on the dance floor, every breath she took, she heard his voice, low and husky, telling her over and over again how much he wanted to kiss her and touch her and . . . and more.

The warmth of his hand on her back soothed her taut nerves, yet, at the same time, played havoc with them. A few times she thought she'd collapse right at his feet, but he held her up—her rock, her strength.

"May I?" Mac's voice sounded behind her.

Levi stopped moving, his gaze shifting between Jo and Mac. "Sorry, Mac," he said, "but Joanna promised me every dance tonight."

A sly smile spread across her uncle's face as he

leaned closer. "Even if I let her stand on *my* toes, too?"

Jo laughed, feeling very foolish all of a sudden.

"Just one," Mac continued. "I'll give her right back, I promise."

When Levi made to protest again, Jo stopped him. "It's okay, Levi. Just this once." She gave him a meaningful look. "Why don't you go, uh, cool off for a minute?"

His warm brown eyes crinkled at the corners, the beginnings of a smile tugging at his mouth. "Good idea."

Jo took Mac's hand and continued the dance—now standing on his boots instead. As she watched Levi walk toward Ginny, she saw him mouth the same question he'd asked too often already: Where's Carrie?

"You look real pretty, Joey," Mac said. "Are you having a good time?"

"Yes," she answered, a little too quickly. "Are you?"

"How couldn't a fellow have fun here? Lots of good food, fiddle music, and the McCaine women—it just don't get any better than that, does it?"

"I don't know about that."

"I do." He nodded for emphasis. "Now tell me—how's Travers treating you?"

Out of nowhere, tears burned against her eyes and her bottom lip trembled.

"That bad?" Mac asked with a wink. "Or that good?"

"Oh, Mac," she breathed. "I know you don't like him, but he's not what you think. He'd never do anything to hurt me."

He squeezed her hand a little tighter. "Listen."

His voice was tighter. "I'm not sure what I think about Travers. Knowing he's not responsible for the Pearson girl makes it a little easier to like him. Not much, but a little."

He chuckled softly. "Doesn't mean I'm going to abide him messin' with you, though. You be real sure before you let yourself get too close. D'you hear me?"

"Yes."

"Good. In the meantime, though, enjoy every minute of tonight. And if he wants to treat you like a queen, then you darn well let him!"

Jo laughed again and let him twirl her around the floor until the music stopped.

"Time's up, Mac." Levi stood at the edge of the floor, arms crossed, trying his best to look stern through his smile. "She's mine."

Color flooded his cheeks the moment the words were out.

Mac scoffed. "She ain't yours yet, Travers."

"Not yet," Levi agreed. "But soon."

Jo stood between the two, not knowing where to look or what to do with her hands. With a low chuckle, Mac kissed her cheek, then shook Levi's hand.

"Take care of her," he said. "'Cuz I hear ol' Newt's looking for a reason to hurt you."

"I'll do my best," Levi said.

"Hell, Travers," Mac grinned as he backed away. "You're gonna have to do a lot better than that."

The music started again and Jo stepped into Levi's arms, laughing at his quiet stories about the people dancing around them.

Four more times other men asked to dance with Jo, and each time, Levi politely but firmly denied them. And each time, her heart warmed a little more until she was sure it would burst. Even though she was probably breaking every one of his toes, he was keeping his promise.

They danced in silence, but the hold they had on each other said everything they didn't. And if the whole town noticed they danced all night, all the better.

Bill called another break and everyone made their way to the tables for refreshments. Jo had never been doted on before, but that's precisely what Levi had done all night, filling her cup as soon as she emptied it and bringing her tasty morsels from the food tables.

As they moved through the crowd, Levi seemed to keep one eye on her and one searching the yard. At first, she thought he was watching for the Carlsons, but after walking past them twice, it was clear that wasn't the problem at all.

Carrie. Everything always came down to her.

Levi jerked away from her, muttering curses below his breath.

"Wha . . ?" Jo stepped back, staring at him. He turned in a slow circle until she saw the growing wet spot on his shirt.

"Jeez, Travers," mumbled Big Bill. "I'm sorry as hell."

"It's okay," he said, watching as the spot from Bill's spilled drink made its way around to the front of his shirt. "I'd better go change," he grumbled, then turned to Jo. "Will you be okay here or do you want me to take you to Ginny 'til I get back?"

"No," she answered with more conviction than she felt. "I'll wait for you here."

With an apologetic smile, he hurried off toward his cabin, leaving her to feel all alone in the middle of the crowd.

People moved around her, stopping briefly to chat, then moving on. It seemed like she spoke with everyone while she waited for Levi to return. Everyone except Carrie. And what was taking Levi so long, anyway?

"Come on, Bill," Mac called above the crowd, "let's get these people dancing."

Several men whooped and whistled and before she could catch her breath, the dance floor was full again. Still Levi didn't return. She dared a glance toward his cabin, but couldn't even tell if he was inside.

Maybe he'd fallen. Maybe he was hurt. Maybe . . .

Fear clutched Jo's heart. It couldn't be. He wouldn't. Would he?

Fearing her knees would buckle beneath her, she made her way carefully up to the house, keeping her hands clutched together to keep them from shaking so.

Widow Burke stopped her at the bottom of the stairs, a glass of punch in one hand and a tiny pastry in the other.

"Where's that sister of yours, Joanna?" Her voice grated against Jo's spine. "Haven't seen her all night."

"Oh, I'm sure she's here," Jo answered, trying to sound sure when her heart already knew the truth. "Excuse me, please, Mrs. Burke. I must go check on something."

"Of course, of course." The widow had already started walking away, anyway.

Gripping the rail in her hand, Joanna forced her

feet up each and every step until she was inside the door. It was quiet. Too quiet.

"Carrie?"

Nothing.

Jo moved through the parlor and the kitchen, but her sister wasn't there.

"Carrie?" she called a little louder. Again, nothing.

With her heart pounding in her throat and her eyes already burning behind unshed tears, she mounted the stairs, dreading each step she took down the hall until she reached Carrie's room.

She palmed the door handle, swallowed twice, and forced her hand to turn it. Empty. She knew it would be. The problem was, it was emptier than she'd hoped. Gone was Carrie's doll from her bed, gone were all the primping products she usually stored on her vanity, and, even without looking, Joanna knew all would be gone from the wardrobe, too.

In the middle of the bed lay a single sheet of rose-colored paper. She didn't want to read it, didn't even want to look at it, yet there she was, lifting it from the quilt with fingers that trembled too hard to hold the page steady.

Dear Joanna

We've gone on to San Francisco as planned. I'll write once I'm settled at Aunt Meredith's. I hope you won't hate me forever.

Carrie

No. She wanted to scream, to cry, to throw something. But Carrie had taken everything with her.

How could she do this? How could *he* do it? He'd
told her he loved her, said he wanted to marry her.
He'd even convinced Mac—again—that he was
trustworthy. And now he was on his way to San
Francisco with her sister. Her younger, much prettier, sister.

Oh, how she hated him. How she hated herself
for being so stupid. She knew better than to think
any man would choose her over Carrie, yet she'd let
him fool her. And he was good, too. Pretending he
didn't want to bed her—it was probably because he
was having his way with Carrie the whole time.

She'd never be able to face anyone again. The
whole town had seen how she'd carried on with
him out on the dance floor, how he'd only danced
with her, how she'd come out of hiding for the first
time in years to dance with him. With Levi Travers.

The thought of their pity made her hate him
more. She made a dash for the chamber set and
threw up into the bowl. Over and over she retched,
until there was nothing left, and still her stomach
heaved.

Her throat, nose, and eyes burned with the re-
lentless flow of huge, hot tears. How long she sat
there, up against the wall with the chamber bowl in
her lap, she had no idea, but it was long after Big
Bill called the last dance, and long after the sounds
of wagons driving off down the road filtered up
through the open windows.

She didn't care. She just didn't care. Travers had
humiliated her worse than she could have ever
imagined—and he'd planned the whole thing.

Darkness swallowed the room. And her heart.
Twice the door downstairs opened and closed, but

Jo stayed where she was. The thought of facing anyone—and God forbid Mac—was enough to make her retch again.

It was much later when Ginny's voice called up the stairs.

"Girls—are you up there?"

She didn't answer, just pressed herself tighter against the wall. When Ginny's foot sounded against the bottom step, a sob broke from Jo's throat before she could stop it.

"Joanna?" The footsteps sped up, then stopped at Carrie's door. Ginny's face appeared in the light of her oil lamp. "What on earth?"

"Don't," Jo sobbed. "Stay over there."

"Nonsense," Ginny said, setting the lamp down on the vanity and turning to look at her niece. "Good Lord, Joanna, what's wrong?"

Jo shook her head. "Nothing. I'm just more stupid than I thought." She tried to force out a laugh, but it came out as an even louder sob.

Ginny moved closer, her arms out, but Jo leapt to her feet and scrambled away.

"Don't, Ginny. Don't touch me."

Ginny stopped, clasped her hands at her belly, and spoke slowly. "What is it, Joanna? And why are you in Carrie's room?"

Jo shook her head harder and moved farther away from her aunt. She couldn't let Ginny hug her or she'd never get control of herself again.

"Where's Carrie?" Ginny asked, yet the sound of her niece's name seemed to put everything in place. "Where is she, Joanna?"

"G-gone."

"Gone where?" Ginny stepped into the doorway and yelled like Jo had never heard before. "Mac!"

"Sh-she's gone."

"Yes, Joanna, you've said that." She moved back into the room and inched a little closer to Jo. "Where did she go?"

Mac's feet pounded up the stairs. "What's going . . . holy hell, Joanna, what's wrong?"

Both women ignored him.

"You have to tell me, Joanna." Ginny's voice was so calm. How could she be calm at a time like this? "Where did Carrie go?"

Unable to find her voice, Jo lifted a shaky hand and pointed to the floor near the vanity where she'd thrown Carrie's balled-up note. Mac reached it first.

"Jesus Christ." He blew out a long breath, his face turning every shade of red under the sun. "I'm gonna kill that sonuvabitch."

Ginny grabbed the paper away, read it quickly, then handed it back to Mac.

"You've not seen Levi?" she asked quietly.

Jo shook her head. "H-he went to ch-change his shirt."

"When?" Mac demanded.

"I . . . I don't know. Long time ago."

"How long?" He moved toward her, but Ginny held him back.

"I-I don't kn-know," she repeated, wishing the bowl was closer.

"Joey—"

"No, Mac." Ginny put her hand out. "Go to Levi's cabin and see if there's anything down there to explain this. And no matter what you find, bring it back here."

"I'm taking my gun."

Neither Jo nor Ginny put up an argument. He stormed out of the house, slamming the door behind him. Minutes passed—long, deafening minutes in the quiet room.

Jo finally came out of her corner long enough to grab the pitcher of the chamber set and retch into it, but Ginny didn't touch her, didn't rub her back or bring her water like she normally did when Jo was sick.

No amount of touching or water was going to make this better.

Finally, and slowly, Mac's feet sounded on the floor downstairs. Jo clung to the pitcher, praying for a miracle, a miracle she knew wouldn't happen. Not for her.

Mac stepped into the room looking absolutely gray. His shotgun hung over his shoulder, his fists tight against his thighs. For a moment, Jo thought she'd have to pass him the pitcher, but then he spoke and she knew she'd never give the thing up.

"He's gone."

"How do you know?" Ginny asked weakly.

He uncurled his left fist and handed her a scrap of paper. Oh God—not another note.

Ginny read it quickly, her eyes darting from Mac to Jo.

"Give it to me, Ginny."

"Joanna," Ginny began, but Mac cut her off this time.

"Give it to her."

272   *Laura Drewry*

With great reluctance, Ginny held out the paper; Jo snatched it away and scrambled back to her corner.

Gone to S.F.

That's all it said, yet it meant more than any other words ever had. She slumped to the floor, her whole body aching with every breath. Her mind went blank, her heart shattered into millions of tiny pieces.

"Joanna." Ginny stepped toward her, but Jo held her off with a raised hand.

"Don't touch me, Ginny," she sobbed. "Just leave me alone."

"But—"

"For God's sake, Ginny, please," she cried, her voice hoarse and choked, "just go away."

No one moved for what seemed like a lifetime. Then Mac slipped his arm around Ginny and led her back downstairs.

More hours passed. The lamp flickered out, leaving Jo in darkness again, but she didn't care. She didn't care about anything anymore.

She'd let a skunk like Levi Travers crush her and let her own sister betray her, but she was stronger than that.

She *had* to be stronger than that. There was a ranch to run and hands that needed to be paid. And now that Carrie was gone, someone was going to have to take over the book work.

Before first light, Jo forced herself to stand. Then she forced her feet to move; with each step her heart broke all over again, but she continued on.

Standing in her own room, she didn't even try to stop the new course of tears flooding her eyes as she stepped out of her dress. Stupid thing—it should have been her first clue. No man likes a girl in a plain dress; they all like ruffles and lace and all that crap.

As she belted her heavy denim pants around her waist, she knew what she had to do. She balled up the dress and Travers's old belt, picked up the two notes she'd left strewn on Carrie's floor, and made her way downstairs.

It was too early for Mac and Ginny to be up yet, so Jo stoked the fire in the stove and then pushed in everything: the belt, the notes, the dress and crinolines, even the stockings and the emerald satin shoes.

For a long moment, she stood and watched it all burn, then she closed the door and went outside. Broken heart or not, there was work to be done.

"You're gonna get sour milk if you keep pumping that hard." Newt stood behind her, clicking his tongue as she continued to yank on the poor animal's udder.

"I don't need you telling me how to do this," she snapped. "I've done it before, you know."

"I know what you done before, missy," he growled. "And I know why you're yankin' on them so hard, but it ain't their fault what happened, so quit takin' it out on them."

Jo's hands stilled.

"I'm sorry, Newt. You're right." She adjusted the upturned pail she sat on, gave the cow's flank a good pat, then set back to work on milking the animal. It wasn't any use, she couldn't find her rhythm.

"Get away from that animal," Newt leaned over her shoulder. "I'll get Clay to do it."

"Clay?" she choked.

"He tol' me he wants to learn how and if you keep up that way, we'll never get another drop of milk from any of these animals." He pushed against her arm. "Move."

Jo clicked her tongue, but moved off the pail and let Clay take the spot.

Newt threw her a harsh look. "Go find something else to take your temper out on."

"M-Miss Joanna?" Clay's nervous eyes turned to look at her, but she gave him a smile she sure didn't feel and nodded.

"It's okay, Clay. These cows will be a lot happier to have you milking them."

Though he didn't look convinced, he squatted on the pail and set his hands as Newt instructed.

Jo watched for a few seconds before walking out. There were always other jobs needing to be done. If only she could find one that required a lot of hammering.

With her horse saddled, she rode out to check the herd. It was going to take the animals a while to get used to the barbs, but in the meantime, they'd be suffering from nicks and cuts as they walked into the sharp twists.

Jimmy and Simon were nowhere to be found, given that it was Sunday, and she hadn't seen Mac yet this morning. Just as well. If she could get through the next few days without seeing him, maybe she'd be able to get over her humiliation and look him in the eye again.

Doubtful, but maybe.

She spent the rest of the morning tending the cattle, cleaning their cuts and scrapes and applying a creamy white ointment she'd found at the feed store last month. None of the animals seemed any worse for wear, thank goodness. It would just be one more thing Mac could give her his "I told you so" look about.

When she was done, she climbed back on her horse and headed back toward the house. She'd missed both breakfast and lunch, but she'd run out of water, too. She'd just fill her canteen, then head back out.

As she rode, she studied the land around her. This was hers—all hers. It was the only home she'd ever known. The only place she'd ever wanted to be. Yet now, she felt nothing for it.

The endless blue sky no longer made her heart ache; the acres of rolling fields no longer filled her with pride. Not even the cattle, one of the best herds in the state, made her feel any sense of accomplishment.

Nothing.

She was completely empty inside.

It didn't even make her curse when she spotted the windmill spinning crazily again. She just didn't care.

Back at the house, she filled her canteen quickly, then scurried to the stable to saddle up another horse. She loaded its pack down with all the tools she needed, then hurried away before anyone—okay, Mac—spotted her.

She set the block and tackle, hobbled the horses, then started up the ladder again. She was bent over almost double, fishing around for the plunger, when his voice stopped her heart in mid-beat.

"Thought I told you to come and find me the next time that needed fixing."

Jo had been wrong. She wasn't completely empty inside. She was filled with a rage so deep, a hatred so thick, it nearly sent her tumbling back down the ladder.

It hurt to breathe, yet she forced the air in and out of her lungs. And only when she'd fixed the stupid windmill again did she climb down the ladder and face Travers.

"Joanna." His voice was so soft, so tempting.

Her right fist slammed into his nose. "You sonuvabitch. How dare you show your face here after what you've done?" She stormed around the ground, picking up her tools and throwing them back in the saddlebag while he lay flat on his back, blood pouring from his nose.

"I—"

"Shut up, Travers." She removed the hobbles, threw the bags over the second horse, and jumped into her saddle. "You best get off my land. If Mac doesn't shoot you, I will."

"M-Mac's the one who sent me out here," he groaned.

She held her reins tight. "Mac wants you dead. He sure as hell wouldn't send you out here to me."

Travers rolled up to a sitting position and continued to mop his nose with the sleeve of his shirt.

"I swear. He did."

"You're a lying bastard, Travers. I don't know what the hell you were thinking by coming back here, but

you've got about five minutes to disappear again."
Jo kneed her horse into a run, pulling the other
animal behind her.

Tears streamed from her eyes and twice she
leaned over her horse and threw up. Damn Levi
Travers. May he and Carrie rot in hell together.

Chapter 15

"Joanna." Mac's voice sounded his surprise. "Where's Travers?"

Fury flamed in her belly; slicing pain ripped through the heart she thought had died the night before. Jo slid from her saddle and threw the reins to Clay, who was waiting at the stable door. "You knew he was here?"

"Didn't he tell you?"

"Of course," she stomped past him toward the house. "What the hell were you thinking by letting him back on our land? And where the hell's that shotgun you're so fond of?"

Mac hurried to catch up to her. "Joey, didn't he tell you what happened?"

"I know what happened, Mac," she grunted, stuffing her gloves in her back pocket. "He took my sister to San Francisco—or at least part of the way. God only knows what else he's done with her."

"Hold on a second." He grabbed her by the arm, but she yanked away. "Joanna!"

"What?" she cried. "What do you want? You're

the one who told me he was no good. You're the one who told me he couldn't be trusted, that he was just messing with me." She swiped at the tears flowing down her face. "And you were right. There, are you happy? You were right, I was wrong."

She turned back to the house, dreading every step, but needing the comfort of her own room, of the peace and quiet of her own bed.

"I'm the one who was wrong, Joey." Mac's quiet voice split the air between them. "You were right."

She followed where his finger pointed, to the front porch. There stood Carrie. And Will. And Reverend Walters.

What the hell was going on? She glanced back at Mac, who urged her forward.

"They'll explain everything."

Oh God, where was that chamber set?

Carrie came down the steps and met her halfway, her face crumpling beneath tears.

"Oh, Joanna, I'm so sorry. I never thought in a million years that you'd think I . . . that we . . . that Levi and I . . ."

"What are you doing here?" Jo's voice came out in hardly a whisper. "I thought you . . ."

"Please," Carrie pleaded. "Come in the house and let me explain."

Jo's feet remained planted. "No. Tell me now. What's going on?"

"Where's Travers?" Mac asked again. "I thought you said he was with you."

A deep pool of dread filled Jo's stomach. "He was."

"Where is he now?"

"Shut up, Mac, and tell me what's going on." She couldn't swallow and it was getting even harder to breathe.

"Joanna." It was Ginny's voice, coming from the kitchen door. "Come inside. We'll explain everything."

"Someone better start talking fast," she snarled, "or I'm going to start punching more of you."

Mac gaped. "You didn't—"

"Mac, please." Ginny took Jo's arm and led her to the kitchen table. Nobody spoke until every chair was filled.

"Start talking." Jo pointed at Carrie, then shot a long, hard glare at Will.

"First of all, Joanna, you have to know how much Levi loves you. You. Not anyone else. Just you."

The pool of dread got deeper.

Carrie's face flushed almost scarlet as she continued. "You know I've never liked being here on the ranch. I've always wanted to live in a city—a big city with lots of excitement."

Jo rolled her eyes and sighed. "I don't care about any of that, Carrie."

"But you must—it's the reason all this happened." Carrie wiped her eyes and sniffed, but as far as Jo could tell, it was all real, not a bit of acting put in it.

"Go on."

"When Levi told us all how much he loved you and that he was going to stay here, I was furious. I knew neither of you would ever allow me to go west by myself."

Jo's eyes nearly popped out of their sockets when

Will reached over and took both of Carrie's hands in his.

"So I went to Will and begged him to take me with him." She chuckled sadly. "You know how I am, Joanna. When I want something badly enough . . ."

"You didn't!" Jo growled, reaching across the table at Will, but Mac pulled her back.

"Just listen, girl."

She sat back down, but kept her glare fixed on Will.

"He finally agreed to take me with him, but we both knew we'd have to leave in quiet because you'd have tied me up in my room."

"Again," Jo couldn't help but add.

"Yes, again." Carrie offered her a small smile. "The dance last night was our best opportunity. With so many people here, no one would notice if we weren't here."

"But we did notice."

"Yes," she agreed, "but not until we were already gone."

"So you got all dressed up for nothing?"

"Not for nothing, Joanna. It was part of the plan." Her face flushed even deeper, as did Will's.

What the hell was going on? Jo's eyes flicked over to Reverend Walters, who'd yet to say a word.

"And what does he have to do with any of this?"

Will cleared his throat and finally spoke up. "I know you think I'm a dog," he said. "And I haven't given you much cause to think otherwise." He ducked his head, then looked up at Jo and held her gaze. "But I love your sister, Joanna, and—"

"You what?" Jo nearly fell backward off her chair. Mac steadied her, then patted her arm.

"Shush, girl. Let him explain."

"I'm listening, Mac, but my head's beginning to spin from all this."

"Tell me about it," he muttered.

"We got married." Carrie's announcement sucked the breath from Jo's lungs. "This morning. We rode out to the Scully place last night—"

"That's like thirty miles from here," Jo said.

Will rolled his eyes. "Don't have to tell me that," he grumbled. "She insisted."

"Yes, I insisted," Carrie said. "Reverend Walters was out there and I knew I couldn't leave with you all thinking I'd shamed you."

"So you rode half the night instead?"

"Yes." Carrie nodded, and even though Will grumbled again, the light in his eye when he looked at Carrie made Jo's heart soften. A little.

"And where does Travers fit into all this?" Jo asked quietly. "Your note said—"

"I'm so sorry," Carried gushed. "I worded that silly thing all wrong. I didn't mean you'd hate me because I left with Levi, just that you'd hate me for leaving without saying good-bye."

"But . . ." The pool of dread overflowed in her stomach. Jo raced out of the house and retched on the ground. She took her time going back into the kitchen, knowing what she'd have to face.

Ginny patted her back and handed her a glass of water.

"Is there any whiskey?" she rasped.

Reverend Walters hissed out a breath, then smiled. "Sounds like a grand idea."

"Travers had nothing to do with this," Will said. "When he found my note, I guess he—"

"*Your* note?" Jo croaked.

Mac patted her hand softly. "It was his note I found in Travers's cabin."

"I think I'm going to be sick again."

"No you're not," Ginny said. "Now sit down and listen to the rest of this." As she spoke, she slid Jo a glass with two fingers of whiskey in it, then set the bottle down beside her. She handed the reverend a cup of coffee.

"Anyway," Will continued. "Once he saw the note, I guess he thought the worst and came tearing after us."

Jo downed half the glass in one swallow. "But why didn't he tell me?"

"Dunno." Will shrugged. "Hell, I don't even know how he trailed us all the way to the Scullys', but he did. Fit to be tied by the time he got there, too."

"I imagine," she murmured.

"Was too late, anyway. The reverend had already married us."

Jo rubbed her pounding head, then swallowed the rest of her whiskey.

"Why are you here?" she asked. "Why come all the way back here now instead of going straight on to San Francisco?"

Will and Carrie laughed. They laughed hard. And the harder they laughed, the angrier Jo became.

"What is so goddamned funny?"

"Miss McCaine." Reverend Walters frowned over his coffee at her, but she ignored him.

"Oh my goodness, Joanna," Carrie continued to laugh as she spoke. "You should have seen Levi. Once he found out it was all innocent, he said he'd rather ride on to California with us than have to come back here and face you alone. He knew you were going to be mad."

"So he made you . . ."

"Yes," Will whined. "He made us ride all the way back here just to prove to you that he wasn't the lying bastard—sorry, Reverend—that you and Mac probably thought he was."

Jo's eyes rounded on Mac, who shrugged guiltily and smiled. "Told you I was wrong."

"What about San Francisco?" she asked, turning back to Carrie.

"Oh, we're still going," she said. "In a few days."

"Oh my God." Jo slumped over on the table, her head resting on her arms. "What have I done?"

"I don't know," Will said slowly. "What *have* you done?"

The kitchen door opened and everyone gasped except Jo. She knew who it was. And she knew how he looked, too.

"Ginny," Travers said thickly. "Could I borrow a couple rags?"

"Jeez, Joey," Mac whistled. "What d'you do to him?"

Jo kept her head down, but shook it against her arms.

"Seems her right hook is just as good as she claimed it was," Travers said, sliding into Ginny's vacant seat.

"That's my girl," Mac said with pride. "Taught her everything I know."

"I believe it."

She listened to Travers shuffle in his seat, trying to get comfortable, but for the life of her, she couldn't look at him. She just couldn't.

"Tell me she knows what's happened," he groaned. "'Cuz she wouldn't listen to a thing I had to say."

Will snorted. "She knows."

"Yes," Ginny hurried to add. "She knows. So why don't all of us leave these two alone for a while and let them talk?"

No. Don't go. Don't leave me with him now. Shoot me instead.

Chairs scraped against the floor, boots and shoes tapped out a hurried exit, and the door closed. Then there was silence. The most agonizing silence she'd ever listened to.

"So," Travers finally said, "about that windmill."

A huge sob broke from her throat. "I'm so sorry," she cried. "So so sorry. I—"

Warm hands closed around her arms, making her cry harder.

"Joanna. Look at me."

"N-no."

More chair legs scraped against the floor, more boots scuffled around the table. Another chair scraping, then squeaking beneath his weight.

Oh God, he was right beside her now.

"Look at me."

She shook her head. How could she look at him? Not after the things she'd thought about him, the hate she'd felt for him, and the pain she'd caused him. Again.

"I'm sorry," he murmured. His arms were around her, his head resting on hers. "I'm sorry I made you think . . ." He stopped. "And I'm really sorry I didn't believe you when you warned me about your right hook."

He smiled against her head, but she couldn't laugh. All she could do was cry harder.

"Oh, come on Joanna—that was a little bit funny."

"No it wasn't."

"Yeah," he chuckled, "it was."

He turned her chair, with her still sitting in it, so their knees touched. Then he eased her twisted body up and off the table.

"Look at me."

"No."

"What can I do to make it up to you?" His soft, beautiful voice broke. "I'll do anything, Joanna. Just tell me."

"Y-you . . ." She pulled her head up, inch by inch, and forced herself to face him. Though blood still oozed from his nose, plenty more had dried beneath it and around his upper lip. "Oh, Travers, I—"

She reached out to touch him, but he caught her wrist in his hand and held her fast.

"I don't care about that," he said, then grinned. "Sort of expected it, actually."

"I'm so sorry," she said again, finally looking into his eyes.

"Don't be," he murmured, caressing her cheek. "Wasn't your fault. I should have told you what was going on."

"You knew?" she pulled back a bit, but he brought her back.

"No. I mean once I found Will's note, I should have told you straight away. But I thought if I could bring Carrie back here, without too much fuss, that Mac would . . . well . . . I don't know what I thought."

"You thought you'd finally earn his respect."

Levi shrugged.

"I've, um, thought some pretty horrible things about you since last night," she admitted, her eyes cast down again. "I'm sorry about that."

"I knew you'd be upset."

"Upset?" she snorted. "Mac was walking around here with his shotgun last night."

"I knew how you felt about Carrie," he said. "About always feeling second best with her around. But I thought I'd made it plain enough it was you I wanted. Not her."

If she could only curl up into a tiny little ball and roll away somewhere.

"Look at me." Why did he keep making her do that?

Reluctantly, she lifted her head again. He took her hand and pressed its palm beneath his shirt, right above his heart.

"Feel that?" he asked.

Jo didn't dare open her mouth for fear of blubbering all over him again, so she gave him a quick nod.

"That beats for you, Joanna McCaine. Only you."

When she began to shake her head, he used his other hand to stop her.

"Yes," he murmured. "If you want me to leave, then

you may as well rip it out of my chest right now because it sure as hell isn't going to beat without you."

"Oh, Travers," she said, her fingers warming to the touch of his skin.

"Levi."

Her lips moved of their own accord, smiling up at him. "When I thought you'd left with Carrie, I wanted to die."

"I know. I'm sorry."

"And then, when she told me what had happened, I wanted to die all over again."

"I'm sorry." He pulled her hand out and kissed each knuckle, slowly, deliberately. When he'd reached the last one, Jo tucked it right back inside his shirt and smiled a little bigger. With her free hand, she lifted his hand and slid it inside her own shirt, resting his rough fingers over her left breast.

Levi's eyes shot open, as did his mouth.

"Feel that?" She giggled when he only nodded. "That beats for you, Levi Travers. Only you."

His Adam's apple bobbed. Twice.

"And if you ever leave me again, you may as well rip it out of my chest because it sure as hell isn't going to beat without you."

Levi groaned as he reached to pull her closer. "Hot damn, but I love you."

"Say it again." She reached for the wet rag and began to gently wipe the blood away from his nose.

"I love you."

"Me?" She moved the cloth over his mouth, gently rubbing away the last bits from each lip.

"Only you."

She poured a shot of whiskey into her glass and

held it to his mouth. He swallowed slowly, his gaze seeping through her entire being.

When he'd finished, she lowered the glass to the table and cupped his face between her hands.

"I promise I'll never hit you again."

His smile warmed her through. "I promise I'll never give you reason to want to."

"You really love me?" she asked again. Would she ever believe it?

"I really do."

"Make me believe it," she whispered against his whiskey-soaked lips. "Show me."

A whoosh of cold air blew between them as he pushed back his chair and stepped away from her.

"Wha—"

"Come on, then." He hauled her to her feet and half-pulled her outside. "Where the hell is everyone?" he muttered. "Want some privacy and there's a million people around. Today, when I'm looking for someone, they all disappear."

"Where are we going?" Jo stumbled after him, barely able to keep up with his long strides. "Travers, will you slow down?"

"Hello!" His voice echoed through the air, but no one answered. By this time they were clearing the stand of trees and heading toward the barns. "Hello!"

Mac stepped around the corner of the bunkhouse. "Over here."

Levi dragged Jo around the building and there they all were—even Carrie, who'd never in her life set foot near the bunkhouse, let alone sat on the porch.

"Reverend," Levi said. "Got your bible?"

"Of course." Reverend Walters pulled his small black book from the pocket of his coat.

"Good. Marry us."

"What?" the cry came from almost everyone on the porch. Everyone except Mac. He just nodded.

"Right here, right now. Just do it."

Jo stared at him, wide-eyed. "Right here?" she repeated. "Right *now?*"

"Yes, by God," he said, determination blazing in his eyes. "Right now."

"But she's not dressed," Ginny protested.

"She doesn't have any flowers," Carrie said.

"And jeez, Travers. You look like shit," Will added.

Levi turned to Jo. "Do you care? Do you want a fancy dress, some flowers, and a better looking groom?"

Joanna stepped closer and wrapped her arms around him. "Do you care? Do you want me in a fancy dress, with flowers, and do you want a better looking bride?"

The love in Levi's eyes smoldered as he gazed down into her upturned face. He caressed her cheek, then reached around and released the string from her braid.

"You know how I feel about you in dresses, flowers don't mean a thing to me, unless they do to you, and there isn't a better looking bride anywhere in the world."

Someone behind them sniffed, then sobbed. Carrie?

"Reverend," Jo said, never taking her eyes from Levi's beautiful face. "Marry us. Right here, right now."

* * *

"We're married now." Levi slid the lock on the cabin door and leaned back against it.

"So we are." She threw him a slow, teasing grin that set his blood pumping a little faster.

"And you know what that means, right?" He pulled the stupid string tie from his neck and tossed it across the room.

"Of course." She stepped further into the room until her hand brushed against his bed. *Their* bed. "It means you get to take over running this ranch and I get to sit up at the house reading books and having long, hot baths. With bubbles."

"Uh, no." He toed off one boot and left it by the door. "I was thinking of something else."

"Hmm." She slid her finger along the edge of the quilt, glancing back at him over her shoulder. "Did you mean now that we're married, you're going to attend church?"

"Uh, really no." He toed off the other boot and padded across the floor behind her.

"Well, I just don't know then." When she batted her eyelashes at him, he lunged, caught her up in his arms, and pressed her back against the wall.

"God, I've missed you," he murmured, burying his face into her neck. "And you still smell like strawberries."

A soft sigh slipped from her lips a breath before he kissed her, long and deep, until she shuddered in his arms.

Her fingers curled through what was left of his hair, holding him against her, making him drunk with lust.

"You're growing this back, right?" she whispered,

her lips tickling his earlobe, her breath warm against his skin.

"Anything you want," he moaned. "Anything."

"Mmmm," she purred. "I like the sound of that."

He took her wrists above her head and held them there, pinning her to the wall with his hips. Her eyes widened, then smoldered, burning with the need he felt.

"Joanna," he breathed against her neck. "Tell me what you want."

"I-I . . ." she swallowed beneath his lips. "I don't know."

He slid his tongue down to the small hollow at the base of her throat. "Some of that?"

"Mm-hmm." She squirmed in his hold, but he held her fast.

"What about this?" He moved lower, following the V in her shirt until the top button stopped him. With one hand, he made quick work of each one, leaving her shirt open to him, to whatever he wanted, and whatever she wanted.

He kissed the gentle curve of her breast, then slid his tongue over the top until he reached the tip. His hand slipped around her back, pulling her closer, as he captured her already stiff peak in his mouth and teased another long, throaty cry from her.

"I can't do this," she groaned. "I think I'm gonna die."

"Not yet," he chuckled. "Not until I'm good and done with you."

"I don't know how much more I can take. Will it be long?"

"Oh yeah," he whispered against her breast. "We're going to be here for a long while yet."

"But I can't stand up anymore." Her breath came in short gasps. "My legs are so—"

In one swift move, he had her on the bed, her eyes wide again, her gorgeous lips trembling.

"D-do it again," she pleaded, reaching for him. "Please."

"If I must." He eased her shirt from her shoulders, amazed at how soft her skin was. One arm at a time, he released her until she lay bare from the waist up. Levi let out a low whistle. "Might not be here as long as I thought."

Jo squirmed beneath his mouth; nothing had ever felt so glorious, nothing had ever made her entire being feel like hot, molten lava. She needed more, but didn't know how to tell him. Or what to tell him.

What she did know was that he had far too much clothing on. As he pulled moan after moan from her, she grasped the edges of his shirt and pulled as hard as she could. Buttons flew everywhere.

"That's two shirts now," he laughed. "You're going to have to learn to sew."

"Don't count on it." She shoved his shirt back and down until he shrugged out of it and let it fall behind him. Then she set to work on his belt buckle.

"Whoa." Levi sat up so fast, she thought he'd land on the floor beside his shirt. "You don't want to do that."

"Oh yeah," she nodded, grinning and reaching for him again. "I do."

"Not yet." He gripped her hands again and held them above her head. "Later."

"No," she whined, but he just nodded and kissed her again, draining every thought from her head.

When he reached for her belt, she stopped him, too. "I thought that was later."

"No, Joanna," he grinned down at her. Damn that smile of his was sexy. "I'm later. You're now."

"Right now?" she asked, suddenly a little nervous.

"Right now." He took his sweet time easing the belt apart, then even more time unfastening her heavy pants. By the time his fingers curled around the waistband, Jo was sure she was going to explode right there on the bed.

"Jesus, Travers."

"Levi," he murmured, planting small wet kisses around her belly. "Say it."

"L-L—"

His tongue dipped into her belly button.

"Levi!"

"That's it," he said. "Just like that."

"Yeah," she agreed. "Just like that."

With agonizing slowness, he eased her pants and drawers down at the same time. When he kissed the inside of her thigh, her whole body convulsed and she grabbed him by the hair to control it.

"Let it go, Joanna. Let it go." He made short work of her boots, then slid her pants the rest of the way down. "Oh my God, you're beautiful."

"Come here," she begged. "I need to touch you."

He stretched out beside her, his lips finding hers, and he took his time loving each lip, then dipping his tongue inside to dance with hers. He tasted of whiskey, salt, and something musky. Something that nearly drove her mad.

She couldn't feel enough of him beneath her hands. They moved across his chest, down his stomach, up his back and over his arms, but it wasn't enough. He was touching her in ways she'd never imagined, but she had no idea how to touch him the same way.

"Levi," she rasped out, "I want to touch you."

"You are," he chuckled.

"No, I want to touch you the way you touch me."

He rolled onto his back and pulled her on top. "Do whatever you like."

She straddled his hips, sitting squarely on top of his iron-hard desire. Her body moved on its own, pressing harder against him as she moved in slow circles.

"I thought . . . you just wanted . . . to touch me."

"I am." She leaned over him and kissed his very stubbled chin. "Don't distract me."

His only answer was a long groan.

Jo moved his arms until they lay straight out, then she danced her fingers up each one, taking her time to feel the muscles and marvel at his strength. Next she moved over his chest, loving the rough patch of hair that led lower. She followed it down to his waistband, smiled again when he groaned, then traced the line back up.

She'd nearly collapsed when he took her nipple in his mouth; would he feel the same? With her eyes locked on his, she lowered her mouth and took him in the same way as he'd done. His eyes rolled back in his head, his mouth opened slightly, and his hands gripped her around the waist.

"Joanna," he murmured. "Oh, Joanna." His hands slid lower until they cupped her bottom. Lightening bolts raced through her veins.

"Oh," she gasped, wiggling against his fingers. His hands moved again, one up her back and the other beneath her, sliding closer toward her aching core. Surely he wouldn't . . .

Surely he did. At his first touch, Jo nearly leapt right off the bed, but he brought her back down, held her with one hand, and slid his fingers toward her again.

His thumb moved in slow circles against her sensitive nub, making her arch and squirm against his hand. He rubbed again, slower, then slipped his long finger inside.

Jo bucked against him, begging him to stop, to *please* stop, to go deeper, to stop the ache deep inside.

He didn't stop. Instead, he flipped them over so she was on her back again, reaching for him, panting out a need she'd never known before.

He withdrew his finger, almost to the tip, but she arched into his hand again, then pressed her own over top, begging for more. He pulled her breast into his mouth, sucking, caressing, driving her mad until something snapped inside her and she cried out, her back arched against his hand, her voice rasping out his name.

"That's it," he murmured against her cheek. "Let it go, Joanna. Let it go."

When her body finally stopped trembling and

her breathing had evened out enough to speak, she almost cried when she asked, "What was that?"

"That," Levi chuckled, "was only the beginning."

He stood up, his long, lean body making her want him all over again.

"But I don't think I can move anymore," she sighed.

"Don't then. Let me do all the moving." He shucked his pants and stretched out beside her, very hard and very erect.

"Oh my."

He kissed her, long, deep, and wet, while his hands moved over her body again. How could she possibly want more of him after what had just happened? But he must have been right, because that low burn deep in her belly was already flaming out of control.

"Touch me," he said.

She didn't even think twice. Following his lead, she danced her fingers down his rib cage and across his belly. At first, she wasn't sure how to touch him. What if he didn't like what she did?

"Joanna," Levi ground out. "Please, darlin'."

Very gently, she ran her finger down the length of him, astounded at the size. Levi gripped the blanket beside him. Next, she slid her finger over the tip, keeping one eye on the way his knuckles tightened with every move she made.

Feeling much bolder, she wrapped her hand around him and slid it up and down his length slowly at first, then faster.

"God yeah," he rasped. A second later, he was

pressing her back against the blanket, easing his body over hers, and nudging her legs apart.

But he didn't enter her. He kissed her lips, softly and gently, then caressed her arms, neck, and finally her breasts with his strong, calloused hands. Jo chomped down on her lip to keep from crying out, but he smoothed his finger against her mouth, easing her lip out.

Her tongue darted out, licked at his finger, then pulled it inside her mouth where she sucked it, teased it, and caressed it with her tongue.

Levi closed his eyes then leaned forward and replaced his finger with his own tongue, darting in and out of her mouth until she was crazy with needing him again.

"Please," she begged, "fill me, make it stop."

"Make what stop, darlin'?"

"Oh, Levi. The ache. Make it stop." She arched against him, pressing his stiffness against her own flaming desire.

"You mean this ache?" He slid his finger back inside her, then out, then two fingers, slowly pumping in and out.

"Yes," she whimpered. "Yes."

Levi raised himself up, keeping his weight off her, and pressed his tip against her opening.

"This what you want?" he asked, sliding in a little farther, then out again.

"Yes. Don't . . . the ache."

"I ache too, Joanna."

"Stop it," she cried. "Make it stop."

He eased in a bit more, then pulled almost all the

way out. His teeth ground together, the vein in his neck throbbed.

"Do you want me to make it stop?" He slid in again, then retreated. "Or do you want me to make you ache more?"

"Oh," she writhed beneath his glorious torture. "I can't . . . I . . . oh!"

Levi slid in again, this time pressing his thumb against her when he did, moving in the same small circles as he had before. Joanna caught his hand in hers and slid his finger in beside his hardness. Both of them gasped. She could feel the end coming; it was close, closer.

Then Levi was inside, filling her, moving inside her, and she came undone in his arms. Her body opened to take him in, her legs wrapped around his waist and she cried out his name over and over. He throbbed deep inside her, once, twice, a long, delicious third time, then collapsed on top of her, his chest slick, his lips seeking hers.

He rolled to the side, dragging her with him, until she lay flat on top of him, her hair a tangled mess over her face and his hands caressing the small of her back.

"Levi," she whispered.

"Mmm?" The touch of his hand on her hip sent shivers down her spine.

"I had no idea."

His hand stilled, so she wiggled against his hand to get him moving again.

Something strange was happening, and it took her a minute to realize what. Still buried inside her,

Levi was growing hard again, and from the grin on his face, he wasn't nearly as exhausted as she was.

"Are you serious?" she squeaked.

"Oh yeah." That sexy, dazzling smile of his turned positively wicked. "I told you we were gonna be a long while yet."

"But aren't you . . . I mean, can we really . . ." she wiggled against him again, marveling at the whole thing. "I never would have believed it."

Levi's chuckle rasped from his throat. "You didn't believe I could charm you, either." His smile sent warmth pooling through Jo's system. "But look at you now."

"Yeah." She sighed against his chest. "I've been charmed all right."

"Took long enough," he growled, rolling her onto her back. "But now that we're here, let's concentrate on the benefits of the whole thing."

Levi flicked her nipple with his tongue and grinned. "Best thing I ever did was spend all these weeks trying to charm you, Miss Joanna."

"I don't know about that." She arched into him, pressing herself against his mouth. "You seem to be outdoing yourself here tonight, Travers."

"It's Levi." He flashed her the sexiest smile she'd ever seen. "And you ain't seen nothin' yet."

Complete Your Collection Today
Janelle Taylor